ADVANCE PRAISE FOR COLBY HODGE!

"Talented Colby Hodge delivers space adventure at a breathtaking clip! Fans of *Star Wars* and *Riddick* will love *Stargazer*."

—Susan Grant,
Author of *The Scarlet Empress*

UNDER NORMAL CIRCUMSTANCES

"I can arrange it so you go straight to prison if that is your desire," she ground out.

"That's just like a woman," he spat out in disgust. "What happened to all those promises you made concerning my freedom if I helped you?"

"You did help me and I'm grateful, but now you're just turning everything around," Lilly cried out in frustration.

"Prove it."

"Prove what?" Lilly felt like crying but refused to do so.

"That you're not controlling me. Plant a suggestion in my head, something that I wouldn't do under normal circumstances."

"It doesn't always work that way," she whispered.

"Do it." The words were forceful; his face so close that she could feel the puff of his breath.

Lilly closed her eyes and tried to clear her mind, but it was difficult; it had been difficult to concentrate since she had walked into the cryo bay. *Something he wouldn't normally do,* she thought to herself. She felt his presence; she knew if she opened her eyes, she would see his staring back at her. Taking a deep breath, she emptied her mind of the turmoil and reached out with the first thought that came to her.

Shaun's eyebrows flew up in surprise as he felt her mind enter his like a cool breeze. He slowly leaned in, tilting his head to the side as their noses touched. Lilly's eyes opened in surprise and she saw herself reflected in the mirrors of his eyes. His lips were a breath away from hers.

"You want me to kiss you?" He said it so softly that she felt the question instead of hearing the words. Her lips trembled in anticipation. "Where did you get that idea?"

Stargazer

Colby Hodge

LOVE SPELL NEW YORK CITY

LOVE SPELL®

April 2005

Published by

Dorchester Publishing Co., Inc.
200 Madison Avenue
New York, NY 10016

ISBN 0-505-52627-1

Printed in the United States of America.

Stargazer

Prologue

Michael clutched the newborn infant closer to his body even as her mother reached out her arms for the babe.

"Let me see my daughter," the mother cried as she fought against the women who were hastily cleaning up evidence of the birth.

Michael looked down at the tiny face that stared up at him with pale gray eyes beneath long dark lashes. She had eyes just like her mother. Was he wrong to think that was a bad thing?

"Please," the mother begged, tears streaming down her cheeks. Was she crying for her child or for herself?

He couldn't risk the child's life by finding out. He wrapped the blanket tighter around the perfectly formed little body and left the chambers, ignoring the anguished cries of the mother.

The child should be spared the sentence of her mother. Hadn't the Sovereign waited all these long months just to spare the child? The Sovereign had hoped for a male, an heir to take the place of the one who had been lost. Instead there was this girl, who was the image of her mother.

What would he do if the Sovereign ordered that this babe must die with her mother? Surely he wouldn't. The man could not be so maddened by grief that he would condemn an innocent child to death. Could he?

Michael heard the hushed whispers as he carried the infant through the corridors. "It's a girl, a female," he heard as he held the precious bundle close.

What would he do? He had sworn himself to protect the child's father at all costs but had failed miserably. Victor, brother of Sovereign Alexander, had died saving the Sovereign's life. Michael knew it should have been he who died that day, giving up his life as he had sworn to do, but the witch had tricked him again.

Could he allow this innocent child to die for the sins of her mother? For the sins of her father?

"The child is born?" Sovereign Alexander asked as Michael entered the room with the baby girl. Without a word Michael kneeled before his Sovereign and opened the blanket so Alexander could see the soft perfection of the child. Surely his heart would soften as he looked upon his niece.

"I had hoped for a male," Alexander commented without emotion as he looked on the babe with bitterness in his eyes. "No doubt Zania thinks this her final revenge upon me."

Michael held his breath as the Sovereign continued, but his face revealed nothing of the emotion that was tearing at his gut. He had always been skilled at hiding what he was thinking.

"Still, she may have her uses if she is trained properly." He dismissed the child with a wave of his hand. "See to it that she is taken care of," the Sovereign said.

Michael quietly released the air he had been holding in his lungs and stood, careful of his burden.

"Take the woman now!" Alexander let out the command in a burst of frustration and outrage, knowing that the horrendous ending he had planned for the witch would not change what had happened. But still he looked forward to her suffering. He looked forward to hearing her scream.

"The child needs a name," Michael said quietly as the guards rushed to do their Sovereign's bidding.

"I care not what you call her," Alexander said. His eyes were already looking toward the square where the execution would take place.

Michael bowed and backed away, keeping the child close. He considered it a miracle that the baby had not cried out yet. But now he did not know where to take her. Provisions had not been made beyond the moment of her birth. He dared not take her back to her mother's quarters, where even now the guards were dragging the doomed witch down the corridors to her death.

Michael ducked into a small courtyard and sat down on a bench. Water softly gurgled from a fountain placed along the wall and the smell of the great stargazer lilies filled the air. The burst of vivid pinks and magentas was so intense against the pristine white of the outer walls that it hurt his eyes. He looked down at the child and saw that she was captivated by the bright flowers that towered behind his head. Her light gray eyes swam back and forth as she searched for a focal point in the swirl of color.

A horrible scream rent the air. The first of many to come. Zania's skin was to be cut from her body with lasers, one minuscule section at a time. It was an execution destined to last an infinite amount of time while causing an immeasurable amount of pain.

The child jumped in his arms, startled by the horrible sound. Michael rocked her, giving comfort with a song from his childhood, hoping the tune would distract the babe from the noise. Once again her eyes went to the lilies behind his head, and Michael stopped his song long enough to glance over his shoulder at the fantastic blooms.

"Lilly," he said as he looked back down into the pale gray eyes. "We will call you Lilly."

The baby girl closed her eyes, finally lulled to sleep by the peace in the courtyard as her mother's screams faded to moans, her voice gone long before her life would mercifully end.

Chapter One

Twenty years later

Lilly could feel him as she entered the cryo bay of the ship, a presence that reached out to her as she followed the solid back of Krebbs up the ramp. It teased the edges of her mind, causing her to look furtively from side to side as if she were being watched. There was always a chance she'd been spotted, but Krebbs was good at his job and had hidden their tracks well; they blended inconspicuously with the other passengers that were even now lining up in front of their tubes. Once she was inside the bay, her head flew up in shock, her dark-lashed light gray eyes quickly scanning the length of the narrow passage that would hold their bodies suspended in a barely conscious state for the next month. She was searching, drawn, without even knowing she was moving, to a tube directly across from the one she had been assigned. The clear plexi cylinder already held a passenger: a man, his eyes covered with a dark mask and his wrists and ankles bound with heavy cable. The bulging muscles of his arms made her wonder, briefly, if the bonds would hold him once he awakened from the enforced sleep that he was already under. The Seal of the Legion was affixed to the front of his tube. "Do not revive without authorization" it warned any and all who cared to read.

Lilly closed her eyes and willed herself into a state of total relaxation, reaching with her mind into the thoughts of the one before her. Intense emotion hit her with the force of a blow, but none watching her noticed the impact. A wave of frustration from the one who was within washed over her; then her mind filled with anguish so deep that she wanted to cry out. She didn't, her years of training taking over automatically whenever her emotions went out of control. Her training was not strong enough, however, to keep her from being startled by a sudden flash of bright light that resembled a flare. She gained the impression of sunlight bouncing off highly polished metal, then darkness.

"I wouldn't get too close if I were you," someone warned her.

"He seems to be quite harmless." Lilly's voice did not betray the turmoil she had just experienced as she turned to find a Legion officer standing next to the occupied tube. He seemed young enough to still hold the Legion's high ideals of glory, but experienced enough to be cautious. He could have been from any one of the hundreds of planets that made up the Senate. He casually lounged against the cryo tube, ready to impress Lilly with his tales of conquest.

"Oh, he is now, but when he awakes it's a different story." The officer rubbed his hand over the smooth plexi of the tube while gripping his side arm with the other. Lilly had the impression that he wanted to use it on his prisoner but something or someone held him back.

"What did he do?"

"Murdered five soldiers of the Senate who were only doing their duty," the officer spat out in disgust.

"He must have disagreed with their orders." Why was she so concerned about the prisoner's side of the story?

"Words such as that could be considered treasonous if heard in another place." The threat was vague and his tone condescending. But why should his attitude be otherwise? She was of no consequence, just a poor passenger on a slow-moving cargo ship, nothing more.

Lilly ignored the remark. She didn't feel the need to play the game with this soldier. "And his sentence?" She gave the officer what he wanted, a moment to glory in.

"Life, in the deepest hole we can find." He seemed to enjoy that prospect.

"Rykers?" The prison planet had long been used as a threat to keep small children on the path to good.

"Yes, Rykers, the dark star, where he will never again see the light of day." The officer leaned back against the plexi and casually crossed his arms. "The funny thing is, it shouldn't bother him a bit. He's like a cat—he can see in the dark."

Lilly looked up at the mask that hid the prisoner's eyes. Dark rich hair curled out from under the sides and down the back of his neck, the shine and softness of it contrasting sharply with the strongly corded muscles that stood out in the dim light. The skin was heavily bronzed; obviously he'd spent a lot of time under the rays of a strong sun. Lilly wondered how long it would take the deep tan to pale once he was thrown into the depths of the prison planet. *"He can see in the dark"* rang in her mind, and she saw the flash of sunlight on metal again.

"Don't worry about him hurting you; he's in a deep sleep now," the officer assured her, his chest all but swelling as he considered Lilly's slim, youthful frame. She turned away from his intent stare, but as she turned she caught a movement from the corner of her eye in the darkness of the cryo tube. Had the prisoner twitched his finger?

"You can hear our voices," she said in surprise, using the voice that formed in her mind as she perused the still form of the prisoner.

"I can," a deep voice whispered back, and Lilly's light gray eyes widened in shock. She had momentarily forgotten her training. *"Why?"* the deep voice asked in confusion.

Krebbs gently touched her arm. "It's time, my lady," he said in a whisper, inclining his head toward their tubes. He would not take his until he was sure she was safe inside her own, so she let him lead her across the corridor to the container that would hold her in a suspended state of sleep until they reached their destination.

"*Who are you?*" the deep voice said inside her mind as she stepped into her tube. She turned and faced the opposite wall and saw the legion seal on the prisoner's tube glowing in the dimming light; the man behind had faded into the darkness. The flight attendant gave her a friendly wave as he initiated her cryo state, and she felt instead of saw Krebbs's frown while he watched the proceedings closely. Lilly closed her eyes as she felt herself lose consciousness, but before all went black, she saw another flash of light.

The noise was deafening. Lilly felt it all around her, even though she could not actually hear it. The heavy machinery churned until the area around seemed to vibrate. Lilly knew she was deep in the bowels of the earth in some sort of cavern, even though the heavy shadows made it hard to see where the great generators ended and the walls of the massive cave began. She felt herself floating within the dream toward a sound that was not quite drowned out by the roar of the engines. A baby was crying, a baby young enough to be held in a woman's arms, but old enough to try to escape from the pain that was being inflicted upon him.

"I'm sorry," the lovely woman sobbed above the screaming child. The little boy was lying facedown across her bloodstained lap, struggling mightily against the hand that held him firmly in place. Tears streamed down the woman's face as she held the needle-sharp point of a dagger against the child's neck, right below the line of soft dark curls. The agony showing on her face made it clear that the tears were not from the pain of her own wound, but for the pain she was inflicting upon the child. Trickles of blood were streaming from the cuts that marred the tender skin of the child's neck, but the woman did not stop, not even to wipe her tear-filled eyes as she repeated the words over and over again. "I'm sorry, I'm sorry, please forgive me."

Lilly longed to scoop up the child and run with him, but she was helpless in the dream. She felt tears stream down her own face as she watched the woman, who she knew was the child's mother, hold the dagger against his soft flesh. "Why, oh why?" she asked herself over and over again as she floated within the dream. "What am I doing here, what am I supposed to see, what does this mean?" No one answered her except the generators, whose roar proclaimed loudly that they brought life to this strange, dark place and shelter to the two crying out in pain and anguish.

The vision before her vanished as the roar of the engines became louder and louder until Lilly's ears were ringing with the sound. She wanted to clamp her hands over her ears to block out the noise, but the cryo sleep held her paralyzed. She felt the vibration from the noise, and her body began to shake with it. Slowly, her conscious mind began to take over, warning her that she was no longer dreaming. As her mind began its swim to the surface, she felt the life force that was Krebbs leave his body. She felt grief well up inside her, but she suppressed it as her arms reached out to brace her body against the bone-shattering vibration. Lilly's light gray eyes finally opened and she blinked at the flashing red light that alerted everyone the ship was in peril. To her left, Krebbs was slumped in his tube, his soul gone from his body, the unsuspecting victim of whatever was attacking the ship. She felt an impact against her tube, a jolt that nearly knocked her down, except there was no place for her to fall within its narrow confines. A struggle was going on at her feet, but her eyes could not focus on it. She scratched at the smooth plexi until she found the release button and then stumbled out, landing in the middle of the melee in the corridor.

She was greeted with a snarl, and pushed away by a strong pair of manacled hands. Lilly's mind began to race as the situation became apparent. The ship was under attack, which meant they had found her. Her bodyguard was dead, which meant she was alone. She must not be captured; too many people were counting on her.

The struggle before her had become one-sided. The Legion officer had taken advantage of the bonds that still held the prisoner and was now pressing the heavy metal bar that connected the manacles against the bronzed skin of the prisoner's throat. The cords of his muscles stood out as he strained against the bar that was choking the life from his body. Lilly picked up a heavy pipe that rolled up against her and, without a second thought, brought it down hard against the back of the Legion officer's head. The prisoner pushed the unconscious form off his chest and blinked through the smoke and flashing light at his savior, who was even now searching the man's uniform pockets. Lilly pulled out a key and hastily fitted it in the manacles. They opened with a distinctive pop and slid away.

"The escape pods are that way," she said as he jumped to his feet. He grabbed her arm and pulled her after him as they joined the other passengers who had come to the same realization that the ship was breaking apart. Some had enough sense to make their way to the pods, while others just added to the confusion of chaotic light, sound, and smoke by screaming and running aimlessly.

Lilly stuck close to the solid form that parted the way for them. His grip on her arm was solid but not painful; she felt his steady control and let herself trust him to get them away from the ship. The dark head ducked under a hatch and then backed out.

"It's jammed!" He pressed the release lever, which did nothing, then punched it with his fist. The door slid open, and he swept his arm aside as if he were opening the door to an elegant carriage. Lilly bolted into the escape pod, and he closed the hatch behind them. She pressed her face against the window while her companion threw the release lever that catapulted them away from the dying ship. She felt his solid presence behind her as they both gazed upward.

"Why would Ravigans attack a cargo ship?" he asked no one in particular as they observed the attack vessel hovering over the large craft that was even now breaking apart.

Lilly shook her head as a shiver went down her spine. "They're after something; they're sending out Falcons."

His eyes ran over her back as he considered the situation. He sat down in the small nav chair and began punching up charts. "I haven't done anything to make them mad, at least not lately. How about you?"

Lilly didn't answer, just continued to watch as the commercial ship broke up above them while escape pods jettisoned away, the small fighters called Falcons taking up pursuit.

"We're close to Cathra. If we're lucky, its gravity will pick us up." He had found their position on the charts.

"Cathra?" Lilly turned, unfamiliar with the planet, and froze as she looked into a set of eyes exactly the same color as her own. *Only women are permitted to have eyes that color*, she thought to herself. Then she caught a flash of silver, like the flash that had filled her mind, a flash like that of sunlight bouncing off metal, except there was no sunlight here, just a dimly lighted escape pod that was being pursued and fired upon by Falcons. The pod vibrated when the shot missed, the brightness of the flash telling them how close they had come to being blown to pieces.

He switched off the autopilot and took the controls in a firm grip. "Hold on." The pod lurched forward as they accelerated, the sudden movement taking the Falcon pilot by surprise. Lilly stumbled into a seat and strapped herself in as he maneuvered the ship directly toward another pod.

"Where are you going?" she gasped as she saw his intent. She closed her eyes against the death that she was certain was imminent.

"We can't outrun them," he tossed over his shoulder. His hands on the controls were steady as he flew the pod into the space between another pod and its pursuing Falcon. They had no more than passed when an explosion sent them spinning wildly.

"What happened?" Lilly asked when she was able to take a breath again and he had regained control of the pod.

"Our friends out there had a meeting of the minds."

Lilly unbuckled herself and, with amazement, pressed her face to the window again. Debris from the Falcons was caught in their energy trail, the bigger pieces spiraling away into space.

"Meeting of the minds." She heard his deep voice inside her head. She turned back to look at him, but he was focused on the controls. *"Who are you?"* His voice asked again, inside her mind, as his eyes focused on the console with serious intent. Lilly studied the handsome dark head, the curve of his neck, the heavily muscled arms that were bronzed from the sun.

The arms crossed as he swiveled his chair around to look at her. "I think now would be a good time for you to let me in on your secret." His light gray eyes seemed to look right through her.

"Secret?"

"Yes, Princess, your secret." He was certain she had not belonged on that cargo ship, but he had no idea where she came from or what she was doing. She had saved his life, of that he was sure, but now he wanted some answers. He leveled his gaze on her casually, as if he had all the time in the world.

The term "Princess" caused another shiver to go through her. There was no way he could know about her. She was sure she had not given anything away.

Certainly her clothing was common enough, and they had not had enough of a conversation for him to gauge her level of education.

He continued. "The Ravigans attacked a common cargo carrier. You saved me from a Legionnaire, which means you would rather be in the company of a convict than a soldier. I have a hunch the Ravigans are after you, and since I am now sharing your company, they are after me. I would like to know why I am about to die."

The sound of his speech surprised her more than the content. He was a convict, someone she had supposed to be a common criminal raised in the poorest of circumstances, but he sounded educated, was almost refined in his manner. *No wonder that Legionnaire hated him,* Lilly said to herself.

"They really don't need you as an excuse to kill me," he retorted as if he heard her thoughts.

Lilly arched a delicate eyebrow at him. "So I heard."

A sheepish grin crossed his handsome face and he leaned back to study her. "Why were you on that ship?"

"The same as everyone else: I was traveling."

"Where were you going?"

"It doesn't matter now; I'm obviously not going to get there." Lilly's mind went into overdrive. He was not going to be easily manipulated.

"Why did you help me?"

"I was hoping maybe you would return the favor." She willed her body to relax. She needed all her wits about her now.

His eyes narrowed and he sat up as he saw they were getting to the heart of the matter. "You saved my life on the ship, I saved yours by getting you away from there; it seems like we're even. I might even be ahead, if you think about it."

Oh, he's good, Lilly thought as she felt another shiver slide down her spine. This one felt different, however. It felt exciting. *Concentrate on your task!* she chided herself. "Perhaps we could come to an arrangement." She decided to get directly to the point.

He leaned back in the chair again and waited for her next move.

"You are a convicted murderer," she stated as a matter of fact.

"Yes."

"And you will be hunted throughout the galaxy."

"Possibly." He was not ready to give anything away. He almost seemed to be amused at the prospect.

Lilly gave him a doubtful look but continued. "I can protect you from that."

That statement brought a hearty chuckle to his lips as he closely examined her. Average height, a slim build, a lovely heart-shaped face with full lips, a pert nose, and light gray eyes under dark lashes that had an upward tilt at the corners. Her light ash-brown hair was tied back away from her face, but a few tendrils had escaped and his hand had a sudden desire to smooth them back into the long tail that hung down to the middle of her back. He recalled the look on her face when she had struck the Legionnaire who had been choking him, and then he imagined her staring down an entire squadron of soldiers with those extraordinary eyes of hers. *Our eyes are the same color.* It suddenly dawned on him. He had never seen another person with eyes like his. The impact of the light color beneath the dark lashes made him more conscious of his own odd coloring. His eyes had always been an asset for him, especially where women were concerned. But when he looked into her eyes, their color set him off balance. As a matter of fact, he had felt like this ever since she walked onto the passenger ship. He had felt her presence in his state of suspended animation and it had awakened something deep within him. He couldn't put his finger on it yet, but something in him had recognized her. "Who are you?" he asked, curiosity overcoming his usual cautious nature.

"Lilly." It was all she could give him for the present time. She had seen his realization about their eyes.

"And how are you going to protect me, Lilly?" He realized she had not given him her full name, but let it go.

"I can change your identity, so no one will question who you are."

A dark eyebrow questioned the validity of her statement, but he decided to play along. "And what do I have to do?"

"Be my protector."

He waved a hand toward the empty space behind them, where bodies and pieces of ship were floating. "That might be a little more than I can handle."

"This attack was as much a shock to me as it was to you." She felt responsible for the deaths but refused to dwell on the pain they caused her; too many people were still depending on her.

"Imagine the shock it must have been to the poor souls that are dead now."

"I never dreamed the Ravigans would go to such lengths." Her eyes clouded with the grief she had felt when Krebbs's soul left his body, but there still wasn't time for it, so she locked it away.

A sudden lurch of the pod interrupted his reply. "We're in the gravity field," he said as he spun back around to the controls. "Hold on, it's going to get bumpy." Lilly had no doubts about his skills as a pilot as he negotiated the pod through the atmosphere of the planet. They soon were flying through darkening skies as their tiny ship arced across the horizon.

"What is this place?" Lilly asked as she peered down at the green and brown landscape.

"Cathra. It's mostly a swamp on the surface, but underneath it has lots of resources."

"Mines?"

"Yes, a few."

"So there's a settlement?"

He laughed out loud. "I guess you could call it that."

"Can you find it?"

"Right now my main concern is finding someplace to land where we won't sink." The treetops were starting to take shape beneath them as the pod continued its descent. They seemed to go on forever, and Lilly briefly wondered if they would even see the surface through the dense branches. He seemed to know what he was doing, however, and they were soon hovering over a small mound that looked black in the dimming light. He gently lowered the pod between the trees into a space that was not much bigger than the craft itself. They landed somewhat at a tilt, and he hastily kicked the hatch open. "This won't last forever," he said as he extended a hand toward Lilly. She looked down in disgust at the mud that was sucking at the landing gear of the pod, but she had no choice. She landed on her feet and immediately sank up to her ankles.

"Make your way to the trees," he yelled from the confines of the pod. Lilly pulled her booted foot up and shook the mud away before she buried it again it the muck. The mud begrudgingly let her move, protesting each step with a great sucking sound. She soon heard her companion's solid presence behind her as she made her way into the murky water that came up to her knees. Lilly wrapped her arms around a tree and waited for him.

He came toward her grinning, slopping his way through the mud, a weapon now strapped to his side and a small pack slung over his shoulder. Lilly canted her head to the side as he splashed up beside her. There was something about him that unsettled her mind, but she put it down to the circumstances. "You look like you are enjoying this," she said when he had joined her.

"It beats the alternative." He turned back as the pod groaned and settled down into the mud, the muck pouring into the still-open hatch as it sank down. "If we're lucky, the mud will smother the homing beacon."

"Next thing you'll be telling me you planned it that way."

"I do what I can." He sloshed into the trees.

"Wait!" Lilly called after him. He stopped and turned with a questioning look on his face. "I don't know your name."

"Phoenix." He turned and took another step.

"Phoenix?" Lilly came splashing up behind him.

"Yes, Lilly, Phoenix." He almost sneered when he said her name, letting her know that he realized she was being vague about her identity. "And try not to make so much noise." Lilly immediately froze in her tracks and looked around. Phoenix turned back again and grinned, shaking his head. "You won't see them coming." He took off again, and she scampered after him.

Chapter Two

Lilly felt as if she had been trudging for hours. The swampy water made it hard to take each step. She concentrated on keeping up, her eyes focused on the strong back before her, the black of Phoenix's shirt almost invisible in the darkness that surrounded them. Above her head there was light—she could see it through the treetops—coming from two full moons hanging high in the sky. Occasionally there was enough of a break in the canopy above that the reflection would catch in the water, but then the branches would close in on them and all would be dark again. She was tired, she was thirsty, and she did not have a clue as to where they were going or when they were going to get there. Phoenix seemed perfectly content to drag along through the swamp; he had not said a word since his vague warning before, and he had not even turned to check on her.

Lilly was stopped by his broad back as she came up

against it. His head turned and she was taken aback by the silver glow of his eyes in the darkness. It was as if both moons above had taken up residence in his face. He looked beyond her, concentrating on something behind them. Lilly stayed frozen where she was, his warning from earlier echoing in her ears. Then she heard it, the sloshing sound of the water. Someone was behind them.

Phoenix swung his head back and slowly surveyed the landscape before them. Apparently he had found what he was looking for, because he started forward again, this time slower, barely making a sound as he moved through the water. "Can you swim?" he asked casually.

"Yes."

"Good." The water was getting deeper, now coming up to the middle of Lilly's thighs, and even though the air was warm and muggy, she shivered. When it was waist deep, he stopped her and handed her the pack. The trees were not as dense now, and the twin moons reflecting off the surface of the water gave the air about them a strange white glow. "Swim straight across and then climb to the top of that tree." He pointed across the way into the darkness.

"I can't see it." Lilly's teeth were chattering.

"It's there, it's on an island. The branches are low. Go on." He turned away from her.

"Wait," Lilly whispered into the darkness. "What about you?"

"I'll find you. Now, go!" He seemed to disappear before her eyes without a sound. Lilly blinked, her mind knowing he was there but her eyes not seeing him. The night sounds closed in on her, the creatures that lived above in the trees giving voice to their eternal chorus. She felt the sensation of living things swimming about her booted feet, and his words rang again in her ears: *You won't see them coming.*

Lilly started out in the direction he had indicated. After a few steps, she was swimming, keeping her arms below the surface so she wouldn't make noise that would attract unwanted attention. The darkness loomed before her like a black hole, but soon she was able to make out the shapes of the trees and found one that looked different from the rest—bigger and spread out, instead of straight and tall like the others. Her feet found the bottom of the lake and she ran up the bank. She wondered briefly what else she might meet on her way up among the branches and hoped that Phoenix had taken that into consideration when he gave her his instructions. A few birds took flight when she disturbed them, but for the most part she seemed to be alone. She was up high enough now that she could see with the help of the moonlight, and she took time to survey the area. In the distance she saw lights among the treetops and hoped they were signs of the settlement. If they were, then Phoenix had been leading them in the right direction, and if he did not come back, she would at least know which way to go. She looked back at where they had been, trying to see some sign of anything; there was nothing but darkness. Lilly settled her back against the trunk of the tree and waited.

* * *

Phoenix knew that the beacon had given them away. It had only been a matter of time, really. He had hoped they would make the settlement before they were found. There they might hop a transport and disappear without a trace, but that would require incredible luck and he had been short of that lately. Right now he was just grateful to be free instead of facing life imprisonment in the bowels of another planet. He had been underground before and was not looking forward to living that way again. His experience had been good for one thing, however, and he was glad to have the ability that allowed him to see in the dark. It would give him an advantage over whoever was following them.

Lilly, he immediately thought. What made her so important that dozens of people had been killed to get her? And what was it about her that affected his mind so much? It was almost as if doors were opening inside of him. He could feel a presence that wasn't there before, and there had been times in the past few hours when he had heard her voice even though she hadn't said a word.

He saw the movement ahead of him, the soft ripple over the surface of the water. He could hear a steady splashing beyond—two, possibly three, the crew from a Falcon perhaps. No doubt they were tracking down all the escape pods. He wondered briefly what they did when they found the others who had survived. Destroyed the evidence probably. The Senate would not be happy with the planet Raviga if it was discovered they were out haphazardly destroying slow-moving cargo ships. There was no profit in it.

The ripple drew his attention again. It was almost as if it were circling. Phoenix knew that the creature had heard the noise beyond; he could use a little help if there were indeed three Ravigans. He had not had a chance to test the weapon he had found in the pod and was not sure of the charge on it. He quietly backed away, melting against the trunk of a tree.

The creature took the first one under before the man had a chance to realize what was happening. It was a simple kill. The tail wrapped around the victim's legs and the head rose up out of the water, undulating as it towered above its prey, the mouth wide open, the tongue flicking as the jaws stretched. The man screamed in panic and raised his weapon, but he was swallowed, head first and whole, before he could fire a shot. His companions gave fire, but the creature was gone, the eighty-foot length coiling among the trunks as it swam off to its den to digest its dinner.

Lilly heard the scream and the shots. She rose up, holding on to the branch above as she leaned out, trying to see anything that would give her a clue, but all she could discern was the darkness and the disturbed sounds of the night creatures.

Phoenix saw the heat scanner that one of the soldiers was holding and lowered himself into the water, his eyes just breaking the surface. If it had not given any indication of the monster, then perhaps the water would protect him also. The two men were obviously frightened by what had just happened, and he could not say that he blamed them. It had frightened him also, and he had known what to expect. The two soldiers scanned the area and tentatively set out again.

They walked right by him. He didn't breathe, nor did he blink when the water they stirred up in their passage splashed into his eyes. He rose up when they were safely past and cautiously followed. Phoenix could see the scanner blinking, catching all of the wildlife that lived in the treetops above. He hoped Lilly would be nothing but another blip on the scanner.

Why is she so important? Phoenix asked himself again as he moved from tree to tree, barely making a sound as he moved through the water, edging closer and closer to the pair. They were moving into the deeper water, motioning ahead toward the island where she was hiding. When they were swimming, he took a deep breath and went under.

The light of the twin moons danced under the water, giving the plants a neon glow. He saw a pair of legs in motion and came up behind them, grabbing the ankles and pulling the man under. Phoenix held him down, surfaced for a breath, then pushed the man deeper into the murky water. The Ravigan struggled against him as his companion took off, afraid that the creature had struck again.

The fight was nearly out of his victim when Phoenix felt the brush along his legs. He spun away in sudden realization and pushed the body of the man toward the coils that were rolling around him. The snake instantly compressed around the body and Phoenix shot to the surface, hoping that the dead man was enough to satisfy the creature's appetite. The snake rolled across the surface, taking the body with him in its churning wake, and Phoenix took off toward the island, where the last of the Ravigans had left a trail of water in the sand.

Lilly heard the splashing in the water; it was close enough that it sounded as if it was right beneath her. The constant sounds of the night creatures grew still as the death struggle occurred, then came back louder, as if warning her of approaching danger. She couldn't see anything below her and dared not move, afraid it would give her position away. She leaned back against the tree, closed her eyes, and with a deep breath cleared her mind.

Phoenix felt her presence as he came out of the water. She was inside his head, making sure he was still there, still alive. "I guess it's good to be needed," he said in a whisper as he caught sight of the man running under the trees.

Lilly opened her eyes in shock. He had known she was in his mind and had responded to her. That had never happened before; she had always gone in as a spy, reading intent, sometimes even making suggestions to those who were of a weak will. This was almost like a conversation. At least she knew he was alive, for the moment, but she had also seen what his eyes had seen and knew that the enemy was approaching fast.

The soldier regained his confidence now that he was on firm ground again and stopped to take stock of his surroundings. The reward for her capture was great and worth the risks, but never in his wildest dreams had he imagined coming up against anything like the creature that had taken his companions. At least now he wouldn't have to share the reward. With that thought, he once again turned to the sensor, holding it in one hand while he held his weapon ready in the other. He scanned the trees, ignoring the small blips of birds and smaller animals that roosted above. But then he found a larger mass just above that had taken shelter in the spreading branches of a huge tree.

Phoenix took aim with his weapon and pulled the trigger, but nothing happened. The charge had expired or the water had ruined it. He did not know and did not have time to think about it. The man was now under the tree that held Lilly with his scanner pointed up, his weapon aimed into the tree. One shot would either kill her or knock her to the ground, and that was something he could not allow.

The impact of his feet churning across the earth was enough to alert the soldier to the coming danger. He turned just as Phoenix threw his body at him, reaching for the weapon with one hand and for the Ravigan's throat with his other. They rolled to the ground, each one fighting for his life as they came up against the tree. Lilly knew the struggle was going on beneath her. She couldn't stand by and wait any longer, so she made her way down the branches, jumping down one by one. The lower she got, the louder the fight became. She heard the impact of a bare fist on skin, heard the grunts and snarls of the two men as they tried to overpower each other. She was close enough to see now; they were on the ground, each one with a hold on the weapon. Both arms brought it up, and it fired right at her. Instinct took over and she leaned back, flipping gracefully off the lowest branch and landing lightly on her feet. She recognized Phoenix as the man on top. He was smashing the other man's arm into the ground until the weapon bounced away. Phoenix pulled the soldier up by the jacket collar and then smashed his fist into the man's face. Lilly picked up the weapon and held it ready in case the soldier moved, but he stayed where he had landed.

Phoenix stood, wiped the blood from his lip, and reached for the pack that Lilly was still carrying. He took a bottle of water out, drank from it, then handed it to Lilly. He ran his hands through his still-dripping hair and then tested his jaw where a few blows had landed.

"Are you all right?" he asked.

"Yes."

"Then would you mind telling me why half the galaxy is trying to kill you?"

Lilly took a step toward him. "I have to know if I can trust you first."

"I just killed a man to protect you." Lilly looked down at the Ravigan, who was still breathing. "Back there, in the water." Phoenix waved behind him. "The natural order of things took the other." Lilly looked back into the darkness, where the sounds of the night creatures were returning.

"You knew they would be after you also."

Phoenix snorted in disgust. "Look, Princess, I don't know what your problem is, but you chose me, remember? Now, if I'm going to get us out of this swamp, I would like to have an idea of what I'm up against."

Lilly took another step toward him and lifted her hand toward his face. Her light gray eyes asked permission, and then she extended two fingers and laid them against his temple. His eyes glowed silver as her mind asked a simple question of his. "*Can I trust you?*" A vision filled her mind, his face full of anguish, a dead woman in his arms, and rage, a rage so great that he had killed for it.

He pushed her hand away. "Did you find what you were looking for?" The steely glow of his eyes raked her face.

"Yes."

"Then let's go." He took off in the direction of the settlement, with Lilly following as she had before.

Chapter Three

Phoenix had been right: It was not much of a settlement. Mostly prefabricated housing placed on platforms next to a rocky outcropping that held the entrance to the mines. There were ships, however. That was a good sign, it meant a way off the planet, if they could find someone they could deal with. Lilly was aware that money bought a lot of loyalty, and she knew help would not come cheaply. For now she would see where Phoenix led them. He had not spoken a word to her since the exchange under the tree, just stopped occasionally to let her drink, then plodded onward, anxious to leave the swampy place of death behind them.

Phoenix had not stopped thinking about her since they had left the big tree. When she had touched his temple, a flood of memories had poured forth, things that he did not want to think about anymore. He was not proud of what he had done, but he'd had his reasons and he would do it again if the opportunity presented itself. He was puzzled more by the control she seemed to have over him. He had always been accused of having too strong a will, but Lilly was able to just pop into his head at a moments' notice. His father had told him of women like that—the Witches of Circe, he had called them. They were treacherous and manipulative and should be avoided at all costs. Now here he was trudging through a swamp with one. Wouldn't his father be proud? Thinking of his father brought forth his grief again, and he shook his head to drive it away. At least she didn't whine and complain, as a lot of women would under these circumstances. Not that he had ever been with a woman under such conditions. Usually the women and the surroundings were . . . easy. He took a moment to look behind him to see if she had read his thoughts, but her eyes were focused on the settlement. It had not changed much since his last visit; he hoped the people were the same as well.

It was not every day that strangers came up out of the swamp, and the local populace gave them strange looks as they climbed up onto the suspended platform that held an odd collection of buildings. Phoenix gently took Lilly's arm as they made their way through the settlement and guided her into what appeared to be a tavern, where he settled her at a corner table.

"Got any credits on you, Princess?" he asked as she gratefully sat down. "I didn't have any need for them where I was going." Lilly ignored his sarcasm and dug some coins from her pocket. "Is this all you have?" he asked as he surveyed the small sum she handed him.

"No, but it should be enough for some food and drink." Her eyes dared him to ask for more.

"And how do you propose to pay for a ticket off this rock?"

"You find us a ride; I'll come up with the credits."

A dark eyebrow went up in approval at her retort, and he sauntered off to the bar. He returned, after a deep conversation with the bartender, with some sandwiches and drinks.

"We're in luck," he announced as Lilly looked up questioningly at him. "I have a friend who owns a transport, and he just happens to be here."

Lilly was suddenly very curious about what type of friends he had. Phoenix, however, didn't seem to be in much of a hurry. He just sat there calmly eating his sandwich. When he saw that she was done with hers, he casually inclined his head toward the back of the bar, where an occasional cheer could be heard.

The room they entered was filled with the working class of the settlement, who were obviously involved in some heavy drinking and gambling. One area had been cleared, and a tall, lean, young man with a mass of curly brown hair was showing off his expertise with a series of knives. Lilly watched in amazement along with the rest of the crowd as the man hit the center of his target time after time, then with a flick of his wrist summoned the knives back into his hand, where they seemed to melt together into one deadly dagger. He held the weapon over his head for the crowd to see, and they cheered him once again as he collected the credits he had won off the skeptics.

Phoenix watched the proceedings with a look of boredom; obviously he had seen this all before. His handsome face stretched into a grin, however, when the man spotted his dark head towering over the rest and he made his way to where the two of them were standing while accepting congratulatory handshakes along the way.

"Shaun!" he exclaimed as he grabbed the hand of Lilly's companion and pulled him into a bear hug.

I'm one name up on him now, Lilly thought to herself as she watched the reunion.

"I heard about your parents," the man was saying. "I feel . . ." Phoenix stopped him with an upraised hand. The man inclined his head toward a table in the corner where they could talk in private. "I also heard about your sentence," he said when they were seated. "What are you doing here?"

"The princess here promised to help me out of my predicament if I can get her where she needs to go."

"Princess?" The man looked Lilly over with smiling blue eyes and lifted a brow in bemusement. "I'm always ready to help a friend of Shaun's if they have the money." The man leaned back in his chair and crossed his arms. "Where is it you need to go?"

Lilly took a deep breath as she examined the two faces before her. It was time to get to the heart of the matter. "Oasis."

The front legs of the man's chair hit the floor with a solid thump and he leaned forward on the table, serious about the business at hand. "Oasis!" He glanced at Shaun, then back at Lilly. "Aren't you at war right now?"

"Yes, I was on my way to the Senate to stand in for Sovereign Alexander."

"Why would the leader of the garden planet send you to speak for him?" the man asked skeptically.

"I'm his niece." Shaun and his friend exchanged looks, then turned as one to Lilly. She leaned over the table and pulled the sleeve of her jacket back. The white shirt she wore underneath was sleeveless, so the motion revealed her tattoo, the lion. It was a symbol of her bloodline and had been personalized with a lily blossom for her name.

"So you really are a princess," Shaun observed.

"Good guess," she replied as she adjusted her clothing.

"So what were you doing on a primitive cargo transport? Why didn't you just go by hyperdrive?"

"The Senate was on hiatus, so I had time to travel, plus the Ravigans have our hyperports under siege. Krebbs and I were smuggled out on a grain transport. We were hoping to travel in secret."

"I guess your secret got out," Shaun commented dryly.

"Yes, it did." Lilly was not sure if she appreciated his humor. "That's why I need to get back. Someone gave me away. I have to warn my uncle."

"So your uncle would pay well for your safe return." Shaun's friend seemed to be practical if nothing else.

"Get me there safely and you can name your price." Lilly knew when to be direct.

"Just call me Ruben, Your Highness." Ruben grinned widely. "Time is money, so how soon do you want to leave?"

* * *

Ruben's ship was stripped down to the basics, most of it devoted to cargo space, but it did have a few amenities, like a hot shower, which Lilly took advantage of as soon as they were under way.

"So how did you hook up with the princess?" Ruben asked Shaun after he had set the autopilot.

"She saved me from being choked to death by my personal escort."

"Where were they taking you?"

"Rykers."

"Ouch!"

"I haven't decided yet if she did me a favor." Shaun leaned back in the copilot's seat and smiled at the sound of singing coming from the shower. "What is the story with this war?"

"Did you just get out of prison?" Ruben had a knack for being cynical. "This war has been the talk of the universe."

"My parents were hiding from current events, remember? While I am well educated, thanks to my mother, we didn't get a lot of news flashes on Partin Five."

"You weren't on Partin Five that long and you've spent a lot of time traveling around. As a matter of fact, you've done a lot of traveling with me."

"Okay, so I have heard about the war. I just haven't paid attention to the details."

Ruben gave him a look of exasperation but proceeded with the story. "Raviga and Oasis share the same sun. Oasis is the fourth planet, Raviga, the third. The entire planet of Oasis is like a huge garden, enough plant life to feed a solar system. The people there have really taken care of their planet. The wildlife is abundant but controlled, and they never had much industry, so there's been no problem with pollution. The entire planet is mostly made up of farmers, and those who don't want to farm go into the service. Raviga, on the other hand, is a desert. That's why so many of their people go into the Legion, or the Senate guard; there's nothing for them at home. Their forefathers abused the planet and now there is nothing left. The Ravigans have decided that they want Oasis, and what they want, they have a habit of just taking." Ruben loved a good story.

"And since Oasis is inhabited by farmers . . ." Shaun began.

"Don't take those farmers for granted. They can fight, that's why it's been going on so long. But Raviga has more fighters than Oasis to throw into the fray, and the only posture Oasis takes is a defensive one. I guess that's why your princess was going to the Senate."

"And what is the Senate's position on this?"

"The Senators will stay out of it until it makes them look bad. The Senate will step in when the people of the universe start going hungry because the grain shipments aren't coming through. Of course, by then there might not by anyone left on Oasis, and the only problem the Senate will have is making a new deal with Raviga."

"Why doesn't Oasis attack Raviga, instead of just defending itself?"

"Serious lack of leadership."

"What about Lilly's uncle?"

"He was a great leader many years ago, before he lost his family."

"How did he lose his family?" Shaun asked, now caught up in the story.

Ruben was a good storyteller along with being a great smuggler, and he appreciated a captive audience. "Sovereign Alexander is the older of two brothers whose family had ruled Oasis for generations. He was educated at the finest universities and well trained in all the arts. He made a great marriage, albeit a political one, but it also turned out to be a love match. Have you heard of the Witches of Circe?"

"Yes." Shaun almost laughed out loud. He was sure he was keeping company with one at the present time.

"Alexander married one. A very beautiful woman, they say. Her name was Ariel, and she gave birth to a son, Nicholas. The witches have great power, and according to their code, all male offspring must be killed. Ariel rebelled and refused to do it. She and her husband kept the boy under heavy guard to protect him. That's where Alexander's brother Victor came into play."

"He killed the boy?"

"No, he was seduced by another witch. They all have those light-colored eyes, but this one disguised hers somehow. Victor brought her home as his wife. It wasn't too long before she was with child, and then she went after Alexander, Ariel, and the boy. Her plan was to remove them and have Victor take over as Sovereign with their daughter as the heir. Victor found out her plan and died saving Alexander. They never found Ariel or the boy. There's been a rumor floating around for years that they got away and the boy is waiting to come back and reclaim his destiny. Alexander waited until after Victor's baby was born, then put the witch to a horrifying death."

"My uncle was hoping for another boy child." Lilly was done with her shower, dressed again, and tying back her freshly washed hair. "You seem to have studied the history of my planet quite a bit, Ruben."

"You hear a lot of things hanging around warehouses and bars."

"So you were going to the Senate to ask for help?" Shaun asked.

"Something like that." Lilly stood between the two seats to check the nav chart. "Is this our position?" She pointed a finger at the chart.

"Yes, we're about one cycle from Oasis," Ruben replied. Lilly leaned over the console and began punching buttons on the com. "What are you doing?"

"Code, so they'll know it's me."

"How do you know that you won't be given away again?" Shaun asked.

"This code is known only by one other person. And that person I trust with my life."

Shaun and Ruben exchanged looks as she went back toward the living quarters on the ship. "The Sovereign was never the same after his family disappeared, and there's no heir, except for your princess, and she's cursed with her mother's blood." Ruben finished his story in a much quieter tone.

Shaun pondered what he had heard while he watched the stars fly by them at light speed. "I have a feeling I might have been better off in prison." Ruben did not argue with him.

Lilly was stretched out on a narrow bunk when Shaun finished his shower. Ruben was dozing, his feet propped up on the console while the autopilot guided the ship. As he studied her, he scrubbed his hands through his wet hair, setting the dark rich ends up in spikes. She had taken off her boots and jacket and was lying toward the wall with one arm flung over her face as if to shield her eyes. The tattoo on her arm was visible, and he leaned over to study it more closely. She moved her arm down with a soft sigh, barely audible despite his close proximity. Her hair flowed back away from her temple and he remembered the touch of her fingers on his face. *Should I?* Shaun hesitated just for a moment before he tentatively reached out with his own fingers and placed them against the side of her face in the same manner in which she had touched him.

Because of the numerous thoughts flooding his mind, he did not have a chance to be amazed by what was happening to him. He saw images, flashes of faces and places; he was overwhelmed by the feelings flowing from within her mind. His hand moved back and smoothed her hair. "You're carrying a lot of guilt inside you, Lilly. It wasn't your fault." He caught the glimpse of a smile at the corner of her mouth, and then it was gone.

There was only one bunk. Ruben had worked alone since Shaun's troubles had begun. The chair did not look comfortable enough to ease Shaun's weariness, so he stretched out next to Lilly on the bunk, gently easing her over toward the wall. Shaun lay on his back, his arms folded over his chest, and let the soft sound of her breathing lull him to sleep.

Shaun knew it was a memory instead of a dream; he just did not know whom it belonged to. He saw a child, a toddler who'd just learned to walk. There was blood running down the child's back, leaving dark stains on his clothing, and he was crying as he wandered through darkened tunnels where huge machinery roared. He could see the child clearly, because he could see in the dark as well as most people could in the light. The dream troubled him, because he felt sorry for the child and angry because of his predicament, yet he did not know why.

The dream stirred him to awareness; he became conscious of a body pressed up against his, the feel of a soft breast under his hand. He opened his eyes and saw a mass of soft ash-brown hair. He had rolled over in his sleep, his arm coming around Lilly, and she had spooned up against him with her slim arm wrapped around his. His nostrils took in the scent of her and his body responded to the feel of hers. Shaun pulled his hand away, and Lilly murmured a protest. In the next second he rose from the bunk.

It was his absence that awakened her. Lilly had felt his warmth, his protection. Before, Krebbs had always reassured her, but now, she felt an even stronger sense of protection from Shaun. She stretched and opened her eyes. She could see him now, sitting in the cockpit with Ruben, his dark head tilted toward Ruben's lighter one as they conversed. "Shaun Phoenix." She tried the name out in her mind and smiled. He turned his head toward her as she perused him, as if he had actually heard her call his name. She wondered again at his unusual response to her mental abilities. Lilly felt a great need to find out more about him.

Ruben rose with a great deal of yawning and stretching when she joined them in the cockpit, then made his way to the cabin, turning the controls over to Shaun with a sly wink. Lilly slid into the vacant seat and watched the stars slide by at an amazing speed.

"How long did I sleep?"

"Quite a while."

"I guess I was pretty tired, then."

"I imagine casting all those spells would be tiring." Shaun had not meant to be sarcastic, but he was beginning to worry about the effect she was having on his mind and body.

"I am not a witch." She was suddenly annoyed with him. "That is a myth."

"What are you, then?"

"I am a telepath. I can read people's minds and also send messages."

"That must be convenient for you. How did you come by this amazing ability?" he asked sarcastically.

Lilly decided that patience was the best tactic at this point, although she had the urge to send several disturbing images into his brain. "A long time ago, the women of the planet Circe were under the strictest control by their husbands. They were not allowed to appear in public unless they were completely covered from head to toe. They wore transparent veils over their eyes so they could see where they were going, but no other part of them was allowed to be exposed. Their husbands controlled every aspect of their lives. They could not eat or drink unless their husbands allowed it. The daughters were sold in marriage to men they had never seen before. The control became so oppressive that the women were not allowed to speak unless so directed by their husbands. Some men even went so far as to cut out the tongues of their wives.

"As the generations passed, however, something began to happen. At first it was told that the women could communicate with their eyes, and then they began to reach out to one another with their minds. They did so until they were able to control the men by suggestion. Probably it was a latent ability, lying undiscovered until it was needed. The men become complacent because they felt no challenge; the women had found an alternate way to communicate. Eventually the women became politically stronger than the men and took control."

"And they kept control by killing off all the male offspring?"

"That's another myth. Not all women have the mental powers; they appear only in women with pale gray eyes."

"So you kill only the boys who have eyes your color."

"Yes." Lilly hated to admit it, but it was true. She hated that truth. She was ashamed of it. "The women of Circe are afraid of men having the same power they do."

"I guess I never would have made it if I'd been born

to a Circe witch." His light gray eyes turned on her with a sudden intensity. "Would I?"

Lilly found that she was profoundly curious about his origins. "Where do you come from?" she asked since he had brought up the subject.

"I spent the first part of my life on Pristo, deep in the mines."

"Isn't that planet covered with a poisonous gas?"

"Yes, I never saw sunlight until I was almost grown. I guess that's why I can see so well in the dark; my eyes adapted. It took a while for me to get used to the brightness, and I still have to wear shields when the sun is high." Shaun leaned back in the chair, surprised at how much he was revealing about himself. "When we left Pristo, we settled on Partin Five. My parents sent me to the academy, but I never really fit in there, so I left after a few years. I met Ruben soon after, started running supplies with him to the far outposts, and earned enough credits so my parents could live out their lives in peace." Shaun stopped his story abruptly.

"Where are they now?"

"Dead." He leaned forward to check the settings on the autopilot. "The Senate decided it didn't want settlers on Partin Five when they discovered the riches that were beneath its surface. My father didn't feel like moving again." He couldn't believe he was telling her all this.

"So they were killed?" Lilly asked incredulously.

"Something like that." Shaun dismissed her question with a shrug of his shoulders. "So tell me,

Princess, what's it like being able to read people's minds?"

"It's a gift that I use for the good of my people and my planet."

"And you get no personal pleasure out of telling people what to think and do?" What was it about her that made him so suddenly antagonistic? He had spent most of his adult years maintaining a calm and cool facade, but ever since he had met Lilly, his insides were in turmoil and he was having trouble controlling his emotions.

"I don't tell people what to think, and I certainly don't tell them what to do."

Shaun was pleased to see that Lilly seemed to be experiencing the same tumult that he felt inside. "You mean to sit there and tell me that you don't practice a little mind control on whoever happens to be around?" Shaun laughed just to see her reaction. "You've been doing it to me ever since we met."

"I have not!" Lilly became indignant. "I couldn't control your mind even if I wanted to; that's only possible with the weak-willed."

"So you do tell people what to do." He quickly pounced on her statement, strangely excited that he had bested her in the exchange.

"I make suggestions. And that's all I do." Lilly could not imagine why she was feeling the need to defend herself.

"You've been trying to control me since we met." It was the only explanation he could think of for the way he had felt since their paths had crossed.

"I merely offered you an alternative to prison." Their voices were loud enough now to cause a disturbance in the steady flow of Ruben's snoring.

"Some alternative. Either my body is a prisoner, or my brain."

"I can arrange it so you go straight to prison if that is your desire," she ground out.

"That's just like a woman," he spat out in disgust. "What happened to all those promises you made concerning my freedom if I helped you?"

"You did help me, and I'm grateful, but now you're just turning everything around," Lilly cried out in frustration.

"Prove it." Shaun turned his chair around so that he was facing her. He grabbed the arms of her chair and spun her around to him.

"Prove what?" Lilly felt like crying but refused to do so.

"That you're not controlling me. Plant a suggestion in my head, something that I wouldn't do under normal circumstances."

Lilly tried hard to control the trembling of her lower lip as she looked into his dark-lashed, light gray eyes. Just being in the same room with him disrupted her mind. "It doesn't always work that way," she whispered.

"Do it." The words were forceful, his face so close that she could feel the puff of his breath.

Lilly closed her eyes and tried to clear her mind, but it was difficult; it had been difficult to concentrate since she had walked into the cryo bay. *Something he wouldn't normally do*, she thought to herself. She felt his presence; she knew if she opened her eyes she would see his staring back at her. Taking a deep breath, she emptied her mind of the turmoil and reached out with the first thought that came to her.

Shaun's eyebrows flew up in surprise as he felt her mind enter his like a cool breeze. She was sitting before him, her eyes closed, her breathing so slight that he was hardly aware of it. Her forehead was furrowed in concentration, a slight line showing in the space above her nose. He slowly leaned in, tilting his head to the side as their noses touched. Lilly's eyes opened in surprise and she saw herself reflected in the mirrors of his eyes. His lips were a breath away from hers.

"You want me to kiss you?" He said it so softly that she felt the question instead of hearing the words. Her lips trembled in anticipation. "Where did you get that idea?" he asked.

Lilly flung herself back in the chair as shock set in. He had entered her mind and offered that suggestion, his voice had said *"Kiss me"* inside of her head when she had tried to take control of his mind. Her eyes were wide with fear as she looked at him.

"Who are you?"

"I thought I knew until you came along." He was almost snarling at her. "Why don't you tell me?" Lilly shook her head as if to deny everything that had just happened. "I've certainly never been able to do this before I met you, Princess."

"I don't understand," Lilly whispered, more to herself than to the man who was sitting next to her.

"I don't either." He turned back around to the console. "All I do know is that you're the one with the answers, and I'm sticking close to you until I get them."

Lilly's mind began to whirl in confusion. Did she really want him to stay? What would happen if he did? "So this means you're going to remain with me?" She couldn't let him see her confusion.

"As your protector?"

"Yes."

"How many protectors have you had?"

"Just Krebbs." Her voice almost broke; she needed time to get her mind back under control.

Her face looked so sad. She must have been close to the guy, Shaun thought. He felt compassion for her, but he decided not to act on it. Things were confusing enough as it was without that complication. "I'll take the position, for now. But tell me, Princess, are you sure that I'm qualified?"

"I'm sure." She knew he would protect her from the Ravigans, but who would protect her from him? "There's one thing you should know. When we get to Oasis, there will be questions."

"About my past?"

"Yes, they'll want to know they can trust you."

Shaun gave her a cocky grin. "How can you be sure you can trust me?"

Lilly tapped a slim finger against her forehead. "I asked, remember?"

She had asked, back in the swamp under the tree. He remembered the moment and the images that had come unbidden to his mind. *What's done is done*, he reminded himself, and wondered how long it would be before the bad memories would fade away and the good ones would come back.

Chapter Four

An alarm sounded on the console, a reminder that they were approaching the hyperport. Shaun turned off the beacon as Ruben, yawning, came into the cockpit. Lilly vacated her seat and Ruben joined Shaun in making sure of the coordinates. The ship suddenly lurched a bit as it dropped out of light speed. A moment later, when they burst through the port, lights and alarms went off.

"It's a destroyer!" Ruben identified the ship that was waiting at the gateway. "Ravigan."

"You still have the smuggler's box?" Shaun asked as he jumped out of his seat.

"Like I always say, if it works, don't mess with it," Ruben called after him as he pulled Lilly from the cockpit.

"Where are we going?" Lilly asked as they ran through the cabin and out into the hold of the ship.

"Ruben has been known to transport some things

that are slightly, let's say, illegal." Shaun was pulling her along toward the back of the hold. They lost their footing and fell to the metal floor when a tractor beam captured the ship, but he hastily pulled her up and dragged her along. "But he does have a nice little hiding place for things that he doesn't want found." Shaun found what he was looking for and popped the floor grid from its place. He pointed, and Lilly jumped down into a hole barely tall enough for her to sit up in. Shaun came down behind her and pulled the grid over their heads just as they heard the echoing sound of the destroyer surrounding them. "It's pulled us into the hold." Shaun wrapped his arms around her and guided her down so they were facing each other, lying side by side in the small space.

"Won't they find us with heat sensors?" Lilly whispered.

"We're over the reactor; it will take hours for it to cool down to body temperature." *Or maybe it won't*, he observed quietly as Lilly squirmed around trying to find a comfortable position.

"This is not much bigger than a coffin," Lilly whispered. The light was dim, but there was enough for her to make out the walls surrounding them. Shaun's knees were slightly bent; he was too tall to stretch out, which put her own legs at a strange angle.

"He didn't have us in mind when he made it."

Lilly nodded in agreement. One arm was in an awkward position beneath her, so she shifted a bit, moving it up, but then the only place to put it was around his neck. Her legs were cramped, so she lifted the top one and, since she could not find a better place for it, placed it on top of his, which let his knees slide between hers. The intimacy of their position hit her at the same time they felt the gentle whoosh of the outside hatch opening.

"Don't worry; he'll die before he gives us away." Shaun was inside her mind, talking to her.

"I'm not worth Ruben losing his life," she responded.

"He'll talk his way out of it," Shaun reassured her.

Her light gray eyes looked into his. There was no doubt in them, only trust, and even as his head screamed for him to stop, he pulled her closer and kissed her.

The first touch of his lips went through her like a knife. She felt it deep inside of her, felt the impact of his lips like a blow. She wrapped her fingers around the back of his neck, wound them in the curls of rich dark hair and felt the ridges that marred his skin. His knee slid up between her legs and his hands moved against her back, pressing her body against his. The ring of footsteps on the floor grids above echoed in their ears, and Shaun growled deep in his throat. The thought of capture made him more desperate; he couldn't give her up now that he had just found her. He would die before he let them take her, and his desperation poured out into the kiss. His mouth plundered hers, daring anyone else to claim her. Lilly couldn't breathe, but she also couldn't let go, so she hung on for dear life while the men walked above and Ruben talked about his rights according to Senate Law to transport supplies for the outlying mines. The footsteps faded. Lilly pulled her head back and sucked in air, filling her lungs again. Her mind was whirling, trying to find some order, and she felt his doing the same. She focused on his eyes, and he bent his head until their foreheads were touching.

"You're stuck with me now," he whispered.

"I know."

"And it frightens you?"

She was shaking. "Yes. When we get to Oasis, this will make it . . ."

"Complicated?" He was grinning at her, his teeth flashing white in the dim light.

"Dangerous."

"More dangerous than having every Legionnaire in the galaxy hunting me down?"

Lilly tried to pull away, but his arms were still holding her close. "Don't make light of it, Shaun. You can't do this on Oasis; it's forbidden."

"It's forbidden to kiss a beautiful woman?"

"It's forbidden for a protector to engage in a physical relationship with the one he has sworn to protect."

"Is that straight from the protector rule book?" He couldn't resist teasing her while she was being so serious. He brought his lips down on hers again. "Am I or am I not supposed to obey your commands?" he murmured against her mouth.

"Yes."

"So if you command me to kiss you, I would just be doing what you commanded." His lips closed over hers again.

"I would never tell you do to that."

Shaun moved his head back to get a look at her face. "Really?" His eyes glowed silver in the dim light.

"I think you would." He captured her mouth again. "Tell me to stop, Lilly." The engines beneath them fired and they felt the vibration of the ship as it lifted from the hold of the destroyer.

"We're moving." Lilly managed to tear herself away from his mouth.

"We'll stay here until we're safely away." Shaun continued his assault on her senses. Her mind and body were in a frenzy. She had never been kissed like this, never. Her duty, her honor, had never permitted it. Her purpose was to serve her father's people, to aid her uncle, to somehow make up for the terrible things her mother had done. Her entire life had been molded to that purpose; there was no place in it for this whirlwind of emotion. She knew that someday she would marry, when the time was right, but it would be a strictly political alliance. She hoped she would be happy when the time came, knowing that she had done the best she could for Oasis. This could not go on, this rush of heat that consumed her body. Yet she was powerless against it. For the first time in her life, her body was controlling her actions instead of her mind. Footsteps rang above them; they were safely away from the Ravigan destroyer and Ruben was coming to set them free.

Shaun popped the grid before Ruben had a chance to reach for it, taking his frustration at the interruption out on the covering. Ruben was startled by the impact of the grid, then saw the look on his friend's face and grinned. "Apparently you weren't bored during your wait."

Shaun shot him a quelling look and lifted Lilly up

to the floor of the hold. She stood there for a moment, blinking like an owl against the bright light, then had the presence of mind to smooth her clothing.

"Any problems?" Shaun's snarl was an indication of his mood.

"No. They're looking for her, but I don't think they have a clue as to what to do with her when they find her."

"Then we'd better get her home."

Lilly was already making her way to the cockpit, anxious to get a glimpse of her home planet. The console was flashing with a response to her earlier code, and she punched in the reply as Shaun and Ruben joined her.

"Welcome, visitor. Are you a trader?" a familiar voice asked her over the console.

"No, I'm a sailor who's been lost at sea," she replied. Shaun and Ruben exchanged looks.

"Lilly," the voice replied. "We've been worried."

"I'm home now, Michael, with the help of some new friends."

"I'll be waiting for you." The voice was as cool as ice as it signed off.

"Follow those coordinates," she instructed as they slid into the chairs. Shaun's mouth was set in a grim line as he helped Ruben with the prelanding ritual. His body was still aching from the heat that had started inside while he was kissing Lilly. As far as he could see, there would be no immediate relief. She was standing between them, looking very calm, but he felt her eyes on him and wondered if she was feeling the same way.

Lilly felt his mind try to reach out to hers, but she had thrown up a wall against him by falling back on a litany from her schooling. She repeated it over and over, partly to cool the fires he had started, but mostly to get herself back under control.

They soon came out of the darkness of space and into the clear blue skies of Oasis. Shaun found a set of eye shields; the air was so clean that it made the color more intense, and his eyes were still not accustomed to the brightness. They were soon flying over fields that were abundant with crops. The landscape was a myriad of bright color as the greens and golds of grains contrasted sharply with the pinks, purples, and reds of fields of flowers. In the distance glittered what looked like a huge diamond. It turned out to be a city of pure white granite that rose up from the landscape as if it had been carved from a mountain. It was surrounded by lush gardens full of flowers of every possible color, which stood out in sharp contrast against the pure whiteness of the walls of the city.

"We use every part of our planet; nothing goes to waste," Lilly said, proud of her homeland.

"It is impressive," Shaun agreed. Oasis was breathtakingly beautiful. He had never seen anything like it in all his travels.

Lilly pointed out the landing port to Ruben, who gracefully maneuvered the ship into position. "I'll have your hold filled with whatever you want for trade." Lilly's eyes remained on the port they were entering as she spoke. "My uncle will reward you, and then you can be on your way, both of you." She turned to make her way toward the hatch.

"Wait just a minute there, Princess!" Shaun was out of his seat in a flash, quickly catching up to Lilly. His hand on her shoulder stopped her advance and turned her to him. "You're not getting rid of me that easily."

"I'm safe now. You did your part, so there is no reason for you to stay."

"And there's no place for me to go. Remember, I'm a wanted man."

"I can arrange for you to have a new identity."

"You offered me a job."

"Yes, but under the circumstances, I don't think you should take it."

Shaun placed his arms on either side of her, leaning against the hull, trapping her in between. "You've changed your mind?"

"Yes."

"So you are not to be trusted?"

"What? Yes, I can be trusted."

"Trusted until you change your mind?" Shaun ran a finger down her cheek. "When it suited you, you offered me a job. Now that you're back home and surrounded by your royal subjects, the job offer is gone. Seems to me like you were just using me, Princess."

"No, I wasn't." Lilly was aware of how he was twisting the situation, but at the moment all she could think about was the feel of his hand on her face. "I don't use people." She said it softly so he had to lean in to hear her. "I just don't want you to get hurt."

"Hurt by you?" His mouth was next to her ear, his breath softly stirring her hair.

"By those who want to protect me." She turned her

face away from his mouth. The sounds of the docking filled the air around them. "They'll never allow it."

"Never allow what?"

No matter which way she turned, she couldn't escape his words, so she looked directly at him, trying to see what his eyes held behind the shields. "They will never allow us, you and me. We can't be together."

"Do you want us to be together?" An image filled her mind: two bodies, skin touching, pressed close together, his face hovering over hers, their foreheads touching as a whirlwind carried them away into the heavens . . . The whoosh of the hatch opening drove the image from her mind, and Shaun took a step away from her. *"It's your decision, Lilly, not theirs."* She heard his voice in her head as she turned to Michael, who was plowing his way onto the ship.

Lilly was soon crushed against a wide chest, folded into the arms of the handsome soldier who was her uncle's right hand and the closest thing to a father she had ever known.

"We thought we had lost you." Michael's deep voice almost broke on the words, and then he realized they were not alone and quickly drew himself up into a commanding pose.

"You would have, if not for this man." Lilly quickly explained, "Krebbs was killed in the attack, and Phoenix saved me." Ruben was coming toward them. "And Ruben helped us escape from Cartha, where we had crashed."

Michael extended a hand to both men. "Whatever you want is yours. We can't thank you enough."

Ruben began calculating in his head the riches he could expect. Shaun, meanwhile, looked at Lilly expectantly.

"Michael," she began, her mind whirling as the words came without thought. "I have taken Phoenix as my protector." She hadn't meant to say that.

Michael arched a dark eyebrow in surprise. "Your uncle is waiting; he has a lot of questions for you." Lilly fell into step beside him, Shaun taking his place behind her as if it were the most natural thing in the world, with Ruben following along.

The air around them actually seemed to sparkle as they came out of the ship. Ruben let out a low whistle as he saw that the granite walls seemed to be encrusted with precious stones. Several soldiers stood at attention as they passed by, each one giving a slight bow as Lilly passed them with a genuine smile, her love for her people evident for all to see. She was very conscious of Shaun behind her, his usual casual stance replaced by an erect bearing. He had been to the academy, she remembered him telling her; she just hoped he would know how to conduct himself when they reached her uncle.

"Afraid I'll embarrass you?" She heard him in her mind, and fought back the laughter that threatened to overcome her. What was it about him that made her forget everything she had ever learned about protocol and control? Michael caught the tiny smile on her mouth and frowned. They made their way through several passageways, some of them open to the city beyond, where the view was of lush gardens and clean streets. They soon came into what appeared to be the

center of the city. The corridors opened up into a central courtyard with a huge fountain surrounded by flowers. They went across and entered beneath an ornately carved arch, with the words "Strength, Honor, Obedience, Unity and Nobility" scrolled around the entrance, the first letter of each word larger than the rest. Lilly recited the words to herself as she walked through. They were the first words she had learned to read as a small child. Michael had taught her the letters, holding her up on his shoulders so she could trace them with her small hand. It was the code they lived by, foremost in their thoughts and in everything they did. There was no room for anything else.

She's been brainwashed, Shaun thought as they walked through the arch. The words had not escaped his notice; you would have to be blind not to see them. He felt as if he were going blind, even with his shields; the brilliance of the city was almost too much for his eyes. He felt better when they walked beneath the arch. He hoped that wherever they were going, the windows would be covered.

They were soon at the entrance to a large room. Lilly continued in as Michael blocked the entrance with his body, stopping Shaun and Ruben from following. Michael kept his eyes on Shaun, his arms folded across his chest, almost daring Shaun to make a move on him. Shaun felt the benefit of his shields; they allowed him to study Michael as he moved his own body into an at-ease position. Ruben took advantage of the rest to recalculate his coming riches in his head.

Shaun decided to test his newfound powers of the

mind. He reached out to probe Michael's thought, and was met with a fierce need to protect Lilly. *"I feel the same."* He sent out the thought and saw Michael's eyes narrow in response. The older man's military training was stronger than the stray thought, however, and his cautious stance remained unaltered.

Alexander was reading several papers when Lilly came into his chambers. He opened his arms to welcome her, but as usual, something was missing from the greeting he gave her. There was no warmth such as she had felt when Michael swept her into his arms. Lilly wished again, as she had all her life, that she had not been cursed with her mother's looks, that there was something of her father in her, that every time Alexander looked at her, he would not see the woman who had destroyed his family. The tender smile that was present beneath his graying beard did not quite reach his sad brown eyes as he kissed her forehead. "I am glad you are safe, niece. We were afraid we had lost you forever."

"You would have, Uncle, if not for Phoenix."

"Phoenix?"

"He was a passenger on the ship. When Krebbs was killed, he helped me. He saved my life several times over."

"Then his reward will be great," he said indulgently, making her feel like a child.

"He has not asked for a reward," Lilly replied. "I've asked him to be my protector, since Krebbs is now gone." She was not usually so direct.

Alexander was surprised by her request, but hid his

opposition to it, a talent that served him well as the leader of their planet. "Michael will have to approve his appointment. We shall have to make sure he is suitable."

"He suits me, and that is all that matters." Why was she suddenly so assertive? she wondered. Alexander patted her hand as if to placate her, so Lilly decided not to push any further. "How goes the war?" she asked. She could see her uncle was weary and had noticed the alert status of their guard.

"Not well." Alexander pinched the bridge of his nose between two fingers. "Raviga has stepped up the attack on our outgoing ships. The next move may be an attack on the planet itself. If it happens before the harvest, it will be devastating."

"Surely they will wait. They're starving. They don't want to destroy the very thing they're after."

"That logic did not stop them from destroying their own planet, now did it?" Alexander shuffled the papers at his desk. "We must get you to the Senate. You are the only one who can go. If I leave, the people will see it as an act of cowardice. I must remain here."

"Someone betrayed us, Uncle. Someone here does not want me to reach the Senate."

"Don't be ridiculous, child. It was a coincidence, nothing more."

Lilly knew better than to argue with him. "I'll go, Uncle. As soon as you bid me, I will go."

"There is time—for the moment, anyway. Now, let me meet the man you say saved your life."

His words rang in her ears as Michael entered, followed by Shaun and Ruben. *You say saved your life.*

Her mother's treachery would always be between them. Someday she would make up for it, she promised herself again. She felt Shaun's eyes on her from behind his shields, and she flashed him a quick smile that Michael noticed immediately.

Alexander greeted the two men with warm smiles and generous overtures, and several questions about what exactly had happened. Shaun was direct and concise in his answers, his only omission being the circumstances that had put him on the ship with Lilly in the first place. Then Michael started in on him, grilling him about his past, not able to conceal his surprise when Shaun informed him that his father had been an officer of the Senate Court and his mother a teacher, both of them dead now. He told about his years at the Academy, where he had been first in his class. He wouldn't lie about that; it could easily be checked out. Lilly arched a delicate eyebrow in surprise at that, but as he had told her earlier, he had left because he didn't fit in, not because he flunked out. They did not ask him if he had a criminal record, if he had ever been charged and found guilty of murder, and he did not volunteer the information.

That went well. Shaun allowed himself a moment of dry humor after the interrogation as they made their way through the corridors. Lilly was gone, dismissed from the interview after her uncle had made assurances that he would reward them well for saving her life. Ruben was on his way to guest quarters, where he would enjoy the hospitality of the court of Alexander. Shaun had been turned over to Michael, who was now taking him to be outfitted in garments befitting his role as Lilly's protector. Shaun knew that it had been too easy so far. The set of Michael's jaw was proof enough of that. He would be tested—and tested hard—until he passed or was dead, he was sure of it. *You should have taken the reward and left this planet.* The thought ran through his head again and was gone, driven away by the strange feelings that had overcome him since he'd first laid eyes on Lilly.

Chapter Five

Michael could not determine what it was about Phoenix that disturbed him so. On the surface, he seemed more than qualified for the role of Lilly's protector. He could not deny that the man was strong enough; that was evident to all who happened to glance his way. He also comported himself quite well, a result of his years at the Academy, no doubt. As for the rest, Michael would have to see for himself his weapons skills and what type of pilot he was. The eye shields bothered him also. Were they just vanity, or did the shields serve a purpose? The man was an enigma, and Lilly's determination to have him by her side even more perplexing. It would cause problems all around if there was something going on between them. It would be better to stop it now.

Michael felt a pang of regret as his mind began to formulate a plan. What if she did have feelings for this man? It was only natural for her to feel gratitude, and from what she'd told them of their time on Cartha, he had risked his life to save hers. She would just have to understand. She was born to a purpose. Her sense of honor would conquer any rebelliousness of her heart. He would talk to her. After all, hadn't he put duty ahead of everything else for all these years? He would convince the man to leave, and if he couldn't be convinced, he would be forced.

Lilly was frantic as soon as she reached her quarters. Somehow Michael had maneuvered her out of the picture and Shaun was now at his mercy. She knew Michael was trying to protect her, but she was a grown woman not lacking in intelligence and able to make her own choices. They had sent her to her quarters, supposedly to prepare for dinner to celebrate the men who had returned her safely home. Her attendants had greeted her, exclaiming their happiness at her arrival, but she had hastily dismissed them after they had prepared a bath for her. Her mind was overcome with worry about Shaun.

Lilly paced through the luxurious rooms, even going to the outer chamber, where her attendants were anxiously awaiting her slightest whim. She ignored them and stopped at the doorway of the room that had housed Krebbs. His belongings were gone already, probably dispersed to his friends, as he was without family. *This will be Shaun's room now*, she thought to herself, and then imagined the look on his face when he saw the door that would separate them. *There cannot be anything more between us*, she told herself again as she imagined Michael's response to Shaun's lecherous gaze.

She went back into her rooms, locking the door behind her before making her way to her bathing chamber. She stripped off her clothes and sank into the huge tub that was her one self-indulgent luxury. She slid under the water, staying submerged until she was desperate for breath. Then she laid her head back against the edge and cleared her mind, reaching out with her thoughts for Shaun.

"So you miss me." He felt her slide into his mind.

"Don't flatter yourself," she replied.

"You miss me." She saw with his eyes. He was being fitted for a uniform, the standard olive-green jacket and pants along with a black sleeveless shirt that seemed to enhance the width of his chest. *"How do I look?"* he asked her. He was admiring his reflection in a mirror; she could see Michael's disapproving stare reflected in the glass. Her head began to throb; he was too far away to maintain the connection. He felt her waver, and then she was gone. *I'm going to have to try that sometime*, he said to himself as he turned back to Michael.

"Do you ever take those off?" Michael waved a hand toward the eye shields.

"When it suits me," Shaun replied. He could take them off now—the light inside the manor would not bother him—but he did not want anyone here to see the color of his eyes. "I spent the first part of my life underground," he explained, not wanting Michael to think he was being difficult. "And your planet is pretty bright."

"What were you doing underground?" Michael asked. "You said your father was a Senate Officer."

"He was. He left the service before I was born. They did not look kindly on his marriage."

"Your mother was a teacher, you said?" It began to make sense to Michael. "She was in the service of the Prefect's family? The Senate frowns upon those types of relationships, I have heard."

"They chose to be together, so they had to leave. It was either that or suffer the consequences. They spent the rest of their lives in hiding."

Something clicked in Michael's mind.

"Your father was Ryan Phoenix?"

"Yes."

"He was a great soldier; we studied him when I was at the Academy."

"He was almost past his prime when I was born, but he taught me well." Shaun meant it as a warning, but the memories of the years when his father had trained him in the art of combat came unbidden to his mind. He had been a great warrior; he'd deserved a better death than the one that had been dealt him.

"It was a great loss to the Senate when he left."

"He had no choice. It was the only way they could be together." Shaun couldn't resist adding, "I know I wouldn't be here now if he had stayed where he was."

Michael caught the jab, was actually amused by the younger man's sense of irony. It was almost a shame that he would have to leave. He might actually grow to like Phoenix if it weren't for Lilly. He would definitely like to delve further into the story of his father. The thought of someone sacrificing his honor and duty for love fascinated him.

* * *

Lilly noticed as she made her entrance into the grand banquet hall that her uncle had not spared any expense. Oasis might be under threat of attack, but the Sovereign would not show fear. The music was gay, the conversation was animated, and the food was abundant. Lilly's stomach growled when she saw the spread before them. It had been a while since she had sat down to a decent meal, and she suddenly felt most anxious to start.

"You are beautiful." It was Shaun, his voice in her mind. Her eyes found him next to Ruben, who had managed to improve his own wardrobe since coming to Oasis.

Shaun had seen her the moment she came in. His mind had been searching for her, so he was ready for her entrance, or so he'd thought. He had found her attractive before, even when she had been wringing wet with swamp water, but now he felt the impact of her natural beauty. The deep amethyst of her dress gave her eyes an almost lavender hue. Her hair had been artfully arranged—one of the benefits of being a princess, he supposed—the mass of it twisted on top of her head, so that the length of her graceful neck beckoned for a kiss.

"You are headed straight for disaster," Ruben managed to say around his drink as they watched Lilly take the extended arm of her uncle. "Why don't you come with me and help me spend my new fortune?"

"I have my eyes on a better reward." Alexander was escorting Lilly around to the assembled guests, who all were exclaiming over her near misfortune.

"Is it worth getting yourself killed over, or worse?"

Shaun turned his shielded eyes onto his friend. "That's what I mean to find out."

Ruben shook his head in mock disgust as a well-endowed lady of the court began to make her way toward the two. "Cast your eyes elsewhere, my friend. I see a reward coming this way that probably could be yours with little effort."

Several women of the court had noticed the newcomers' presence in the room and had begun to center their attention on Shaun and Ruben. The Ravigan blockade had made it difficult for visitors to come to Oasis, and the presence of new faces, especially handsome faces, lent a certain excitement to the proceedings. The pair was soon the center of attention, with some of the women reaching out to touch Shaun's arm as they questioned him about his heroics with Lilly. Somehow he managed to gracefully retreat from each question, turning it all about to make Ruben into the savior, downplaying the incident in the swamp until it seemed like a walk through a puddle. Ruben quickly took over the story, embellishing his part to include a very close escape from several gunships. Some of the women became caught up in Ruben's tale, but some also made it clear they were available to Shaun, who engaged in a bit of mild flirting just to see Lilly's reaction.

"Quite an impressive display." Without the benefit of being in his mind, Lilly could see the cleavage that was so amply displayed under his nose. She had noticed it from across the room. The high-pitched laughter of the woman grated on her already frayed nerves.

"Oasis is a bountiful planet," Shaun replied, and

she could see his smug grin from across the room; she knew the eyes were laughing behind the shields. *"But I prefer a slimmer form."* His voice in her head became softer, almost caressing, almost as if his hands were touching her skin. *"Besides, I don't think she would have fit in Ruben's hiding place."*

The corners of her mouth lifted as she suppressed the laughter that threatened to spring forth. Shaun had planted an image in her mind, one of the lady's generous curves being squashed into the narrow confines of the smuggler's box. Michael noticed the play on her face; saw the merriment in her eyes as she looked past him at Phoenix.

"Damn those shields," Michael muttered to himself. He knew what the man was thinking, however, without seeing his eyes. Phoenix would have to leave before Lilly became too involved with him.

Dinner was announced and the assorted nobles and guests made their way to their seats. Alexander took his place at the head of the table, with Lilly on his left and Michael on his right. Shaun was seated next to Michael and Ruben next to Lilly, as they were the guests of honor. The courses were laid out before them, and Shaun was amazed by the abundance before him.

"I don't think I have ever tasted food like this before," he commented politely to Alexander.

"It's the freshness you taste. Since you grew up in the mining camps, most of your food was processed before it was shipped to you," Alexander explained.

Shaun nodded.

"It amazes me that your father was able to go to a

planet like Pristo," Michael commented. "Life in the employ of the Senate, especially for one of his stature, was very good."

"I'm sure it was extremely difficult for both of them." Shaun did not particularly want to talk about his parents or the hardships they'd faced on the mining planet, but he also did not want to offend.

"Wasn't there a bounty put on him after he left?" One of the guests had joined in the conversation. "If I recall, the Senate considered him a deserter."

"Yes." It was a tactless question, but Shaun felt obliged to answer it. "My father felt that the atmosphere of Pristo would discourage those who were out for the money. He relied on his skill to take care of the rest."

"Apparently so," Alexander chimed in. "You say he died recently?"

"Yes. Recently." Shaun's face did not reveal the rage and grief that surfaced every time he remembered the senseless murder of his parents.

Lilly, however, could feel the suppressed emotion boiling beneath the smooth exterior he presented to the group. It was time to change the subject.

"Uncle, what happened with the disease on the silkworms?"

"We were able to defeat it, luckily."

"Everything on Oasis is perfectly balanced," Lilly explained to Shaun and Ruben. "But occasionally a disease is carried in—"

"And we quickly eradicate it," Michael interrupted, his meaning clear as he turned his eyes on Shaun.

"Oasis is a planet of complete harmony. We do not take kindly to those who would disrupt it."

Shaun did not miss his meaning and decided to return the challenge. "Then why do you continue to let Raviga attack your vessels?"

"I am an old man," Alexander said with a wry smile. "I prefer to settle this matter through diplomacy rather than by battle. Raviga has ten times our population, and its government is more than willing to sacrifice people to acquire our lush planet. It would be the answer to all their problems."

"Oasis has not suffered greatly due to the war; our lives have continued as before," Michael chimed in. "The only ones who are suffering are the people who rely on our shipments to feed themselves."

"Which makes it a problem for the Senate?" Shaun concluded.

"Exactly." Alexander smiled in approval. "This is why Lilly needs to go plead our case. With her special abilities, she is the perfect ambassador."

"Because she will know what they are thinking." Shaun's eyes behind his shields rested on Lilly, who was modestly looking down at her plate. *"He's using you."* His mind entered hers.

"No, he's my uncle. He loves me," she responded. She had quickly grown accustomed to hearing his voice inside her head.

"It must have been interesting when she was growing up, knowing she could read your mind," Shaun commented to Alexander.

"I have never used my ability on my uncle," Lilly said.

Alexander nodded in agreement and smiled benevolently.

"Or Michael." Lilly's light gray eyes looked on the soldier with love and respect.

"We felt that her young mind would be too fragile to absorb the responsibilities of government. So we asked her not to venture there," Alexander explained.

"They commanded, and you obeyed without question," his mind said as he voiced the question. "Weren't you ever tempted?"

"We believe there is strength in honor," Michael explained for Lilly. "Our bond is not easily broken."

"Did you not see the words carved in the doorway as you entered?" Alexander asked. "It is the code we live by. Strength, Honor, Obedience, Unity, Nobility. It helps us to remember why we are here."

Michael and Lilly both nodded at the Sovereign's words, and murmurs of agreement were made down the table.

"It's a fine sentiment," Shaun agreed. "However, it only works when you are dealing with honorable people." His gaze settled on Michael. "There are some who feel that having greater strength is enough."

"That is why we are taking our case to the Senate," Alexander patiently explained. "Raviga must not think that it can just come and take over Oasis."

"But isn't that why most wars start?" Shaun was becoming frustrated with Alexander's noble approach. "And the victor is usually the strongest party."

"We will fight if we must." Michael came to his Sovereign's defense.

"But only if we must," Lilly added. "The Senate will do what's right for us."

"Are you willing to pay the price for their help?" Shaun asked Alexander. It was well known in the galaxy that the Senate was corrupt, often demanding bribes to ensure decisions favorable to a specific planet.

"We are all willing to do what is honorable to save our planet and our way of life." Alexander gave Lilly a reassuring smile that did not reach his eyes. Something about the way he looked at her disturbed Shaun, or perhaps it was the way she seemed to willingly submit to his word. He tried to put himself inside Alexander's head, but found the way blocked.

If he was married to a witch, perhaps she taught him how to block out other people's thoughts, he mused to himself.

Across the table, Lilly's light gray eyes had widened. She had felt his attempt to enter Alexander's mind and was shocked that he had the audacity to try it.

"It's not me he's keeping out, you know," he responded logically. *"Alexander has no reason to think that I could read his mind."*

"I trust him completely," she answered.

"Maybe you shouldn't," his voice said in her mind.

Lilly felt anger at his impudence welling up inside. How dare he come in here and start judging her life and her family? He was an outsider; he had no right. She felt like slapping him. The palm of her hand actually itched with the desire to knock the thought out of his head so the doubt would be out of hers. She quickly summoned up an image of torture to plant in his thoughts; he didn't know what he was playing with, how powerful her mind could be and the imaginary pain that she could place in his mind. She could give him pain that would feel so very real, he would drop in agony before her, begging for his life.

She stopped herself before she went any further. The question of how he came by his powers brought her to an abrupt halt. He was an enigma, and though she had roamed freely inside his mind, she really did not know much about him except for the way he made her feel. His eyes behind the shields were hidden from her, but she knew they were on her, questioning her, trying to force her to question herself and her very existence.

Not a word had been spoken between them, but Michael felt the tension. It was a tangible thing between them, crossing the table, linking the two of them so that he felt he could reach out and touch it. *Damn those shields*, he thought again. Alexander gave him a slight nod; it was time to take care of business.

Alexander reached over and placed his hand on Lilly's. "Come with me, dear one. We need to discuss your meeting with the Senate." Lilly gave him a glorious smile; then they rose as one, with the other guests also rising out of respect. There was silence as they made their exit. Shaun's eyes behind his shields followed the graceful lines of Lilly's back as she left the hall on Alexander's arm. The polite dinner conversation resumed when they were gone, and Shaun turned to find Michael's steely eyes boring into him and a wide grin on his face.

"Uh-oh," Ruben commented. "You're in big trouble now."

"Why don't you come with me, Phoenix?" Michael stood abruptly, ignoring Ruben's comment. He was actually looking forward to this, he realized, but what he was hoping for was not necessarily what he and Alexander had discussed. "I'll show you the barracks." His grinning face turned serious. "And introduce you to some of our best guards."

Shaun turned his own dazzling smile onto Michael. "You are too kind." He inclined his head toward the door, indicating he was ready to follow.

"I wouldn't mind seeing that myself," said Ruben, inviting himself along.

Chapter Six

The corridors rang with the sounds of their boots as Michael set a quick pace toward the outer circle of halls, which housed the barracks. Shaun didn't have to read the mind of the man who walked beside him. The set of his jaw and the look in his eyes were enough to let him know what was in store. A step behind him, Ruben was rapidly making plans to get his friend out safely without jeopardizing the generous rewards that had been loaded into the holds of his ship. *Good luck*, Shaun thought to himself as he caught the quick succession of ideas that were filling Ruben's head. From behind them came the hushed whispers of uniformed men who had seen the procession and were following at a discreet distance. Shaun wondered briefly about Lilly, but he found that he was too anxious about what was going on around him to concentrate on finding her with his mind. They dropped down a level without a word spoken, then turned into a smaller hallway that led to a wide set of doors.

The doors flew open when they approached, almost as if in anticipation of what was to come. Several men were inside, some working on the various machines that were there to enhance their strength and performance, and some watching two men who were engaged in a form of hand-to-hand combat.

Shaun felt himself relax as he watched the two men exchange a series of jabs and kicks. Ruben stood beside him, grinning. They had been in bar fights that made this seem like the play of young children. Surely this could not be the test that Michael had prepared for him. Around the circle of observers, wages were being exchanged as first one then the other combatant seemed to gain the upper hand. Ruben was engrossed by the fight, but Shaun felt uneasy, as if he was being watched. Michael had moved away from him in the crowd, making his way around the circle of men until he was opposite where Shaun and Ruben were standing. The fight was moving to a close, the combatants now taking in great gulps of air as they came to a draw. Shaun felt the muscles in the back of his neck tighten, and then he was shoved into the circle.

He turned with his fists raised and found himself looking directly at a barrel-like chest. He tilted his head up to find an evil grin aimed at him as the giant raised his own fists. He heard Ruben's low whistle and then a sarcastic remark about growing them big on the farm. The two began to circle each other, and Shaun caught Michael's self-satisfied smile from the corner of his eye.

"Why don't you take off those shields?" the giant rumbled. "Or maybe I should take them off for you."

"You have got to be kidding," Shaun couldn't help saying as the crowd of men widened the circle to give them more room. The giant smiled and took a swing.

Lilly could not remember Alexander ever doting on her the way he had tonight, when he had taken her hand after dinner and led her away to discuss their plea to the Senate. It wasn't until he had led her to her rooms and locked her in that she realized it had all been a trick to get her away from Shaun. The code to her room had been changed, none of the override codes were working and her servants were all conveniently missing. She was a victim of Michael and Alexander's plan to eliminate Shaun. They had taken advantage of her promise to stay out of their minds and used it against her. She knew deep in her heart that they were acting out of love for her, but she was still angry, her frustration at being trapped growing as she paced her rooms. She passed a mirror in her circuit and stopped to stare at her reflection, hoping that she could get her emotions under control.

She was surprised at what she saw in the mirror. She had never really thought of herself as a woman before, but her upswept hair and the angry spark in her light gray eyes gave her pause. Her cheekbones were flushed, and she touched them with hands that were trembling. Her entire life had been given in service to her people and her planet, but Shaun had seen something more in her. He wanted her for herself. He had no ulterior motive. She considered her reflection in the mirror and her eyes took on a determined look. Lilly reached out with her mind to Shaun, traveling the corridors of the palace as she searched for his presence.

Shaun felt her enter his mind, and the impact of it was as hard as the blow he had just received to the jaw. He stumbled back against one of the crowd and was shoved forward into the circle. The giant was just standing there, grinning sadistically, and Shaun wondered how many more blows he could take before he suffered a serious injury. His head was ringing and he knew that the man was just toying with him. He shook his head to drive Lilly away—it was all he could manage at the time—but she stayed, her mind questioning. He didn't see the next blow coming; he was still concentrating on Lilly. *"Are you trying to get me killed?"* he demanded, spitting blood from the inside of his cheek. The giant picked him up and threw him across the circle, where Ruben was waiting to catch him before he hit the ground.

"How about a little help?" he asked his friend as he turned back to the fight.

"I'm the brains, you're the brawn, remember." Ruben shoved him back into the circle. "Besides, you got him right where you want him."

Lilly was gone, but she had left an idea behind and Shaun jumped on it. He wearily raised his fists in invitation and jumped into the giant's mind. *"Behind you,"* he suggested. *"Watch out, he has a weapon."* He planted the thought and saw the eyes above him cloud in doubt. The giant turned his head, and Shaun struck. *"There's another one,"* he suggested, and the giant put up his hands as if to ward off a blow to his head. Shaun began to pound his stomach. The giant shoved him away, and Shaun came back with a kick at his knee, which dropped him. The rest of it was fairly simple: A few more blows to the head and he was down, hitting the floor like a felled tree. The crowd was silent in amazement, then let out a cheer, some of the men pounding Shaun on the back in their enthusiasm.

"How did you do that?" Ruben asked, pulling him from the mob.

"I cheated," Shaun replied as his breathing returned to normal. Across the room he saw Michael, who was obviously surprised by what he had seen. He gave Shaun an approving look and ducked out a door. "I'll catch up with you later." Shaun left by the other door.

Lilly had been in a panic since she'd left Shaun's mind. She had seen whom he was fighting. She had seen the giant fight many times, and as far as she knew, he had never lost a bout. She was fairly certain Shaun could handle any normal man in a fair fight, but this was not a fair fight. She needed to get out of her rooms, but the only way out was through Michael or Alexander. Lilly knew she could get the code if she penetrated their minds, but she did not know if she was prepared to take that step.

Shaun was looking for her; she felt his questioning in her mind. "*Where are you?*" he asked, and she felt the impact of his boots in the halls. She went to her door and placed her hands and forehead against it.

"*I'm here.*" She showed him the route in her mind. She felt him coming closer, and the closer he came, the more her mind filled with him, until the only thing she knew was Shaun. The air around her seemed to vibrate with him. *"I'm locked in,"* she told him as he approached her door and his fists struck it with frustration. The blow from his hands was so hard that she felt it, but the intensity of his mind was what drove her from the door. She staggered back against the wall beside it, and her hands searched for something to hold on to as he filled every molecule of her being with his mind. She could not breathe. He was everywhere, his face was before her, and there were sparks flying from his eyes, which had turned silver with the electricity that was circulating through his body, causing his dark, rich hair to float out around him. She felt her own hair rise around her as if caught up in a whirlwind. A burning began deep inside her, a burning so intense that it brought forth a groan from her lips and she slid to the floor.

"Lilly." She heard him in her mind and she heard him through the door. She dropped her head into her hands and then looked up again at the sound of metal buckling. The door was glowing and his hands were shining through it, coming at her as if they were rays from the sun.

The next moment she was pitched over on the floor as an explosion rocked the building, quickly followed by another, then another. Sirens began to scream and another explosion came. "Lilly?" Shaun yelled over the noise.

"Shaun!" Lilly ran to the window and saw the flash of weapons in the sky. "We're under attack! Find Michael!"

Shaun shook his head and blinked as the explosions rocked the building. For a moment he had thought that he was in the same room as Lilly. He could still feel her silky smooth skin beneath his hands. But that was impossible; his hands were still pressed against the door. He heard her scrambling around in her rooms and became conscious of activity behind him. A guard ran past, and he reached out to grab the man's arm. "Give me your weapon," Shaun demanded. The guard shrugged him off, so Shaun dropped him with a punch and removed the weapon. "Lilly," he yelled through her door. "I'm coming through!"

He turned the weapon to full charge and blasted the keypad, which caused the door to slide open and then shut again. The next charge caused a short circuit, and he pulled the door aside with his hands.

Lilly was yanking on her boots when he came through, the gown she had worn tossed aside in her rush to change. The hair that had been so elegantly arranged was tumbling down in her face, and she huffed at it in impatience as she looked up at Shaun.

His face had begun to bruise down one side and his lip was bloody from the fight, but that did not stop him from pulling her up and planting a soul-searching kiss on her trembling lips. The world around them was being rocked as the Ravigan fighters continued their barrage on the capital, but at that exact moment it meant nothing to Shaun and Lilly as his mouth and his mind demanded answers from hers. Her fingertips caressed his face where the bruises were growing, and he felt the pain there subside. The stinging in his lip disappeared also. He pulled his face away from hers and she pushed his eye shields up onto his forehead. Identical sets of light gray eyes searched each other.

"Lilly?" It was Michael, coming through what was left of her door, with Ruben behind him.

"I'm here, I'm fine," she assured him as he grabbed her arms.

"We've got to get you to the Senate. Alexander is leading a counterattack; I need you to get her there safely." Michael turned to Shaun, but stopped when he saw his eyes. "Your eyes . . ."

"We're going to get her there safely," Shaun assured him. "Ruben?"

"Juiced up and ready to go whenever you are."

Michael turned to Lilly. "You're our only hope now. You have to get through."

"I won't let you down," she promised. Michael pulled her to him in a desperate hug, nearly crushing the air from her body.

"Take care of her." Michael extended his hand to Shaun, and when he took it, he felt Michael's pain. The light gray eyes searched the older man's handsome face, and Shaun couldn't stop the widening of those eyes when he saw Michael's secret. *"Don't tell her,"* Michael implored with his mind.

"She can learn it without my telling it," Shaun replied.

Michael watched them as they turned to go down to the launch bay, only turning to help the young guard Shaun had hit when they had disappeared from view.

* * *

Ruben, Shaun, and Lilly ran toward the launch bay as the walls of the building shook from the bombardment. Ruben explained their plan of escape as they went. They were to launch with a group of fighters; it was hoped that Ruben's ship would be ignored as the fighters attacked. If they could make it to the hyperport, they would be safe.

Ruben sent the ship screaming out of the launch bay and punched through a squad of Ravigan fighters who were waiting in ambush. Shaun manned the turret gun, clearing a path for them as the Oasis fighters covered their escape. Lilly wondered how Oasis would ever survive the massive attack as they maneuvered around and through the wall of fighters that were bombarding the capital city. Above them, in the darkness of the outer atmosphere, were the bigger battleships that had launched the fighters. Lilly watched from the copilot's seat in amazement as Ruben flew right at one of the massive ships, then skimmed over it, barely clearing the communication towers.

"What are you doing?" she gasped as he seemed to scrape the surface of the big ship.

"Being a pest." Ruben was grinning as he deftly handled the controls. "We're too close for the fighters to shoot at and too close for the radar to find us. We'll just use these guys as cover and skip right over them to the hyperport." He began punching the Senate coordinates in the nav chart, and Lilly felt the change in the engines that indicated the jump was coming. The hyperport was ahead of them with a cruiser guarding it. A fighter was waiting for them when they came off the cover of the battleship. Ruben rolled the ship as Shaun turned his turret gun on them. As they came up on the cruiser, Ruben dipped the controls, diving underneath just as it began to fire on them. Shaun opened fire on the belly of the ship as the fighter exploded behind them, hit by the cruiser. Ruben punched the hyperdrive at the exact instant they hit the gateway; and they were flung back in the chairs as the g-forces took over, propelled into hyperspace at full speed.

By the time the ship leveled out in the hyperdrive, Shaun had joined them in the cockpit. He took Lilly's hand and led her back into the cargo bay, which had been well stocked during their time on Oasis. He lifted her with strong hands around her waist and deposited her on a crate of farming implements, then stepped back to look at her with his arms crossed.

"Was there something you wanted?" He was acting so strange that Lilly didn't know what to do.

"Why don't you tell me?" One eyebrow lifted as if he were waiting for an answer. "Read my mind and tell me what it is I want to know."

"I don't have to read your mind to know your questions, and I don't have the answers any more than you do."

"But you are the catalyst," he said.

"What do you mean by that?"

"This thing, whatever it is, never happened before I met you. It's almost as if part of my mind was asleep and when you went in and started poking around, you woke it up."

"I haven't been poking around in your mind," Lilly

said indignantly. Shaun graced her with a sarcastic smirk. "I really haven't." Her tone was apologetic now. "I just had to know if I could trust you."

"Do you?"

"Would I be here if I didn't?"

"Yes." Shaun ran his fingers through his hair. "You would come with me if your uncle or Michael commanded it, wouldn't you?"

"Obviously Michael saw something trustworthy in you or he never would have sent me with you."

"Michael saw me as his only choice to save you."

"Save me from what?"

"Answer my question first. Do you trust me?"

"Yes. I've seen what's inside of you and I trust you." Her light gray eyes were shining. He knew when he looked into them that she was holding nothing back.

"You haven't seen everything, Lilly. I wasn't in chains on that ship for nothing."

"No, I haven't seen what happened, but I can see evil and I know there is none in you." That brought a smile to his face.

"What happened in your quarters, at your door—was I imagining that?"

"I don't know. I don't know what happened." Lilly shook her head as if to deny the memory.

"But you did feel something."

"I felt everything," Lilly barely whispered as she looked away from Shaun.

His finger under her chin turned her face back to him. "What did you feel?"

"I felt you, all around me, inside me; it was like you

were inside every cell of my body. I could see you in front of me; you were emitting some kind of energy. I don't understand it."

"There are a lot of things I don't understand."

"Shaun . . . your parents—was your mother from Circe?"

"No, and she did not have my eyes. Neither did my father."

"I thought that might explain it. You see, they don't know what the power would do in a man; they have never let a man-child who has it live."

"If you had a baby boy with eyes the color of yours, the color of mine, would you kill him?" Shaun gripped her arms, and Lilly felt the strength of his body in his hands. "Could you?"

He did not have to read her mind to see the turbulent thoughts that were tumbling about. Her eyes widened in shock as she considered what he had said. "No." Her voice broke. "I could not kill your child."

"My child?" His fingertips brushed the side of her face. "Do you realize what you just said?"

Lilly looked up in shock as the words she'd spoken sank in.

"I'm ready anytime you are." He couldn't help teasing her, but he realized then that she was in a fragile state of mind.

"What am I to do?" Her lip was trembling.

"Just say the word, Lilly. We can go anywhere in the galaxy."

"I can't abandon my people."

Shaun pulled her to his chest and stroked her hair. "Are you so sure that they won't abandon you?"

"Michael would never do that," she said against his chest.

"You said Michael. Does that mean that Alexander would? Or what if he orders Michael to abandon you; what then?"

Lilly's mind whirled with the possibilities that he had placed before her. Surely he was wrong. He was trying to confuse her, to convince her to run off with him. Then she recalled that someone had betrayed her presence on the cryo ship. "I have to go to the Senate." No matter what had happened, Oasis was still depending on her. She had a responsibility to her people and her planet. Nothing else mattered.

"Then we will go."

Chapter Seven

"We have to prepare you," Lilly said.

"Prepare me for what?"

"The Sacrosanct Mistress." Shaun looked confused. "The leader of the Circe. She will surely be present when we address the Senate, and her powers are great."

Shaun crossed his arms and leaned against a crate. "I fail to see what's so scary about your Great Holy Witch, or whatever she is."

"Shaun, she will read your mind. She will know as soon as you appear in her presence that you have abilities." Lilly's light gray eyes revealed her concern at the coming confrontation. "She will not stop until she knows where they come from."

Shaun dismissed Lilly's concerns with a shrug of his shoulders.

"You should not treat this so lightly."

"What can she do?"

Lilly took a cleansing breath and closed her eyes. This was going to be harder than she had originally thought. She did not want to cause him pain, but she also needed to demonstrate to him the seriousness of the situation. She created an image in his mind. One of fire, boiling oil, and horror. She pictured him in flames, his skin melting away, the tissues of his body crusting and falling off. She transplanted the image into his mind. Shaun's eyes widened and he looked down at his body in utter shock. He fell to his knees with his mouth open to scream his agony. Lilly erased the image before he uttered a sound. Shaun collapsed facedown on the floor with a grunt.

Lilly knelt beside him and gently touched the rich dark hair that curled around the nape of his neck. "Now do you understand? She can erase all logic from your mind. You will believe what she wants you to believe, and she will make you suffer until you beg for death."

Shaun pushed himself up from the floor and leaned back against the crate with his legs sprawled before him. "So prepare me." He looked at his hands, splaying the fingers wide as he turned them over for closer examination. They were whole and the skin was clear, but his mind was having trouble accepting that fact. "Do you think you can teach me how to do that?"

"My uncle sent me to the Senate for months at a time to be trained by the Circe delegation there. But I have a feeling you're a quick study. Learning how to control your mind is the first step. The first thing you have to learn is the blocking. You have to block other people's thoughts from entering your mind or else you won't be able to hear your own. The Sacrosanct Mistress will enter your mind as soon as you come into her presence. We have to make sure that she dismisses you as a nonthreat as soon as she sees you."

"Does this Sacred Witchtress have a name?"

"Yes. Why?"

"Well, maybe she wouldn't seem like such a threat if you didn't keep throwing out her high and mighty title all the time."

Lilly smiled in agreement. "Her name is Honora."

"Honora . . . So how do we beat Honora at her own game?"

Lilly sat down before him and crossed her legs, bringing her feet onto her knees. She placed her hands over her feet and opened them with the palms up. "Will you join me?"

Shaun arched an eyebrow and moved away from the crate. He looked dubiously at Lilly's feet, and settled for leaving his beneath his knees.

Lilly waited until he was relaxed. "Now repeat after me. My mind is my own. No other may possess it. I will keep my mind and use it to overcome my enemies."

"I think that goes without saying."

"Yes, it does, but saying it also helps you to believe it."

"My mind is my own . . ." he began dryly.

Lilly sent the image of the flames into his mind.

"My mind is my own. No other may posess it!" Shaun closed his eyes and squeezed them tight. Sweat beaded on his forehead. His hands trembled with the effort of keeping them still. "I will keep my *mind* and use it to *overcome* my enemies."

Lilly fought to keep the flames going in his mind but saw them flickering out as his force became greater. She opened her eyes to look at him. His were still shut, but the look on his handsome face was victorious. She wondered, briefly, how much power he had hidden in the depths of his mind. What would happen if he learned how to tap into it? Even more important, where did he get his power?

Shaun opened his eyes and smiled at her.

"Don't get too sure of yourself," she said when she saw victory dancing in his eyes.

"But I think I'm getting the hang of this game," he replied teasingly.

"It's not a game, Shaun."

"I know." The smile he gave her was devious. She knew without a doubt that he was about to attack her senses. Lilly took a cleansing breath and prepared herself.

Wind caressed her body. She felt her clothing peeling away as if it were made of transparent paper to reveal the smooth skin of her body. She closed her eyes to fight him. *"My mind is my own."* Why did it have to feel so good? She felt the image of his hands holding her face and then moving slowly down her neck and over her shoulders, until he took her hands and then let his drift away from her fingertips. "*No other will possess it . . .*" The hands came again to her hips and slid up her sides, grazing the sides of her breasts before they moved to her back. *"I will keep my mind—"* What was he doing to her? A small sound slipped from between her firmly pressed lips as she saw in her mind the image of his face coming toward hers.

It wasn't enough, Phoenix realized. Although the game felt good, he wanted to have her with his body. He needed to touch her with his hands instead of imagining it with his mind. Shaun opened his eyes and grabbed her arms, pulling her to him. His lips swooped down and plundered hers, drawing her brain from the battle of the minds to the attack on her senses. He growled from deep within his throat, and she responded with a sigh of surrender as she melted against him. He placed a hand under her hips and guided her into his lap without losing contact with her lips. His other hand held the back of her head to keep the contact going. Lilly grabbed on to the opening of his jacket with one hand as the other was crushed against his chest.

He wanted her. He had wanted her since he had first seen her in that moment of awakening while he was still immobilized inside the cryo tube. That was what had kept him from running when his tube crashed to the floor of the ship and freed him from his cryo state. He could have been gone before his guard even realized it. Instead he had gone to her tube and then been attacked by the Legionnaire. He wanted her.

Would he take her on the floor of a cargo hold?

He pulled away.

Lilly looked at him with wide eyes and swollen lips. Shaun touched a finger to her bottom one and she swallowed back a sob. She scrambled from his lap and took off toward the front of the ship.

Shaun dropped his head back against the crate. "Rykers is starting to look better and better," he said to the ceiling of the cargo hold as he thumped his head against the crate again, hoping to drive the feel of her surrender from his mind and body.

Shaun slumped into the seat next to Ruben, whose look was not unsympathetic. "Trouble in paradise, big guy?"

"You could say that." Shaun leaned back in the chair and placed his booted feet on the console.

"Forgot to tell you—I love the look." Ruben waggled his eyebrows and blew a kiss at the uniform that Shaun now wore.

Shaun pounded a fist into his arm.

"Ow!"

"Don't start."

"Just because you didn't take time to get your jollies doesn't mean you should take your frustrations out on me."

"Oh, and you got yours?"

"Yes, I did."

"When?"

"Sometime between the fight and all hell breaking loose. That's were I was when the bombs started dropping. You remember the one with the overbearing laugh and the overflowing bosom?"

"Yeah?" Shaun raised a dubious eyebrow.

Ruben just smiled.

"You are a wonder."

"I'm just trying to do my duty—for mankind and for womankind."

"And a whiz, too."

"Sometimes you have to be fast, my friend. But sometimes it pays to take it slow." Ruben tossed his head back toward the cabin. 'Haven't you heard that old adage 'All things come to those who wait'?"

"Yeah, I've heard it."

"Well then, start thinking with your brain. And I don't mean the one in your pants. Lilly isn't a one-night stand. She's a keeper. She's a forever and a day. You don't want to blow it by being in too much of a hurry."

"Once we get to the Senate, I don't know what's going to happen. I'm afraid she'll find an easy way to get rid of me."

"You mean snap her fingers and off with your head?"

"Something like that."

"Not going to happen. She's crazy about you. If she wasn't, she wouldn't be back there crying right now."

"She's crying?"

"Yes."

"Damn." Shaun looked at the door to the cabin. "I guess I'd better go talk to her."

"Be nice."

"What are you talking about? I'm always nice," Shaun growled.

"Yeah, that's what got you into this predicament."

"Are we going anywhere close to Rykers?"

"No, why?"

"I was hoping maybe you could drop me off."

Ruben laughed as Shaun knocked on the door to the cabin.

* * *

"Come." The tone was imperious. Shaun wasn't surprised to find Lilly standing before him with her shoulders squared and her eyes narrowed. He couldn't help himself; he reached for her with his mind. And came up dead against a wall. She was blocking him.

"I came to apologize . . ."

"Apology accepted."

He looked around the room, not knowing what to say next. Which was in itself a mystery, because he could not recall when words had ever failed him.

"Could you teach me how to do that?"

"What is it you want me to teach you?"

"How to block, like you're blocking me now."

"It requires discipline." Lilly arched a delicate brow at him. "Something you are not inclined to."

He gave her points for that one. He deserved it. "Lilly, you said yourself that I have to block Mother Honora, or whatever it is you call her. Would you please show me how?"

"You already know how."

"I do?"

"Say the litany. Build a wall in your mind. Make the wall out of something you care for. Imagine that if one piece of the wall is breached, then the thing you care for will be lost. She will try to come through your wall. You must not let her."

"Won't she be able to tell that I'm hiding something?"

"Everyone at the Senate is hiding something, Shaun. We just have to make her think that what you're hiding is not important."

It made sense. His father had often told him of the intricacies of Senate life. Layers of politics, he had called it. Motives hiding motives, had been how he explained it. "There's something else we can do."

"What is that?" She was keeping him at a distance.

"They will be expecting you to search their minds. But they won't be expecting anything from me."

"It's too dangerous, Shaun." Her light gray eyes had softened with worry. "If the Sacrosanct Mistress finds out, I won't be able to save you."

"You mean you can't whack her on the head like you did with the Legionnaire?"

Lilly willed the rebellious grin from her lips. "Just as I said earlier, you have no discipline."

"You're not the first one to notice."

Lilly sent the flame image again, but he quickly suppressed it. He was getting better at it every time.

"How about a compromise?" he suggested.

"Compromise? I see no need for a compromise. You are my protector. You will do as I say."

"Unless I feel your life is in danger." Shaun crossed the room to stand in front of her. "Then *you* will do as I say." How quickly he had turned the tables on her. "I promise I won't do any mind gropes . . ."

"Mind gropes?" The grin struggled for supremacy.

"I won't do any mind gropes unless I feel that someone is a threat to you." His light gray eyes bored into hers as he willed her to understand the depth of his feelings for her.

"Agreed?"

"Agreed."

Shaun took off his jacket and sat down on the narrow bed to take off his boots.

"What are you doing?"

"I'm tired. I'm going to get some sleep."

"But . . ."

Shaun patted the bed with an evil grin. "There's room for two, Princess. And it's not like we haven't shared this bed before."

Lilly looked at him in exasperation.

"Oh, I see. You're worried about my lack of discipline." Shaun stretched out on the bed and folded his arms behind his head. "I promise not to touch you with my mind or my body."

Lilly looked doubtful as she pulled off her boots.

"Princess, I am about to teach you the meaning of discipline."

Lilly entered from the foot of the bed, climbing into the space between his body and the wall. She put her back to him and he promptly rolled over and placed an arm around her, pulling her against him.

"You promised . . ." she began.

"Shhh. Go to sleep," he said into her ear. "And see if you're disciplined enough to keep your hands off me."

Lilly threw an elbow into the solid stomach behind her. Shaun wrapped his arms and legs around her body, leaving her totally immobile. "See, you've already lost control, Princess. You have a complete lack of discipline. Now go to sleep."

Shaun walked the caverns of the mine. His eyes, long accustomed to seeing in the dark, recognized the familiar passageways that had been his playground as a child. He had entered into games of hide-and-seek with the children of the miners, along with pretend battles and other imaginary games that filled their days when their schooling was over. His mother had been their teacher, gladly taking on the role of educator. She was good at it. Hadn't she, after all, been the personal teacher for the Prefect's children? She had encouraged their creativity and set no boundaries save one. They were not to go to the chasm.

The chasm was a forbidden place. It was a bottomless pit from which there was no rescue for anyone who fell into its darkness. The way was blocked with a metal grid, but there were ways around it. The older children used it as a test of bravery and a rite of passage. Shaun had been there many times himself as he grew older. He would test his bravery by standing upon the brink and looking down into the darkness. There was nothing visible within the depths, not even for one such as he who could see in the dark as easily as others saw in the generated light that eased the dimness of the caverns they called home.

So why was he standing there now, crying his eyes out? Shaun knew he was dreaming. He had not set foot on Pristo for fourteen years. Leaving there had not been a hardship. For a thirteen-year-old boy who had yet to see daylight, it had been a dream come true. So why the sadness? He could hear a woman crying also. His tears were silent, but hers were gut-wrenching. Her sobs echoed up from the gorge before him and filled the silence of the place, echoing from the walls around him until his head was full of nothing but her cries. He put his hands over his ears to block the sounds, but they grew louder still. He couldn't stand them; they were tearing his heart out. He had to make the crying stop.

Shaun dropped to his knees beside the gorge and let loose a roar that came from deep within. It was the only way to block the cries. He couldn't stand the crying. He looked into the black pit before him. He had to stop the crying. The space opened up before him and he felt himself falling through the darkness, falling toward the crying.

Panic overcame him. He was dreaming. He needed to wake up. But he had to stop the crying. He was getting closer. He could feel it. He needed to see who was crying.

"Shaun. Wake up." Lilly leaned over him and shook him. He had awakened her with his struggles and was still so deeply asleep that he did not respond. Lilly took his face in her hands to still him and laid her forehead against his.

The falling stopped. He was floating now. The cavern disappeared, only to be replaced by a blue sky and a field of grass. Shaun felt the arms around him, felt himself gently being lowered to the ground. The crying was gone, the agony was gone, and a feeling of complete peace filled him. He opened his eyes and found a set that mirrored his own.

"Lilly."

"You were dreaming."

"I was fall—"

"I know . . ."

"Lilly . . ." His hands came up around her back as

she lowered her lips to his. "Don't leave me," he whispered. "I need you."

"Shaun." She buried her face in his neck.

He wrapped his arms around her. "I know."

Chapter Eight

Shaun and Lilly came to an understanding of sorts. He promised not to pressure her about their relationship, and she in turn promised not to get mad at him when he forgot his promise. They had another cycle to go to before they arrived at the Senate. While Ruben slept, Lilly taught Shaun how to block his thoughts from others and the best routes for entering minds. He was a quick student. Or was it because he had so much untapped power? His ability disturbed the balance of her world, and there were no answers for it. She wondered if there had been something on Pristo that had altered his development, but as far as he knew, he was the only child raised there who had ever been able to see in the dark. The development of his eyes and his mind had to be related. Each occurrence on its own was strange enough. To have both happen to one person was strange indeed.

The Offices of the Senate occupied an entire planet.

It had been chosen for its strategic location, and the formerly uninhabitable rock was now the center of the known universe. Domes had been built over the different sectors of the city so atmospheres could be created within. Tunnels connected the domes with moving walkways. Beneath it all was a series of trains that could transport a passenger from one side of the planet to the other in a matter of minutes. And above it, floating in space, were the satellite stations of all the planets represented. The stations were a link to the ambassadors who lived in the sectors below.

Lilly directed Ruben to the satellite belonging to Oasis, and after dropping them off he went on to the free-trade zone to dispose of his cargo, promising to meet up with Shaun at a later time.

"There is one problem we didn't discuss, Princess," Shaun said as they descended the steps from the landing platform to where a reception committee was waiting. "What are you going to call me?"

"What do you mean?"

"Shaun Phoenix is a wanted man, remember?"

Lilly looked up into eyes that were once again covered with shields. "Ryan. Shaun Ryan." She looked down at the waiting committee. "I'll have an immunity chip installed in your hand. That will allow you to pass without question."

She took a misstep on the stairs, and he quickly steadied her with a hand on her arm. "Shaun . . ."

"I know, time to keep my hands to myself."

Lilly was greeted with much ceremony by the Ambassador from Oasis and his committee. The two of them were then rushed to quarters where servants were waiting to prepare their mistress for her coming presentation to the Senate. Shaun was taken away to have the chip planted into the back of his hand, a procedure that he found to be an annoyance. But if it kept the Legionnaires off his back, then it was worth it. Instead of being directed back to her quarters when he was done, he was pointed in the direction of a large room located in the middle of the satellite. The clear dome that served as the roof was at least four stories high and left the occupants exposed to the never-ending expanse of space and stars that were held back by nothing more than a man-made material. Shaun wondered how it would stand up to a meteor storm. He entered the darkened chamber on a balcony that surrounded the circumference of the circular room. He pushed his shields up on his forehead as he surveyed the room.

Lilly was in the center of the chamber with three women attending her. She was wearing a short sleeveless top of deep violet that fit tightly across the chest and left her midriff exposed. Beneath were loose pants of a light gray material that revealed the length of her legs. Her feet were bare and her hair had been tied into a high tail that streamed down between her shoulder blades.

Shaun leaned casually against the wall with arms crossed as she bid the women to leave her side. They disappeared into the darkness beneath the balcony as Lilly took a seat in the middle of the floor with her legs crossed. Shaun playfully thought about sending her an image, but then stopped when he saw how deep in concentration she was. She had turned into her own mind and shut out the rest of the world. He didn't need to test her wall to know it was there. She was preparing herself mentally for the coming presentation.

Lilly bent from the waist, brought her arms out to the side, and touched her forehead to the floor in front of her. She gathered her arms beside her head and pushed up, flaring her legs out into a perfect split and then raising herself into a handstand and bringing her legs together in perfect precision. She let her legs arc slowly behind her and landed on her feet with a delicate grace. She reached behind her back and brought her foot up into her hand, then placed her other hand on it and brought her foot up behind her head. Then she repeated the procedure with the other foot. She took a breath and then took off running, entering into a series of handsprings and flips, spinning and twisting her way across the entire width of the room. Then she repeated the sequence in the opposite direction.

Shaun moved to the rail of the balcony, truly amazed at the grace she displayed as she flew across the floor, her hands and feet barely touching before she sprang away again, ending with a series of twists that carried her through the air in more rotations than his eye could catch. He realized that he was hearing music, a heavy rhythm of drums accompanied by the trilling of flutes. His eyes searched for the source and saw nothing that could be projecting the music, yet he heard it inside his head. Could it be coming from Lilly?

An attendant came out of the darkness and handed Lilly a pair of knives that glowed with silver and gold. The blades were thin, sharp, and as long as her forearm. She twisted and spun them over her head as she went through an intricate routine of cartwheels and kicks. It was beautiful but also deadly. He knew from his own experience that knives such as the ones she held could gut a man in a second.

He was breathless just watching her. How could she keep going on? Her feet and hands became a blur as she went through the sequence again. The knives spun in a whirl of silver and gold. She flew into the air and twisted, flinging one of the knives with a yelp. The other soon followed, and the air reverberated with the sound of the knives embedding themselves in the support beams on opposite ends of the room. Lilly stood with chest heaving and mouth open, drawing in great gulps of air. Her eyes were looking down into the center of the room in the exact spot where she had begun. The attendants came out of the darkness and quickly surrounded her again as they removed her clothing. Lilly raised her arms over her head as they came to her and a large sheet was quickly wrapped around her nude form. Her light gray eyes, colorless in the dim light, moved up and captured his, drawing him closer with every gasp of air she sucked in. He tried to look inside her, but all he could see was the darkness of space and the stars that twinkled above the dome. Her chest was still heaving with her effort as the women moved her toward the darkness beneath the balcony and he heard the closing of a door.

Shaun's hands tingled, and he looked down to find that he was gripping the rail of the balcony so tightly that the blood had ceased to flow. He let go and flexed his fingers as the blood supply returned. He looked at the back of his hand where the chip had been implanted and saw no evidence of its presence. A door opened below him again and he watched as one of the guards came to remove the knives from the posts. He had some difficulty doing it.

Shaun left the room in search once again of Lilly. He wondered what would be waiting for him when he found her.

Lilly was gone. Her body was still present and compliantly beautiful as her attendants dressed her in the royal robes that displayed the riches of her planet. He wondered how her slim body could carry the heaviness of the silver brocaded robe, but as he had seen earlier, her strength was deceiving. Her hair had been woven into an intricate design and jeweled pins sparkled among the ash-colored tresses. Shaun felt he was in the way as the servants rushed hither and yon and the Ambassador from Oasis and his secretary filled Lilly's head with information on who was present, who wasn't, who was on their side, who wasn't, and most important of all, who had made alliances with whom. The Senate was in high chambers, which meant they were still celebrating the opening of the session with all the pageantry that attended it. It also meant that all the players would be assembled. Shaun wondered how she would keep all the information straight in her mind. He watched all the preparation from a position along the wall of her elaborate quarters and wondered once again if Rykers might have been a better choice. Maybe not. He would have been a nonentity there also. At least here he had the freedom to come and go as he pleased.

He was bored, so he let his mind wander. He moved in and out of the thoughts of the men and women who were rushing about the room.

The Ambassador was worried. The Ravigan Prince was present and there were rumors of secret meetings between the Ravigans and the Prefect. It had even been said that the Sacrosanct Mistress had been present at one. That was not good news as far as Shaun was concerned.

The secretary had his own agenda. He mind echoed the same concerns as the Ambassador's, but he was thinking about how he could use the situation to further his career. The man had higher ambitions than the position of secretary to the ambassador of Oasis. He wanted to work for the Senate Prefect himself. *Traitor* . . . Shaun planted the word in his mind and watched as the man looked up from his papers to see if anyone had heard the thought dashing through his brain.

The women were mostly concerned about the impression Lilly's ensemble would make on the gathered masses. It was well known that the lesser population would gather at the gates of the Senate to watch the passage of royalty. It was one of the few entertainments in their days of servicing the great engine that was the city.

The women were moving quickly about the room, and they were all dressed so similarly that Shaun had a hard time telling them apart. The thought of one of them caught his attention, and as she left the room to fetch some forgotten trifle, Shaun focused on her. Mundane thoughts filled his mind: Her feet hurt, she was hungry, she was sleeping with one of the guards—wait . . .

She was blocking! Shaun lowered his shades as she looked up abruptly, her eyes searching his face. She was wondering who was scanning her and looked back over her shoulder at Lilly.

Her eyes were blue, an average shade, although there was something dead about them. There was no spark in the center that spoke of life and soul. Just a flat plane of blue. Ruben had said that Lilly's mother had disguised her eyes somehow. Was this woman doing the same?

"*Lilly.*" She must know; how could she not know?

"Leave me!" she commanded the group gathered around her.

"But the hour is near . . ." the Ambassador protested.

"I know the time, William." She graced him with a smile. "I need a moment alone to prepare myself."

The group filed out of the room with the customary bowing and posturing. Lilly looked in the mirror and found Shaun reflected behind her.

"Your thoughts will betray us." Her eyes met his in the mirror as he raised the shields.

"There's a spy . . ." he began.

"I know. There are spies everywhere." She turned to look at him. "We have a few with other delegations ourselves."

"I'm afraid I'm not very good at all this political intrigue." He moved to stand before her. "That's why I left the Academy."

"You have to control your mind. Not only do you

have to control what's coming in, but you also have to control what's going out. If the Circe detect a stray thought, they will not stop until they know where it's coming from. You must keep your impressions behind your wall and find a decoy thought to throw them off."

"Like your maid does."

"Exactly." Lilly straightened a sleeve of the heavy brocade robe she wore. "She caught your mind grope, as you call it. I had to distract her before she found the source."

Shaun smiled at, the use of his term. "How did you distract her?"

"I sent the image of her lover in another woman's arms. Since she's sleeping with him to get information, it confused her to think that might be doing the same thing."

"I bet he's in for a good time when they get together."

"Shaun, you must be serious. This isn't Oasis, where you can make your little jokes and send me images without anyone knowing it. This is life and death for me and you and the people who depend upon me." She placed a hand on his chest, raising her eyes to look into his. "I need to know I can depend on you. That I can trust you not to do something foolish and impetuous. Because if I can't, then it would be foolish to take you in there with me."

"You've looked inside me, Lilly. You know the answer to that question as well as I do." He placed his hand over hers.

"I do." She pulled her hand away. "I can't protect

you, Shaun. My first obligation is to Oasis." She folded her arms, hiding her hands within the sleeves of the robe. "I would prefer it if you weren't here, but I realize you'd never agree to leave."

"You got that right, Princess."

"I feel that it's safer to have you here with me than out there trying to get in where you don't belong."

"I belong with you."

"Shaun." Lilly raised a hand to stop his progress toward her. "I'm afraid for you."

"As I am for you." He took her hand, conquering her attempts to pull it away. "I would die to protect you." He placed a finger under her chin and looked into her eyes. "I swear that is all they will see when they look into my mind." He guided her hand to his temple. "See for yourself."

The strength of his mind had grown since she had last delved there. The force of his will was sending out one thought and one thought only.

Lilly.

She couldn't respond to what he was thinking. She didn't dare. Why did he have to love her? It was forbidden. She couldn't love him, she must not love him. Her life was given to Oasis, to her people. She had to make up for the evil her mother had done. She had to sacrifice her happiness for her people. There could be no future for them.

She had not accomplished her purpose. She had to make sure his thoughts were secure. She closed her eyes to delve deeper and sift through the layers to find his wall. Against her will they flew open. He had commanded it. He wanted to look into her eyes.

She couldn't allow it. Her will had to be greater. Too much was at stake. She closed them again and almost sighed in relief when they stayed shut. She started the sifting then, moving through the hallways and doors, looking into the cracks and the crevices. She found the wall, and it was strong. There was nothing there to betray him. Relief washed over her and she lifted herself back into her own mind, catching one last message as she returned to herself. *"I allowed you to venture there."*

Her eyes flew open to find him smiling down at her. "Satisfied, Princess?"

"Yes." She found it difficult to speak.

"At your leisure, then." He moved away and bowed with a flourish, letting her take the lead. He fell into step behind her and a little to the left, as was the custom. Right or wrong, the decision had been made. It was time to present her case.

Chapter Nine

The pageantry was overwhelming. From the time the shuttle touched down until they reached the high chambers, the Oasis contingency of Lilly, Shaun, the Ambassador, his secretary, and two women attendants was met with representatives and showered with accolades. Lilly played her role to perfection, posing and posturing with the best of them. Shaun watched quietly and found the entire game to be amusing. The gauntlet they had just run was nothing in comparison to what awaited them within the huge doors of the high chambers.

There was a dais in the center of the room on which a chair was sitting. The chair was occupied by a strong-looking man with iron-gray hair and a barrel-like chest. He wore an ornate robe of the same cut as Lilly's; beneath it a uniform of sorts could be seen. *My father worked for this man . . .* The thought was hidden quickly behind the wall. Gathered to each side of the dais in different positions of authority were the Prefects and counselors. He surmised that the woman with the translucent gray eyes and the ornate headgear was the Sacrosanct Mistress.

As Lilly was presented by the Ambassador and the introductions were made to the critical members of the committee, Shaun felt the presence of the Sacrosanct Mistress in his mind. His eyes behind the shields did not blink as he focused on one thought only.

"Nice hat you got on there."

The slight flaring of her nostrils was the only indication that she had perceived the insult. She quickly moved on to the other members of the delegation. Shaun felt her lingering on the woman whom he had labeled a spy. Confusion passed between them. He saw it as easily as he saw the big hat.

"Honorable Prefect. Please allow me to speak for my planet. And to speak for the people of our universe."

Good tactic, Princess. Get the people on your side.

"Without the crops that Oasis provides, many peoples of the universe will surely starve," Lilly continued. "At the time that I left my beloved homeland, it was under attack by the forces of Raviga." Her eyes fell on the delegation from the dreaded planet. "Our people are not warriors, but they will defend what they love, and they love our planet." Lilly moved away from the Prefect and addressed the tiers of planetary delegations. "As you well know, it is now time to harvest the grains. But we cannot, because Ravigan ships are burning our grain as it stands in the fields. Our men cannot harvest, because they are fighting. Fighting to protect what belongs to you."

Her gesture encompassed the entire room. "So that you and your people will not starve." She stepped back toward the dais. "I have come to ask for your help, Honorable Prefect. Send your ships to guard our ports. Send your troops to Raviga so that the soldiers of that planet may stay home and tend to their own gardens. We promise there will be food for all. Oasis has never withheld its riches from anyone who has need."

"As long as they're willing to pay the price!" the Ravigan delegate shouted.

"Do you not charge for the ores that come from the bowels of your planet?" Lilly arched a delicate eyebrow at the man as he stood in his tier. "Are you saying that we do not have the right to do the same?"

"Honorable Prefect!" the man called. "Does Oasis pay tribute?"

It was a sore point with the Senate. Oasis had power and chose not to pay tribute to the governing body.

"What right does Oasis have to ask for protection when it does not sponsor that protection?"

Several opinions on the matter flew from the tiers. The noise level grew and Lilly took the opportunity to search the minds of the players. Her Ambassador and his secretary were nervous. The advisors around the dais were anxious, too, but their reasons were still hidden from her. The Mistress was a wall, of course. The woman knew she was searching. The Mistress's clear eyes turned to look at the Prefect, who was calling the group to order. She smiled at Lilly and then turned her light eyes to the Prefect.

I am betrayed! Lilly saw it clearly in the Prefect's

mind. He had dealings with Raviga. But how much had they bribed him? There were too many thoughts flowing in his mind to sift through them. She needed time. The man was about to speak, and she needed all her wits to absorb what he was about to say.

"It saddens me to hear all these baseless accusations in my court." He looked at Lilly. "Surely we have the means to conquer this dilemma." The Prefect rose from his chair. "I will meet with representatives of both planets in my personal chambers tomorrow morning. You will each present your case, and we shall see if a compromise is possible."

Dismissed, just like that. Lilly's eyes sought Shaun's as she turned to leave, but of course they were hidden behind the shields.

"Politics." She was glad he could find it all so amusing. They were in serious trouble. But then again, he had no allegiance to Oasis. To him it was just a port where he could enrich his coffers.

He doesn't deserve that, she chastised herself. She was angry, but her demeanor did not betray it. The calm and collected Princess who had entered the chamber was still in evidence as she left it.

"Lilly!" It was the Sacrosanct Mistress. Lilly quickly dipped into a curtsy as the woman approached. Shaun observed the rest of the troop bowing low before the woman and quickly did the same, although he kept his shielded eyes on Lilly the entire time.

"You have grown into a beautiful woman since the last time I saw you," Honora said as she smoothed a tendril of Lilly's hair behind her ear. "You represent your people well."

"Thank you, Mistress," Lilly said, her manner and voice modest. "I only hope that I can do right by them."

"You will," Honora assured her as she once again placed her hands within the opposite sleeves of her ornate robe. "When the time comes, you will do what is right."

She dismissed the group, and Lilly led them away from the chambers.

"We are doomed," the Ambassador cried when they were safely away from listening ears.

"Get your spies out, William," Lilly instructed. "See if you can find out which way the wind is blowing."

"It's blowing right into the Prefect's pocket." Shaun had it figured out, she knew. But why? And who had offered the bribe?

"Are we going back to the satellite?" Shaun asked the secretary.

"No, we have quarters on planet," he answered, and then hurried up to confer with the Ambassador.

"Do you think the Ravigan contingent is going through this mad scramble?" he asked Lilly. She stopped in her tracks.

"Protector!" she called in an imperious tone, and he stepped before her. "Go out into the city and see if you can find us any information." *"Go find Ruben. He'll know what's going on with Raviga."*

She was a genius. Of course Ruben would know. He would have made it his first order of business—that is, after selling his goods, having a good meal, and looking for a prime piece of tail to warm his sheets. *"I shouldn't leave you."*

"Go." Her tone was gentler. She was talking to him, not a protector. *"I'll be fine. My people will protect me."*

Shaun spared a look at the woman he knew was a spy and with a classic Academy bow took his leave.

"He is not of Oasis, my lady?" the woman asked.

"No, Martia, he's not." Lilly watched him as he disappeared into the throng of people who attended the comings and goings of the Senate. It was easy to watch him. He stood taller that most of the population, but eventually his form was lost from sight.

"My lady?"

"Let us go."

Shaun found Ruben in one of the higher-class taverns in the main dome. He was enjoying an expensive bottle of wine, and a tall, buxom blonde was leaning heavily against him in the corner booth that he occupied.

"So how's life in the palace?" Ruben asked as Shaun slid into the opposite side of the booth.

"You tell me." Shaun waved to the bartender and a scantily dressed woman brought him a drink. He waved her away when she wanted to linger. Ruben threw some credits on her tray.

"This is Charla, by the way," Ruben said. The blonde gave Shaun the once-over with heavy-lidded eyes and seemed oblivious to the fact that one shoulder of her dress had slid into a dangerously revealing position. "Shut it down, sweetheart, he's taken." Her hands disappeared under the table, and Ruben grinned across at his friend.

"I take it you're wondering which way the wind is blowing?"

"Let's just say the Princess's reception wasn't favorable."

"From what I hear, Raviga has been doing some heavy politicking lately. The Crown Prince is here, and he's going on like they're the wounded party."

"What's he like?"

"Smarmy." Ruben jerked his head at Charla. "Go warm up the sheets for me, sweetheart. I'll be there in a minute." The blonde slinked off with a pout on her lips and an appetizing sway in her hips.

"I see you've made friends with the natives."

"Charla was just recently seen in the company of one of the personal guards to the Crown Prince of Raviga." Ruben picked up his drink. "Poor thing. I felt sorry for her and decided to show her what it's supposed to be like."

"Think she'll cry when she's overcome with passion?"

"She wouldn't be the first one it's happened to."

"So tell me about the Crown Prince."

"Ramelah? He's a smooth one. The oldest of who knows how many sons. They call him The Ram. You could see for yourself what he's like tonight over in the pits."

"The pits?"

"It's three domes over. Let's just say it's where all the smiling people go to get their jollies. Nothing is taboo there. You think of it and someone over there will do it for you, or to you, and charge you a hefty price in the bargain. There's also a lot of gambling going on. And The Ram is quite handy at the Murlaca."

"He fights the Murlaca?"

"To the death."

The Murlaca was an ancient battle technique that was fought with a series of curved blades that were attached to gauntlets. The gauntlets were worn on the forearms with the blades facing out and away. The only other equipment was a pair of heavy leather gloves. Someone experienced in the game could disembowel his opponent in just a few quick moves. It wasn't many matches that weren't fought to the death, and the Crown Prince of Raviga was out doing it just for fun.

"So I guess we're going to the pits tonight."

"Got some other news for you, too, big guy."

"What's that?"

"The Ram is supposedly here to get a bride. He's marrying for all the right reasons. Politics, alliance, money."

"And?"

"Guess who is number one on his list." Ruben leaned back to watch Shaun's reaction.

"No way." Shaun laughed and took a drink. "Her uncle would never allow it."

"Somebody betrayed her when she was on that ship."

Shaun slammed his drink down on the table. "It's not going to happen, my friend."

Ruben spread his hands in supplication. "Hey, I'm just giving you the high points. What you choose to do with it is up to you." He downed the rest of his drink and stood, throwing more credits on the table. "Charla should have those sheets at about the right temperature now. I'll catch up with you later."

"Here?"

"Here is good." Ruben flashed a smile and went off to find his companion, leaving Shaun to muse over what he had just heard.

It was unthinkable. Why would Ramalah even think he could arrange a marriage with a woman from a planet that he was at war with? Who in his right mind would think that Alexander would agree to such a thing?

Unless . . .

Lilly was Alexander's only heir. And Oasis was a very rich planet. She would have to marry to make an alliance that would strengthen her planet and protect it. Unless her planet was in danger, and her marriage could be an instrument of peace. Raviga had plans to capture Oasis. And the devils were going to get it, except that it wouldn't be by conquest, it would come to them through an alliance. A marriage between Lilly and Ram would establish peace. Raviga had started the war for the express purpose of negotiating a peace contract. That was the only way Lilly would ever consider marriage to the . . . The waitress leaned seductively over the table, interrupting his musings. At any other time or place he would have been tempted. But not now. He hoped never again. She moved away with a pout on her lips.

The Prefect had been paid off to turn a blind eye to the Ravigan attacks. Oasis did not pay tribute. The people of the garden planet had prided themselves for centuries on dealing fairly with the universe, and saw no need to pay for protection. Raviga must have promised the Prefect extra tribute if he would align with the desert planet against Oasis.

But who had betrayed Lilly? Did Raviga have spies on Oasis? Spies close enough to the center of government to know that Lilly had been on that transport ship? Shaun went through the lists of suspects. There was Krebbs, the former protector, who had died in the attack. But he had been with Lilly since she came of age. Michael was the one person she trusted above all others, and Alexander . . . It just didn't make sense that he would hand over his planet to a sworn enemy. Who else was there? Perhaps the witch spy Martia? Had she been on Oasis before Lilly left, or had Alexander notified the Ambassador of her travel plans? Lilly had said the woman had a lover whom she used for information. Maybe Shaun should use Ruben's technique and show her what . . .

His stomach turned at the thought. How could he consider sleeping with another woman when all he could think about was Lilly? Ruben, on the other hand . . . maybe he was up for the challenge.

Shaun grinned at the pun and left the bar before the waitress came by again.

Chapter Ten

"You want me to whore for you?" Ruben asked incredulously. They were riding one of the tunnel transports to the pleasure dome.

"Well, that's one way to put it."

"Just don't tell me she's got a great personality."

"She's a looker, just your type."

"My type?"

"Easy."

"So why don't you just do it?" Ruben grinned knowingly. "Oh wait, I forgot. The Princess wouldn't approve."

"I'm not in the mood for it, Ruben," Shaun growled.

"Lucky for you, I'm always in the mood," Ruben responded playfully. "So what is it I'm supposed to find out?"

"Has she spent any time on Oasis? Does she have contacts with Raviga?"

"You think she might be the one who betrayed Lilly?"

"Possibly." Shaun looked at his friend. "You need to be careful too."

"Why? Can she hurt me? Please say yes."

"I think she might be one of the witches."

Ruben looked concerned, but then a delirious grin covered his face. "I've heard talk that the ones that whore are really good."

"When this is all over, I just might kill you."

"Maybe I'll get lucky and your witch friend will save you the trouble."

Shaun shook his head in disgust.

"So tell me, why are you still wearing those things?" Ruben asked, indicating the eye shields.

"I'm a wanted man, remember?"

"I guess your eyes would give you away," Ruben agreed. Shaun didn't add that if one of the Circes saw him, they would be on him in a flash. He had yet to see anyone with that pale gray eye color but the witches, and himself of course. And Lilly . . .

Shaun and Ruben blended into the flow of pedestrians making their way through the connecting tunnels into the pleasure dome. As soon as they entered the area, their senses were assaulted with the sights and sounds of prostitutes hawking their wares and hustlers looking for their next target. The tawdry mingled with the refined as those seeking pleasure acknowledged their baser instincts. There was a barrage of sight and sound that dulled the senses.

The majority of the crowd was headed to a circular arena that seemed to be carved into the surface of the planet. A series of steps descending to a fenced circle served as the seating for the venue where the present-day gladiators would perform for the bloodthirsty audience. Rich and poor, titled and common, they all longed for the same thing. The sight of blood.

A security force pushed the crowd aside to allow passage for a small group. A woman came forth wearing the same type of embellished robe that the Sacrosant Mistress had worn. Her arms were folded into the sleeves and her light gray eyes scanned the crowd as if she were mentally shoving people out of her way. A masked guard dressed entirely in black led three men with hands linked by a chain. Around their necks they wore a band of silver that blinked with a white light.

"What is that all about?" Shaun asked Ruben as they stepped aside for the procession.

"Circe slaves. All the men on Circe are slaves, or minions. Some of the luckier ones are used for breeding. These three must have displeased their mistress," he answered.

"What do you mean?"

"She's sold them to the games. They will be part of the entertainment."

"What's with the collar?"

"That's part of their control. Once the collar is placed around their necks, their willpower is gone and they are under the control of the Mistress. She could tell them to jump off a tower and they would do it, no questions asked."

Shaun looked at the retreating back of the last man and cast his mind out to search.

He found fear. A cold hard knot of it gathered in his stomach as his mind came into contract with the anguished screams of the man. He knew he was being sent to a horrible death and he was helpless to save himself. His mind was aware of what was happening, but his body was controlled by the Circe witch who led him. The mind cursed the woman and cursed the fear that filled him while his body followed along, humbly doing the bidding of his mistress.

Shaun shook his head as he released the contact. He wished there was something he could do for the helpless man, but saving Lilly must be his first priority. The witch threw up her hand to stop her followers and slowly turned, her nostrils flaring as she scanned the crowd with cold, pale eyes beneath thin, pale lashes. The eyes were frozen and hard as they wandered over the faces. The witch's eyes were a sharp contrast to Lilly's, which sparkled with life and light as if they were cut from a precious gem. This woman's eyes held pure evil. Shaun retreated behind his mind wall and thought of the blood sport that was coming as he pushed by with Ruben. He felt her presence in his mind for a moment and then she was gone, dismissing him as unimportant. The witches were so obsessed with themselves that it never even occurred to them that a man might possess the same talents. They thought they had taken care of that problem eons ago.

Shaun hated her with a passion.

When the two men descended into the arena, Ruben took the lead, bringing them down close to the front, where they took a seat amid the aristocrats who were there to indulge their taste for blood. A few cast glances their way, astounded that commoners had the audacity to rub shoulders with the elite, but the weapons and stance of the two strangers discouraged interference and they took their seats without issue.

"Have you ever seen one of these matches?" Ruben asked as the crowd around them rumbled in anticipation.

"Not in person. I viewed digitals when I was at the Academy."

"And what class was that for?"

"Survival 101," Shaun muttered sarcastically.

"The first few rows usually get covered with blood."

Shaun looked down toward the front, where a young woman with heavy face paint and jewelry awaited the start of the match with eager anticipation. She was there for the blood.

"They'll save Ram for last. He's so quick to kill that they have to," Ruben explained. "By then the crowd will be whipped into a frenzy and will be screaming for him."

"What about those men we saw coming in?"

"They will probably be pitted against other slaves and will have to kill each other off until only one survives. The one left standing will be allowed to stay on as a gladiator if his wounds are not too serious."

"Nice of them to do that," Shaun commented bitterly.

"At least the gladiators have hope."

"I just hope they take the collars off those guys before they throw them in there."

"They will. The crowd wants a real fight."

"And the organizers want the crowd to be happy."

"Give the people what they want."

"And they'll be back with more credits to spend." Shaun felt sick already and the match hadn't even started yet.

The crowd screamed and howled as twenty men were herded into the fenced arena. A blast from a pipe signaled that the battle should begin. At first the combatants were hesitant. It was almost as if they were in shock. They had been dragged to this place and outfitted with weapons that some had never seen before. The crowd screamed in anger, and the men who had shoved the prisoners inside the arena stuck metal prods through the fence to urge the men to battle. One trembling man went berserk after a few stings and jumped into the center, slashing his arms. He struck a man across the face and gore was flung up against the fence, sending the crowd into a frenzied roar. After that it was a matter of kill or be killed, and the floor was soon stained with blood as the contestants slashed at each other while trying to hold their ground on the slippery surface. Several different battles were going on at once as the combatants unknowingly weeded out the weak so that later battles would be more exciting. The crowd wanted the competition to be intense after the initial lust for blood was sated.

Shaun recognized the man he had made mental contact with. He seemed to be holding his own, although he was covered with blood. Of course, it could just be the spray from the men who had gone down with huge gaping tears in their bodies. A combatant had to be quick on his feet to escape with only minor wounds from the evil-looking blades. Shaun was relieved to see that the man could fight after the despair he had seen in his mind. At least he had a chance for survival. Shaun caught sight of the Circe witch on the other side of the arena. She sat as if made of marble amid the wild cheering of the crowd. Her face wore a deep frown; apparently she was disappointed that her prisoner had not met his demise along with the other two.

A blast from a pipe called a sudden halt to the fighting in the arena. Six men were still standing with chests heaving and heads down as they gratefully sucked in air. A crew of workers came in and checked the bodies. Most were already dead; the wounded were quickly dispatched without mercy. The bodies were carried off and the floor hosed down. The workmen splashed the blood onto the screaming crowd as they worked.

"Pretty macabre, isn't it?" Ruben said. "That's why I always sit with the rich folks. They don't like messing up their nice clothes."

Shaun grunted in response. He was grateful that Ruben had taken such things into consideration.

"So what happens next?" he asked as the workers finished their job and left the ring.

"Last one standing gets to walk out of the ring. Then we'll see some balanced matches between real warriors trained in the Murlaca. Then it's Ram's turn."

"Who will he be fighting?"

"One of the lucky winners from tonight. He gets to choose." Ruben pointed to one of the upper rows of seating across the arena. "That's our boy up there. He's watching to find somebody worthy to be his opponent."

Shaun quickly spotted the wide forehead and thick brow that was characteristic of the Ravigans. The bright crimson of his hooded cloak was also a dead giveaway. Ram must enjoy his role as Crown Prince. He wore his pride as overtly as he wore the cloak. He would not be a gracious loser. As far as Shaun was concerned, he could have all the victories he wanted within the arena. But when it came to Lilly, Ram was going to lose.

Shaun watched as one of Ram's companions made a point about the fighters in the arena. Ram threw back his head and laughed, revealing a wide row of perfectly white teeth.

"That's funny," Ruben said. "I expected to see fangs."

"Probably been sawed off," Shaun growled.

"Easy, big guy. Maybe you'll get lucky and the Prince will meet his demise tonight."

Shaun shook his head. He had never been that lucky. He needed to get Lilly away from the Senate, the sooner the better. But who was he kidding? She would never run away as long as Oasis was at risk. Maybe he should just kidnap her. Just take her away from all the scheming and the politics to a forgotten planet and convince her that it was the right thing to do.

She'd have him screaming on his knees in no time. But he was learning some tricks of his own. Maybe he could plant the thought in her head and make her think it was all her idea.

Shaun was disgusted with himself for even thinking

such a thing. He wanted Lilly; she was all he could think about. But he wanted her honestly. He wanted her to need him as much as he needed her.

The crowd started screaming again as the combatants went back to their battle. The Circe prisoner was still holding his own as others fell around him. Soon it was down to two, and he was one of them.

Shaun debated helping him. It would be so easy to plant a thought in the other man's head as he had done when he had fought the giant on Oasis. But did the other man deserve to die? Did Shaun have the right to determine the lives or deaths of these two men who stood gasping for breath as they warily circled each other? Was one more innocent or guilty than the other? Shaun realized that he was gaining an appreciation for what Lilly must go through every day of her life. When was it right to use her powers? Could she justify what she did because it was for the good of her people? Had she ever used her powers to condemn someone to death?

She had used a pipe to lay out his guard and saved his life on the cargo ship. The Legion officer had probably died when the ship broke apart. She must have realized that when she hit the man. She had chosen his life over another's and she had known he was a convicted murderer. What had she seen in him in those few brief moments before she fell into her cryo state?

The crowd went berserk as the other man fell to his knees. The Circe prisoner finished him quickly and with mercy, using his hands to snap the man's neck instead of letting him bleed to death. The witch quickly rose from her seat and went up the aisle to where Ram was still watching.

Shaun did not have to cast out his mind to know what was said between the two. The witch wanted her prisoner dead. And Ram wanted Oasis. A bargain was being made while he watched, and Lilly was part of it.

If only they got lucky and Ram was killed tonight.

The next match was between two women. They both wore helmets and armor that served to enhance their endowments more than to protect them from injury.

"I forgot about this part," Ruben exclaimed as the women shrieked at each other in the cage. "They just fight to first blood. No one wants to see bodies like those damaged."

Shaun looked on in disgust. The women's breasts threatened to spill out of the metal breastplates they wore. The crowd seemed to love it, however, and added laughter to their cries for blood.

"How much longer?" he impatiently asked Ruben, who was more interested in watching for the women's breasts to fall out than the actual battle.

"Not long," Ruben responded without taking his eyes off the ring. "If you're bored, you can go get me some ale."

"I'd be afraid to drink it."

"Don't worry; they sell the good stuff here. Brewed on Oasis, best in the universe."

The women's match suddenly ended when one of the combatants tripped and the other slashed off her hair where it was gathered into a tail high on her head. The crowd booed.

"It's extensions," Ruben confided to Shaun. "They do it all the time."

"How do you know all this stuff?" Shaun asked.

"The same way I know everything else."

"You slept with one of these women?"

"Trust me, my friend. There was no sleeping involved."

"You are unbelievable."

"I prefer to call myself legendary."

Shaun rolled his eyes and seriously considered dipping into his friend's mind for a visit. The appearance of the next set of gladiators changed his mind.

He carefully studied the techniques that the men used as they battled for supremacy over each other. There had to be more to this fighting than just slash and hack. He noticed as the battles continued that each set of warriors was better than the last. They showed artistry with their motions. The movements were made without force, like the motions of a dance. A very deadly dance.

Shaun felt the excitement of the crowd. Anticipation was building throughout the arena. The spectators were becoming impatient to see their champion. They wanted the current battle to be over so they could see the master at work.

"Ram. Ram. Ram. Ram," they chanted. The voices grew louder as the chant spread and circled the arena. Metal slashed and clashed in the arena. The crowd didn't care. They wanted Ram. They wanted to see Ram spill blood.

Shaun looked up at where the prince had been

seated. The area was empty. Ram was preparing for his performance.

One of the combatants slashed through the skin of the other's back as they whirled through the motions of their deadly dance. The crowd roared. The injured man dropped to his knees and bowed his head in submission.

"So he's just going to die?" Shaun asked in disbelief.

"No, he'll have to work his way up again," Ruben explained. "After he heals, he'll be thrown in with the first lot."

"That's nice treatment."

"It's not like they don't know what they're getting into," Ruben said casually.

"I guess the pay is good."

"The pay, the fame and the benefits," Ruben said, and pointed to the new blood-covered young woman in the front row. "I guarantee you that someone who fought in this ring will be warming her sheets tonight."

"No, thanks," Shaun said with disgust.

The lights dimmed as the two warriors left the ring. After a few moments of total darkness, spots of light shot up to the ceiling of the dome and then bounced around as if timed by the chants of the crowd.

"Ram. Ram. Ram," the spectators screamed in their bloodlust. The lights continued to circle and swirl, and then suddenly they were all focused on the center of the ring. The crowd went silent and the atmosphere became charged with tension. Shaun looked around at the faces surrounding him in the dim light of the arena and wondered if he was the only one present who was not holding his breath. Suddenly a red-cloaked figured appeared in the middle of the arena and Shaun scanned the floor to see if there was an opening of some sort that the man had appeared through.

Or maybe it was a Circe trick . . .

Ram threw off his cloak to the wild screams of the audience and held his arms up to the ceiling, revealing the long row of polished curved blades that ran the length of his forearms. Golden bands glistened on his biceps, enhancing the muscle that lay beneath. His torso was covered with a light armor that was detailed with the image of a ram facing forward, head bent, its horns curled toward an unknown foe. The front of his thighs held matching armor that ended right above the knee. Below were heavy black boots. He was dressed in skintight black pants that revealed the long line of the muscle in his legs. His dark hair was closely cropped to his head and stood straight up over his wide forehead. His eyes were dark and set deep over a wide nose and thin lips.

Shaun was sure he saw a red glow coming from the dark eyes as they scanned the crowd, arms upheld as if he were already celebrating his victory. He was also sure of whom the opponent would be.

Just as he expected, it was the Circe prisoner.

The man was afraid. He would be a fool not to be. Shaun admired him for being able to hide it. Ram, on the other hand, looked as if he were getting ready to sit down at a banquet. There was no mistaking the feral look in his face. He was practically salivating.

Ram circled his opponent, who stood quietly and cautiously in the center of the ring. The crowd began its chant again after the cacophony of wild screams at Ram's appearance settled down.

Shaun studied the Ravigan prince as he circled. He stepped lightly and gracefully around the prisoner, as if he were teaching the man a dance. The prisoner turned with him, wisely never exposing his back to the champion. Ram added a few dips and feints as he circled, to the approval of the crowd. Ram was toying with the prisoner. He was confident of his victory.

His confidence was his weakness, Shaun realized as he watched the dance. Ram was playing to the crowd, and each time he did so he exposed the back of his legs and the tendons that ran behind his knees. One quick slice and Ram would be crippled. Why didn't the prisoner see it?

Shaun focused his mind on sending that thought to the prisoner, who warily watched from the center of the ring.

He was too late. Ram whirled and slashed his blades downward, ripping the chest open with one arm and slicing the neck with the other. Blood spurted out as Ram grabbed the man's head between his hands and laughed gleefully as the prisoner gasped in shock while his lifeblood pumped out into the ring. Ram lowered the man to the floor of the arena as the spectators went wild, jumping to their feet and screaming his name.

"I think he just set a new record," Ruben exclaimed above the noise.

Shaun shoved past the people standing to his right. He had to get out of there. Ruben followed on his heels as Shaun fled the arena, the sounds of the chant driving him from the stadium.

Lilly. He had to get to Lilly and warn her. The

thought of Ram leering over her quivering body as he had the man he'd just killed sickened him. He had to get Lilly away from the Senate.

Would she go?

Chapter Eleven

The hour was late, but Lilly was still awake. She had dismissed the Ambassador and his secretary and sent her attendants to bed. She sat by the tall arched window that overlooked the garden behind her suite of apartments on the surface of the planet. Even though rich dark soil had been carried in from Oasis, there could be no substitute for the natural rays of the Oasian sun. The colors of the flowers were not as bright here as the flora that grew naturally on her home planet. Even at night, lit only by the Oasian stars, their vivid hues could be seen. Here they were only varied shades of gray in the dim artificial light that served as a replacement moon under the huge domes.

Varied shades of gray. No black or white, no truth or lies, only layers and layers of politics. Lilly rubbed her temples as she cast about for a solid fact among all the intrigue she had witnessed throughout the long day and evening. There was only one she could come up with. Oasis had been betrayed.

Was greed the reason for her people's difficulties? Oasis paid no tribute and yet the coffers of the Senate were rich. Why hadn't the Prefect asked for tribute instead of selling the planet off to the Ravigans?

A tear trickled unheeded down her cheek as she mourned for her planet. She was not qualified for this job. She did not know whom to bribe or what to offer to save her people. She had been outmaneuvered before she'd even arrived at the Senate. If only Alexander had come with her, or even Michael.

But they were on Oasis, risking their lives in the battle to save the planet. How could she bear to tell her uncle that all was lost?

But perhaps all was not lost. There was still the meeting to be held in the morning in the Prefect's private chambers. There was still a chance to save her planet.

If only she knew what she should do to save Oasis.

"Mistress?" It was Agatha, the attendant who slept outside her door. Lilly had been so engrossed in her thoughts that she had not heard the opening of the wide double doors that guarded her quarters.

"Come," Lilly said, dashing the tear from her cheek as she turned.

"Your protector seeks an audience."

She had left word for Shaun to be brought to her upon his return. She hoped that he had found some hope for her planet. "Show him in and then leave us," she commanded. "Have his quarters been prepared?"

"Yes, mistress," Agatha replied, but made no move to let him in.

"What is it, Agatha?" Lilly asked as she saw the older woman's timid squirming.

"I was wondering, mistress. Why does your protector shield his eyes?"

Lilly smiled to let the woman know that she had not trod on forbidden ground. "He was raised underground. The lights bother his eyes." It was a bold question for the attendant, but not an unreasonable one.

"Do they not handicap him, then?"

The woman was only worried about her safety. "Not a bit. He has more than proven himself."

"I was only concerned because he is not of Oasis."

"He saved my life, Agatha, and I trust him. That is all that need concern you about him."

"Yes, mistress," Agatha said with bowed head. She pulled open the wide door, which swung easily on its hinges despite its great size, and stepped aside to let Shaun enter.

Shaun removed his shields after Agatha left and took a moment to survey the huge room with the tall ceilings and fabric-covered walls. An enormous bed, piled high with thick coverings and hung with heavy drapes, occupied the center of the room. The spacious chamber reminded him of an old digital he had seen of an ancient palace that was rumored to be from an age before the time of their universe.

He had seen Agatha's trepidation at his presence and wondered if it had anything to do with the state of Lilly's dress. She was wearing a simple robe of white that reached to her ankles and wrists. The thread of the fabric was so fine that it was nearly transparent and presented a full view of her silhouette as she stood to greet him before the tall window of her quarters.

"You have news?" she asked.

Even her speech patterns had changed since their arrival on the planet. Shaun was momentarily confused by her abrupt formality, especially when the view of her body beneath the glimmer of her gown was tearing at his insides.

"It's not what you want to hear," he said as he came to her.

"I fear that the news cannot get any worse." She looked up at him with eyes that betrayed she'd been crying, and Shaun once again saw the vulnerability that she had shown on Ruben's ship.

She was to be a sacrifice to Ram and nothing more. The Prince would destroy her beauty as easily as he had killed the Circe prisoner. And she would go to him willingly to save her beloved planet. Because she felt guilty over something her mother had done before she was even born. They had raised her well, her uncle and his protector. They had groomed her to be a sacrifice for the Senate altar.

Rage filled him as he thought of the plan, and Lilly saw it all with her mind without his saying a word. She turned to look out the window at the garden below.

"I wonder where Ram and I will make our home," she said calmly. "We carried the soil from Oasis here to build this garden. I'm sure the same could be done on Raviga."

"I won't let it happen," Shaun managed to choke out between teeth gritted with rage. He wanted to strike out at something, anything, but settled instead for running his hand down the silky length of her hair as she continued to look out the window.

"It's not up to you," Lilly said gently, but he felt the trembling beneath his gentle touch.

"How can you say that?" Her calm acceptance of the situation angered him more than the politics that had led her there.

"It matters not how you feel, or how I . . ." Her voice broke. "It only matters that Oasis be saved." She squared her shoulders and fortified her mind against his coming attack.

"Damn Oasis," he nearly shouted.

"I will not allow that," she replied calmly.

"Lilly!" He grabbed her arms and turned her to face him. Her eyes were as pale as the artificial moonlight that shone upon the garden. His mind dove into hers and he came up against her wall and heard the litany over and over in his head. "Lilly!" he said again, louder, and shook her to awaken her mind from the trance she had put it in. Her face remained impassive, her eyes empty.

His mouth came down on hers hard as his arms wound around her slim form and crushed her body against his chest. His lips slashed across her silent ones, across her expressionless face, over her delicate brow, and down her graceful neck as he desperately sought a reaction from her. It was as if he were holding a likeness of her body in his arms, nothing more. He bent her backward over his arm and moved his mouth down over her breast as his hand splayed across the back of her head.

She was motionless in his arms. Her passivity enraged him. He brought a hand around and ripped the front of the gown, baring her breasts before him. He was desperate for a reaction. He had hoped that she would strike him down, but instead he heard her sharp intake of breath as his mouth moved from one breast to the other. Shaun raised his head and saw her eyes glittering like pale jewels. He thought at first it was passion, and hope and lust flared within his body, but then he saw the jewels slide away and trickle down her cheeks to become lost in her hair.

"Please," she said in a desperate whisper.

Shaun decided in that moment that he hated himself. Rykers would have been paradise compared to this, this torture of the mind, body, and spirit.

He relaxed his hold, allowing her to stand on her own two feet again. Lilly's entire body trembled, violently shivering as she clutched at the torn edges of her gown. Shaun turned away from her, shamed by his assault.

"Go," she said, but it was not the imperious voice of a princess. It was instead a plea from a child.

Shaun turned to look at her, and the anguish of his soul poured out through his eyes.

"I'm sorry," he said, knowing that he still could have her if he tried and hating himself for thinking it. He had to walk away. He couldn't just take her, could he?

"Lilly?"

She turned and stepped away, and as she did her legs would not support her. Shaun scooped her up before she fell and carried her to the bed. She made not a sound as he crossed the room, but her body was rigid as he carried it.

How easy it would be to take her now. He knew he could overpower her body and her mind as he gently laid her on the stack of thick coverings. One hand still clutched the shredded top of her gown as her eyes looked beyond his face to the rich draping overhead.

It was the face she would present to Ram when he took her as his wife. It showed resolution and surrender. Shaun pulled a covering from the foot of the bed up over her body. He turned to leave and stopped before the huge doors.

"Do you want me to go with you in the morning?" he asked, not knowing which answer he would prefer.

"I care not," she replied in a voice vacant of spirit and hope.

Shaun laid a hand on the knob of the door and was not surprised to feel the handle shake. It was merely an extension of the frustration he felt inside. The shaking moved out in a circle from the knob through the door, and the carved wood moved against its hinges as if the sturdy ground beneath it were splitting in two. The rattling increased in sound and movement until the trim around it bowed and splintered. With a shout, Shaun shoved the portal away and it swung back on its hinges, startling poor Agatha, who was looking at the thing as if it were possessed. Shaun moved past her as if she weren't even there, and the woman looked after him in awe before regaining the presence of mind to check on her mistress.

"I am fine, Agatha," Lilly assured her as she pulled the covering close under her chin. "Close the door."

"I cannot. It only opens in, and he has forced it out," she explained.

Lilly sat up to look at the door hanging on its hinges and burst into tears. She pulled the coverings back over her body as she chastised herself for crying over something as foolish as a door when an entire planet's future rested on her slim shoulders.

He had lost his shields. Shaun realized it as soon as he left the cluster of apartments. He also realized that he didn't care. He was sick of hiding behind them. His light gray eyes darted around the neat pathways and carefully manicured miniature gardens that set off the residential area of the Senate. He hoped someone would challenge him. He was aching for a fight. He needed to get rid of the rage that boiled inside him.

The sound of feminine laughter caught his ears and he looked around to see a couple coming his way on one of the paths. He shook his head in amazement when he realized that it was Ruben, which meant the woman wearing the hooded cloak was probably Lilly's maid Martia. He had to hand it to his friend—he worked fast. The last time he had seen Ruben was before he went in to see Lilly. He had left him outside Lilly's apartments with a description of Martia, and here he was cuddled up to her already. Shaun faded into the darkness as the couple approached. Maybe all was not lost. Maybe Martia held the answers to who had betrayed Lilly.

Ruben stumbled as they went past, and Martia steadied him with her shoulder beneath his arm. Was Ruben drunk? He had not been drinking while they were in the pits, and not enough time had passed for his friend to tie one on. Maybe it was an act on his part, but why?

Shaun followed along behind, sticking to the shadows. He knew the couple was going back to the apartments. He had a room there himself, although the thought of sleeping in the narrow bed, while Lilly lay alone and troubled in her own luxurious suite, had been enough to send him back out into the night.

Ruben stumbled again, and Martia's high laugh covered a low rumble from his friend. This was not like Ruben at all. Had the witch found him out?

They were not going to Lilly's apartments. Instead they turned into a pathway between two buildings and disappeared into a passageway that led below the buildings. Shaun quickened his step and caught the door just before it closed. He cautiously looked around before he entered. He caught the flick of Martia's cloak as it moved behind one of the pieces of machinery that inhabited the room. Something definitely was not right about the situation. Ruben was in trouble.

Shaun crept between the machinery, his ears tuned for the slightest sound. Had he misjudged Martia's power? Lilly knew the woman better than he did and had not considered her a threat. What had happened to Ruben to make him into a stumbling drunk in such a short amount of time? Shaun moved in closer to where he could hear the slight sound of feminine voices amid the chugging of the machinery.

Ruben was slumped in a chair, his head lolling. Three women surrounded him; one was Martia and the other two were dressed in the formal robes of the Circe. Ruben was wearing a collar! Shaun caught the glint of the white strobe blinking to life as one of the witches connected the circle.

The witches stepped away and Shaun quickly recognized the cold, expressionless face of the Circe who had led the prisoners into the pits. His fingers ached to curl around her neck and choke the life from her. What were they doing to Ruben?

"What do you know of Oasis?" The cold-faced one asked.

"Bounty . . ." Ruben's voice was slurred and his head wobbled on his neck. Shaun panicked at the word. Surely his friend would not give him up so easily by telling the witches about the Legion bounty on his head.

"Bounty?" The witch leaned in closer. "What kind of bounty?"

"Bounty . . . ful breasts." Ruben was practically giggling like a girl as his head lolled back.

The Circe from the pits grabbed Ruben's jaw with a hiss. "How much of the vial did you give him?" she asked as she looked into the blurry eyes of her captive.

Martia kept her eyes down. "I'm not sure, Mistress Arleta."

"Fool, I can see in your mind that you poured out the vial."

"I am sorry, Mistress. I was in a rush and afraid he would see what I was doing."

"Can we just look inside his mind?" the other witch asked.

The cold-faced witch grabbed Ruben's jaw again

and squeezed it between her fingers as she brought his face into line with her own. "Hear me well, slave. You will answer my questions," she said into his face.

"I don't want to," Ruben said, emphasizing the "to" so that he sprayed spittle into the witch's face. "Punish me," he said with a leer and a snicker. "Please?"

"Bah," Arleta exclaimed, shoving his face away. "He is not capable now of an intelligent thought."

Ruben looked over at Martia and waggled his eyebrows suggestively. Shaun watched the exchange and squeezed the bridge of his nose to keep from laughing out loud. His friend definitely had a one-track mind.

"What do we do now, Mistress?" Martia asked in distress.

"This one was recently on the planet and in Alexander's presence. He left Oasis with a hold full of treasure. We have to find out what he knows."

"But he was rewarded for saving the Princess," Martia declared. "And the other one became her protector."

"Exactly. But who tried to kill the Princess? Alexander assured us that she would come to this marriage willingly. Someone is trying to stop this marriage."

Alexander had arranged the marriage for Lilly? Shaun refused to believe it as he listened to the witches discuss their plans for Oasis. Why would the Sovereign do it? What were his motives? Unless he never intended for the marriage to happen. The words of his father came back to him. *Layers upon layers, motives hiding motives.* What if Alexander had secretly agreed to the wedding so it would appear that he was negotiating for peace and then betrayed Lilly as a way to force the Senate to intervene in the war? But Shaun had seen with his own eyes the Ravigans attacking the cargo ship. Had Alexander purchased their services? It was a mystery, and one that he had no time to unravel right now. He needed to concentrate on Ruben and getting his friend out of this mess.

"The other one?" the third witch said. "We did not know of the other one."

"He came with them to Oasis. He was made her protector," Martia explained.

"Where is he now?" Arleta asked.

"I know not. I was searching for him when this one came to me."

"This one came to you? You did not seek him out?"

Ruben grabbed Arleta's hand and with his other hand rubbed her hip, raising the edge of her gown up with each stroke.

"I've never had a four-way before," he said with a grin and a leer. "There are four of us?" He blinked as he looked around at the three women, who stared at him with mouths hanging open. "Are you two twins?" He looked between the two witches dressed in the robes.

The cold-faced witch pulled her hand away in disgust. "When we're through with him, we shall send him to the pits."

"No, baby, I promise it will be wonderful." Ruben laughed as he reached for her hand again. "I promise."

Shaun shook his head at his friend's antics. Ruben was trying to wink at the women, but he couldn't get his eyelids to cooperate.

"Mistress, we are running short on time." Martia

tried her best not to look at the captive. She was afraid she would laugh at his foolish antics.

"We can wait until the potion wears off or we can persuade him to answer our questions." Arleta placed her hands on Ruben's temples. Ruben tried to blow her a kiss, but then screamed loudly as her mind penetrated his. Shaun was surprised to see what resembled a smile cross her features. The witch was enjoying the fact that she was torturing her captive. Ruben fought against her hands and tried to rise from his chair. "You cannot move, nor can you speak," the witch said, and the collar made it so. Ruben sat motionless with his eyes wide with horror and his mouth open in a silent scream.

Shaun had seen and heard enough. He had to get Ruben away from the witches. He turned his concentration on Martia, who seemed to be nervous in the presence of the higher witches.

"Someone is coming, Mistress," Martia said. "We must leave here at once." Shaun had planted the thought in her head.

The other witch raised her head, but the cold-faced one kept her focus on Ruben as she spoke. "There is no one there, Phyllis. Why do you look?" she said, keeping her hands on Ruben's temples.

Martia nervously looked over her shoulder. "But I can hear footsteps."

Arleta raised her head and looked at Martia. Then she cast her eyes around.

"Fool," she hissed. "Someone is playing with your mind . . ."

Shaun set his mental wall into place as he moved stealthily through the room.

"It's a Circe," Arleta declared. "I can feel her. She has betrayed us."

"Could it be Lilly?" Phyllis asked.

"No," the cold one declared as her eyes scanned the open places between the machinery. "She has not the strength. It is another one, one I cannot see . . ."

Shaun caught the words as he kept moving. He had to lure them away from Ruben. But could he control all three? He dared not try. Too much was at stake. He might not be able to control them with his mind, but surely he could with his fists. All he had to do was take out the most powerful one first. He moved into position behind them and made them look away with one thought. Arleta hissed as she realized the trick. Shaun rose from his hiding place and punched her in the jaw just as she turned to look at him.

"Your eyes!" she exclaimed as her own pale ones rolled back and she sank to the floor. Martia and Phyllis looked down at their mistress in shock.

"The protector," Martia hissed as Shaun quickly knocked her and the other witch unconscious and let them fall to the floor without a second thought.

"Ruben." Shaun shook his friend, who blinked and looked around in shock.

"What happened?" Ruben gasped as he looked at the three women collapsed on the floor.

Shaun worked at the collar around his neck. "You seduced three women at once," he said as he unsnapped the clasp and flung the instrument away.

"You were fantastic." Shaun hauled his friend to his feet and slung his arm over his shoulder.

"I was?" Ruben asked as Shaun carried him away.

"They were falling at your feet begging for more."

"So why do they still have their clothes on?"

"Like I said, buddy, you were fantastic."

Chapter Twelve

"So what you're saying is we're in big trouble," Ruben concluded as he raised his bleary eyes from his third cup of jolt. Shaun had carried his friend to the docking bay and the safety of his ship to recover from his experience with the witches.

"I'd say so. The Circe are curious about us because we just left Oasis with Lilly. Alexander has made a deal with Raviga and the Circe to marry Lilly off to Ram. Apparently Raviga and the Circe have struck a deal with the Senate . . ." Shaun ran through the list of conspirators.

"And Alexander is working on his own agenda that ultimately winds up with Lilly being killed." Ruben rubbed his temples and scrubbed his hands through his hair in an attempt to get his mind working again. "Why?"

"Lilly is the last of her line. Oasis has no one else to offer as part of a peace treaty."

"So if Lilly is killed and it looks as if the Ravigans did it, then the Senate will have to step in and protect Oasis."

"Exactly."

"But I thought you said it was Raviga that attacked the cargo ship?" Ruben asked.

"It was. That's the part that doesn't make sense, unless Alexander bought their services."

Ruben nodded. It was possible.

"Or maybe Raviga found out there was going to be an attempt on her life and sent out ships to capture her instead."

"By blowing a cargo ship apart? That would make it more likely that Lilly would be killed than captured. I don't think they'd take that chance."

Shaun jumped to his feet. "What if instead of sending someone to attack the cargo ship, Alexander planted something on it to make it blow apart? Lilly said that she and her protector were smuggled out with a grain shipment. What if something was planted in the grain . . ."

"And the grain was loaded onto the cargo ship along with the passengers who can't afford to go hyperspace . . ."

"Such as condemned murderers on their way to prison planets," Shaun finished for him. "No matter whether the explosion happened sooner or later, Alexander could blame it on Raviga. All he had to do was leak information to the Ravigans that Lilly was in danger and they would have been after her."

"So they could ensure the safety of their meal ticket."

"Which was why they started the war in the first place," Ruben pointed out. "To get access to the garden planet. So what do we do now?"

"We have to get Lilly away from here."

"Will she go?"

"No. She's determined to do her duty to Oasis."

"Really?"

"That uncle of hers raised her to be a sacrificial lamb, and Lilly doesn't even realize it." Shaun paced the confines of Ruben's cabin. "She's given up. She doesn't seem to consider what she wants at all."

"She's a princess—what did you expect? An invitation for you to warm her sheets?"

"I wish." Shaun laughed hollowly. "No, she's resolved that the only way to save her planet is by marrying Ram. She didn't even realize that was the plan until she saw . . . I told her." Ruben still did not know about his newfound mind powers, and now was not the time to tell him. "As soon as she found out, it was as if everything fell into place in her mind. She's going to go into the Prefect's meeting in the morning and agree to everything they say just to save her planet."

"And her only living relative, who wants her dead."

"The strange thing is that if Lilly's mother's plan had worked, then Lilly would now be ruling Oasis," Shaun mused.

"Maybe that's why Alexander wants her dead. It's his final revenge against Lilly's mother." Ruben rose from his seat and stretched his tall, slim form. "He must hate her violently to forget that Lilly is also his brother's daughter."

Shaun did not comment. He was remembering

something he had seen in Michael's mind before they left Oasis. He cared for Lilly deeply. Surely he would not stand by if he knew Alexander's plans for Lilly. But then again, maybe he would. After all, he had betrayed someone he loved before . . .

Lilly realized in the darkest hours of the night that sleep would be impossible. She might as well rise and prepare herself for the coming meeting. Her mind would need to be strong indeed so as not to betray the emotion that she dared not show. It would be a weakness, and she was determined not to be weak. She had always known this would be her destiny, though she had never thought she would mind it so much.

He had left his shields. Lilly saw them on the table by the window and snatched them up, holding them close against her heart. Without his shields, his eyes would be visible to all. The Circe would want to know who he was, where he came from; they would not stop until they had the answers.

Lilly locked her frantic worry for Shaun in a box and hid it in the deep recesses of her mind. Her thoughts would give him away as readily as the color of his eyes. She was determined that she would not betray him in that way.

Never mind that she would betray him by denying her feelings for him. Never mind that she would betray her own heart by joining in a marriage with the detested Prince of Raviga. It mattered not what she wanted. She had to save her people. She had to do what was best for Oasis. Giving herself in marriage was nothing in comparison to the great evil her mother had brought to the people. If not for her mother, Oasis would have a young and strong leader who could fight its battles. If not for the grace of Alexander in allowing her mother to give birth to her, she would not even be alive. Marrying the Prince was the least she could do.

She would do it. No matter that her heart was breaking. She should have known better. She should not have allowed Shaun to kiss her. She should not have allowed him to come into her mind and haunt her with his wanting. She should not have allowed . . .

"Mistress?" It was Agatha. Of course she would awaken at the slightest sound. The maid stood in the opening left by the destruction of the door. "Have you need of anything?"

"No, Agatha. Go back to sleep. I will summon you when I am ready."

"Yes, Mistress."

When I am ready... How would she ever be ready? Lilly fought the urge to dissolve into hysterical laughter. That would bring Agatha running. Agatha and Martia and William and the secretary, who had his own agenda. They would all come running to watch their mistress give herself up to hysterical laughter and wonder what had caused this strange break with sanity.

Would Shaun come running also? Was he at this moment lying in his narrow cot, waiting for the morrow to come so he could watch her give her life over to the will of the people?

She had told him she cared not what he did. Chances were better that he was sitting in a bar with

Ruben somewhere drowning his sorrows in a huge cup. *Had a shot at a princess, Ruben, and she turned me down flat. Oh well, buy me another drink and find me a willing woman to warm my sheets. . . .*

Lilly shook her head. If she wanted to know what Shaun was doing at the moment, all she had to do was cast out with her mind and search. She could find him readily enough if she wanted to . . .

She must not. Her search would betray him. It was time to erase his memory from her mind. Her decision made, Lilly turned to her chest of clothing and found the gown that she had taken off. Shaun had torn it in his passionate attempt at turning her mind from its course. Her breasts tingled as she recalled the feel of his lips moving down and the feel of his hands . . .

"Enough!" she said out loud. Lilly jerked open her chest and found the clothing she desired. Her knives were in their usual place, and she picked them up as she left her quarters through the door that hung crazily upon its ruined hinge.

They must not find out about him.

"So what are you going to do?" Ruben asked Shaun as he stood and stretched. The unnatural light of the pretend dawn gave the port dome an eerie orange glow.

"I'm her protector. I'm going to protect her," Shaun replied.

"Wait," Ruben said as his friend turned to go. "Take this, in case . . . you know . . ."

Shaun gratefully pocketed the beacon his friend had handed him. He hoped he wouldn't need it.

"I'll have the ship ready and waiting," Ruben assured Shaun as he went down the ramp. "Tell her highness I'll even turn her bed down."

"Just as long as you remember that I'm the one who's going to warm the sheets," Shaun said with a grim smile as he made his way into the growing flow of traffic heading toward the Senate's dome.

Shaun came to the quarters and found Lilly much the same as before her previous meeting. She was an island of calm amid the hustle and bustle of her stewards. How could she look so peaceful when her very life was forfeit to the whims of others? She appeared serene as her attendants dressed her in a long-sleeved white top that crossed in front and tied at the waist, and white pants tucked into boots of the same hue. One of her maids held a long coat of heavy silver brocade, and Lilly held her arms behind her so the maid could guide the coat onto her shoulders.

Shaun noticed that Martia was missing from the group that surrounded Lilly. He didn't know if that was good for him or bad. He had come prepared to deal with the witch spy. He was sure that the three women had recovered by now from his attack. He wondered what their next move would be.

"Put on your shields." She had come into his mind. He saw them where she had left them on the table by the window. No one noticed him as he walked over to the table and covered his eyes with the shades. As soon as they fell into place, the Ambassador addressed him as if he had been waiting for him to come into the room.

"Protector. One of the Princess's attendants is missing. The maid Martia was not in her quarters last night. Have you knowledge of her whereabouts?"

"The last time I saw her, she was asleep," Shaun said with a straight face. *Let them think what they will.* He caught Lilly's slight smile and knew that she saw his meaning in his mind.

"Pay her absence no heed, William," Lilly reassured her ambassador. "I knew her to be a spy, and her job is done. We have no further need of her services."

"My services are still needed, Princess," Shaun told her with his mind.

If she had heard his words, it was not apparent to those who were around her.

"There are things you don't know." His words battered against her wall. *"Hidden layers."*

Her face remained composed and her focus turned inward as William continued on with his notes about the coming meeting.

"I think I've figured out who was behind the attack on the cargo ship, Lilly."

The tilt of her head let him know she was listening.

"Who would profit the most from your death if this arranged marriage could not take place?" he asked, hoping to jar her out of her passive acceptance of her fate. *"Who had the means to betray you?"*

Shaun felt the internal debate in her mind. Years of training and obedience were battling the logic he'd thrust upon her. Her mind was considering his question, and the same answer kept coming to the forefront: Alexander. But she remained as she had before, detached and with no emotion on her carefully composed face.

"Quit being their puppet!" Shaun was angry now. It took every bit of his willpower to stand casually by, watching her, instead of shaking her until her she snapped out of her lassitude. *"You're about to sacrifice your life for someone who wants you dead!"*

Shaun watched as Lilly's chest moved with the effort of taking in a deep gulp of air. She turned her eyes on him and they once again glittered with light and life.

"Alexander wants me dead?"

"Yes, he does," Shaun said out loud.

The Ambassador and his secretary turned to look at Shaun as if he had just made a sudden outburst instead of speaking calmly.

"Leave us," Lilly commanded, her imperious tone ringing out. "I have a need to talk to my protector."

The barriers were down. Shaun felt them fall away as her stewards filed from the chambers. The Ambassador was frantically worried about the time. Shaun sent him a scathing thought involving an impossible feat of contortion. Lilly's eyes danced with her usual humor as she watched the stunned man leave the room.

Shaun crossed the room to Lilly as soon as the assemblage was safely gone. He knew Agatha was poised and waiting outside the damaged portal, but he did not care. He had to have Lilly in his arms.

"You can't," she said as his arms folded around her slim body, pulling her against his solid strength.

"I'm tired of people telling me what I can't do," he said as he pushed his shields up and lowered his lips to hers.

"Nothing has changed," Lilly protested. "I still have to . . ."

His lips silenced hers efficiently as he moved a hand behind her head to keep her pressed against him. Her argument went unheard as he had his way with her lips . . . for the moment. The thought of Ram kissing her in the same manner filled his mind, and it angered him. His lips slashed and trailed across her face as she tried to turn away. He needed to brand her as his possession, his love, his life . . .

Lilly broke loose and pushed him away. "What are you trying to do, place your mark upon me?" She was quite angry with him, and it showed in her flashing gray eyes.

"Do you know what Ram is like?" Shaun asked, surprised and angered at her reaction. "Have you even seen him?"

"I know about Prince Ramelah," she assured him. "Did you think I was just going to walk into this without any knowledge of the man?"

"Yes, I did. You're so determined to stop this war that you would jump off a tower if Alexander told you to." Shaun quickly realized by her expression that his angry words would not go far in convincing her that what she was doing was wrong. "Last night you had given up without a fight."

"I didn't give up, Shaun. I was just resolved to the situation."

"How can you be resolved? Alexander tried to kill you, your esteemed Circe Queen is using you, and your potential bridegroom has struck up a deal with the Prefect to pay him tribute after he steals your home planet. You shouldn't be resolved, you should be angry!"

"I am!" She wanted to scream, but kept her voice down because she knew Agatha was listening. "But being angry doesn't help me and it doesn't help Oasis."

"You're not seriously considering going through with this, are you?"

"I'm willing to listen to an alternative solution to our problem." Lilly turned away from him. "And running off to the far reaches of the galaxy with you doesn't qualify as a solution."

Shaun bit back the *let's run off to the far reaches of the galaxy* plan that had been in his mind. He wondered how far he would get if he just threw her over his shoulder and made a run for the spaceport.

"Don't even think about it," she said, which was a bit late, since he already had.

Shaun rubbed a hand across his forehead. "So what you're saying is even though this alliance was arranged behind your back and without your consent, you are still going to go through with the marriage to Ram?"

"It's the only way to save Oasis."

"What about Alexander?"

"Once I become Ram's wife, it will no longer profit him to kill me. He will lose control of the planet, but our people will be safe."

"But what about us?"

"There *is* no us." Her words were louder than she meant them to be.

"Lilly, you know you can't hide your feelings from me."

Lilly cast a worried look toward the broken door

and Shaun shook his head. He didn't care who knew that he was in love with the Princess.

"I'm not hiding anything, Shaun. I never said that I didn't have feelings for you." Her voice had lowered into a hushed whisper.

"So how can you go through with this?" he demanded.

"Because I'm doing what's best for my people."

"What about what's best for Lilly?" He grabbed her shoulders again, this time determined to shake some sense into her addled brain.

"That's not important, Shaun."

"But it is important. It's important to me."

"And my people are important to me. I was born to royalty, Shaun. That means that I have to accept the responsibility of caring for my people. I have to do what is best for them, no matter what the cost is to me personally. It's my destiny."

"It's a pack of lies that Alexander has fed you for your entire life."

"You don't know . . ."

"Yes, I know. I saw it as clearly as I see you. Alexander has reminded you your entire life of what your mother did and that you are only alive by his grace. And then he's used the guilt that you feel to control you and to make you do his bidding. Now he's ready to throw you away if it will further his needs."

"It doesn't matter. Alexander hasn't been right since his brother's death."

"Mistress, we must go," Agatha interrupted.

Shaun was desperate to stop her. He grabbed her

arm as she turned to her maid. "What if I told you that you're not really Victor's daughter?"

Lilly jerked her arm away. "I'd say that your mind has gone over the edge."

"Have you ever wondered why Alexander and Michael asked you not to probe their minds? We know Alexander's secrets now. What about Michael's?"

"You've spent far too much time delving your mind into places it doesn't belong," Lilly said as she smoothed out the sleeves of her garment. "You have forgotten that power and responsibility go hand in hand." She turned to leave.

"Lilly—" Shaun reached for her sleeve again but pulled his hand back as if it had been burned. "I can play that game, too, if that's what you want."

"That's not what I want." She kept her back to him. "What I want is for you to support me. What I want is to walk into this meeting with you standing beside me as my protector. What I want is to know that I'm not doing this alone."

Shaun took a moment to look inside her mind. She was terrified of what was to come and determined not to show it. She had to be strong. Otherwise her enemies would see her weakness and use it to destroy her. She needed him to help her. Shaun lowered his shields into place and closed his eyes.

"Thank you," she whispered as she felt in her mind his arms circling her, holding her safe, giving her strength.

"Let's go, Princess. It's not polite to keep the Prefect waiting."

* * *

He had been waiting. Impatience showed on several faces when they arrived at the Prefect's personal quarters. Shaun wondered why they were even going through the charade of the meeting. All the arrangements had been made before Lilly had even arrived. Of course, she was not supposed to know that.

He saw Ramelah first, standing before a troop of bodyguards that were armed to the teeth. Perhaps the Prince thought his bride would run and he would need his soldiers to bring her in? The man must really love red, because he was dressed from head to toe in it. Even his soft leather boots had been dyed the color of blood. *So the blood on his hands will blend in,* Shaun thought to himself as the Ravigan Prince's eyes roamed over Lilly's slim body. *He looks at her as if he were buying her in the market.* Shaun sent a piercing thought his way, and the Prince blinked before he rubbed his eyes with thumb and forefinger. Shaun's face and eyes remained impassive behind his shields.

Honora's face remained impassive also. She had not missed the thought sent the Ravigan Prince's way. Nor had she ignored Arleta's report this morning. The protector had strange eyes and strange powers. Powers that were not permitted in a man. As soon as this business with Lilly settled, the Sacrosanct Mistress had plans to delve deeper into the mysterious man who had suddenly appeared in Lilly's life. She was determined to see what he was hiding behind his shields.

Official greetings were exchanged. Hierarchy and history were established. Protocol was served and ceremony satisfied. Then the Prefect had the nerve to speak to Lilly as if she were his daughter.

"My dear, I have spent the past night sleepless over the dilemma that you have laid out for me," he began.

"I beg your forgiveness, honorable Prefect. It was not my intent to trouble you so personally," Lilly responded, the proper look of contrition on her face.

"Poor child, I feel personally responsible for the troubles of all member planets." The man caressed her cheek, and Shaun resisted the urge to pitch him through a wall. "And I am pleased to sacrifice my rest in order to come up with such a compromise as the one I will present to you now."

Shaun watched in disgust as Ram and Honora leaned in to hear the Prefect's words as if they were about to hear them for the first time.

"A compromise?" Lilly asked. Shaun watched the Sacrosanct Mistress's face and knew that she was not fooled by Lilly's question. She knew that her deceit had been discovered and that Lilly was onto the plot.

The Prefect took Lilly's hand in one of his own and motioned for Ram to join him with the other. As Ram approached, the Prefect took his hand as well.

"A joining of your planets," the Prefect announced proudly. "A melding of your kind and your people. A wedding between the Prince of Raviga and the Princess of Oasis. And peace between your planets."

"I shall present the plan to my uncle," Lilly murmured.

"Oh, but your uncle has already agreed to the plan," Honora assured her.

"As my father has," Ram stated. His heavy brow hid the way his dark eyes raked over Lilly's body, and he smiled. Shaun saw it all from behind his shields.

"It seems as if the decision has been made for me," Lilly said. "And so quickly if the Prefect only came to this decision this morning. I doubt that I could scarce have time to get word to Oasis myself in such a short period of time."

Honora's nostrils flared, and the Prefect forced himself to swallow his retort at the impudence the Princess was showing.

"Am I to assume that the ceremony has already been planned and scheduled?" Lilly asked sweetly.

"You overstep yourself, child," Honora warned her.

"She will find that the women of Raviga are expected to be silent when such manners are being discussed," Ram added.

"And you will find that I am always and foremost a woman of Oasis," Lilly reminded the Prince.

"Good for you, Princess."

"Stop!" Honora exclaimed. "We have a spy among us." A murmur rose among the assembled attendants as the witch gathered her robes around her and turned her pale gray eyes toward Lilly's contingent.

"Surely no one would dare!" The Prefect was clearly offended.

"I have been forewarned," Honora replied as she stepped forward with her head held high.

"By the spy you planted in my household?" Lilly asked.

"You dare much, child. Twice this morning you

have shown your impudence." Honora stopped in front of Shaun. "Remove your shields."

Shaun crossed his arms and looked down at the woman.

"Foolish man, have you no fear that I can kill you where you stand?"

"As I can you, bitchtress." He spoke not a word out loud, but his words were clear to Lilly and the Sacrosanct Mistress.

Honora gasped, and Lilly felt her gathering her power. Before the Circe could react to Shaun's challenge, the Sacrosanct Mistress went flying across the room, landing on her back and sliding against a wall.

"How could you?" Lilly gasped.

"It was easy," Shaun replied.

He'd misunderstood her question. Where was his power coming from? Lilly wondered. He had shattered an enormous door with just the touch of his hand, and now he had thrown a woman across the room with the sheer force of his will.

Suddenly the odds in the room were not in their favor. Ram's bodyguards drew their weapons, as did the soldiers that guarded the Prefect.

"We're going to have to run for it," Lilly said into his mind.

"You're going with me?" Shaun asked as the solders cautiously stepped toward them.

"Let it be known that I act now for myself alone," Lilly announced. "Yet I still request amnesty for my people."

"So be it," the Prefect said. "Except for that one." He pointed to Shaun.

"That one is mine," Honora announced as she regained her dignity along with her feet.

Ram's bodyguards made their move. At the same instant, Shaun grabbed Lilly's hand and they bolted through the doors. Shaun slammed the portals shut with his mind, and they could hear the guards pounding on them as they fled.

"How long will the doors hold?" he asked as they ran down the hall.

"You're asking me? How are you doing these things?" she asked breathlessly.

"I don't know. I just think it and it happens." He grabbed onto her hand as they ran.

"So it should hold until you quit thinking it?" Lilly asked.

"Which wasn't long enough," he said as they turned a corner. Honora had opened the doors with her powerful mind. "We've got to get to Ruben."

"If they knew about you, then they're probably watching him," Lilly gasped. The ornate robe she wore was heavy, and she shrugged out of it as they ran.

"Probably," Shaun agreed. They came to the entrance of the building.

"Wait," Lilly said. "They'll have all the security forces after us out there—"

"Make it quick," Shaun interrupted. He could feel Ram's bodyguards breathing down his neck.

"The Prefect has a personal craft on top of the building," Lilly explained.

"Let's go."

They quickly found the lift and were able to distract and overpower the few guards they ran into. The craft was sitting on top of the building, just as Lilly had said it would be.

"How do we get through the dome?" Shaun asked as they entered the craft and he checked the systems.

"It should recognize the Prefect's ship and open automatically for it."

He powered up the ship, and they lifted off just as several guards burst through the rooftop door. Shots were fired as Shaun guided the ship up toward the top of the dome.

"Where's the portal?" he asked as he deftly dodged the blasts coming their way. He knew it was only a matter of seconds before the security force of the planet was onto their escape.

"There," Lilly said, pointing toward an opening. "It's on sensors. Hurry before they override it."

Shaun set the craft toward the opening at full speed. They shot through just as the portal began to close. Outside they were greeted by a security ship. Shaun ignored the hailing from the pilot. He knew that they knew that his cargo was much too valuable to risk her life by shooting them out of the sky. Shaun maneuvered the ship between the satellites that populated the upper atmosphere of the planet as three other ships joined in the chase.

"We've got to make the hyperport before they block it," he said as he calmly handled the controls.

"It will take time for them to shut it down. They can't do it while there's a ship in the port, and it's always backed up."

"Well, we're about to cut in line." Shaun moved the ship toward the waiting line of carriers. Warning shots were fired from the pursuing ships as he streaked toward the port. "Hang on, Princess."

The ship rocked from a blast just as they reached the port. They spiraled into it as Shaun fought for control. He punched in a destination on the nav board just before the ship blasted into hyperdrive.

They had escaped, but they knew they wouldn't get far on their damaged ship. Shaun activated the beacon Ruben had given him and looked over at Lilly, who had settled back into her chair.

"I guess it's safe to assume that the wedding is now off?" he asked with a grin.

Chapter Thirteen

Lilly watched in pensive fascination as the stars stretched into continuous lines of light while they traveled at hyperspeed. The small craft they had stolen seemed frail in comparison to the vast amount of space that stretched before them. It also made the cabin more intimate. She could reach out and touch Shaun if she wanted to, without even trying. It wouldn't take much at all to accidentally brush her arm against his or even lean her head against his shoulder. She knew if she did that, he would respond instantly, even though his hands remained firmly on the stick, fighting to keep control of the damaged craft.

At least Shaun was in control. Even when he was doing something foolish, such as tossing the Sacrosanct Mistress across the Prefect's chamber, he was still in control. Lilly mused that she had lost control of pretty much everything somewhere along the way. Actually she could trace it all back to the time when she had approached Shaun in his cryo tube and realized that he sensed her presence.

She had tried, hadn't she? But she'd never dreamed that her heart would be so . . . rebellious. As soon as she was sure that Shaun would be safe, she would go back and do her duty. She just had to be sure he was safe. Was that too much to ask in exchange for everything she was going to give up?

It was. She knew her duty, and there was no room for personal feelings. She had been foolish. She had been rebellious. She had probably destroyed the only chance Oasis had.

Shaun placed a strong hand over hers. "Everything will be fine. I promise."

"Have you been reading my mind?"

"Couldn't help myself." He lifted her hand to his lips and brushed a gentle kiss against her palm. Lilly felt it down into the pit of her stomach. She was such a fool.

"Ruben will find us."

"So will they. The Sacrosanct Mistress will be especially anxious to talk to you now."

"I guess she will, won't she?" Shaun allowed a delicious grin to cross his face, and Lilly jerked her hand away.

"When are you going to take this seriously?"

"I take all of it seriously. I'm just not going to be morbid about it. There are some things I can't change, and this, unfortunately, is one of them. Believe me when I tell you that there have been times recently when I have seriously considered just going to Rykers and turning myself in."

"So what's stopping you?"

"You are."

"Me? I seem to recall begging you to leave when we went to Oasis."

"I also recall some begging," he said teasingly. Lilly's brows slanted down, and Shaun popped up in his chair as if he'd been jabbed with a stinger. He immediately retaliated in a more devious manner. Lilly's eyes flew open wide as she gasped in shock, her face turning a deep shade of pink.

"Truce?" Shaun asked, his face a mask of innocence.

"Only if you'll listen to me."

"I'm listening."

Lilly settled back into her seat and forced her mind to relax. He was listening. She felt his willingness. She also could feel that he was doing it only to please her. It didn't matter, just as long as he listened.

"How did you do it?"

Shaun knew immediately what she was talking about. "I don't know, it just happens. I wanted to hit her, and it just happened. I don't even remember consciously thinking it."

"And the doors?"

"I wanted us to get away."

"What about the door last night?"

"That was different."

"Why?"

"I wanted you." He stated it so simply, so quickly, that Lilly caught her breath. The previous night seemed more like a dream to her than anything else, but she easily recalled the feel of his mouth on her body. Despite the control Honora was using on her mind, she had felt Shaun.

"We can't."

"Why?"

"You know why."

"That's an excuse, not a reason."

"It's my duty."

"Blast your duty."

"I can't."

"You can," he said earnestly. "All you have to do is walk away. The hard part is over actually; you've already left."

"Shaun."

"Tell me you don't love me and I'll take you back and leave you alone."

She couldn't. Even if she said it, he would know her words for a lie.

He took her hand again. "We'll figure it out."

It would be so easy just to let him take control of everything. It wasn't as if she had ever had control. Her entire life she had done what was expected and done what she'd been told. She had studied under Michael, studied under the Circe, and learned the intrigues of the Senate so she would not upset the intricate subtleties of their world. Her entire life had been a process of obeying orders and learning her duties. She had never expected it to be anything else.

An alarm sounded, a high pinging squeal accompanied by a flashing beacon on the console.

"What is it?" Lilly asked as Shaun flicked a switch and took a firmer hold on the stick.

"One of the reactors is shot. We've lost power on one side. We've got to come out of hyperdrive before we spin out and hit something." He quickly punched up the nav chart with one hand and then typed in coordinates.

"Where are we going?"

"Pristo."

Pristo. The planet he had been raised on. Lilly looked at Shaun's face as he struggled to keep control of the ship. He was going home. So why did he look so sad?

"So this is Pristo?"

Shaun kicked open a gate that had rusted shut from years of disuse. "This is it, Princess." He peered into the darkness that loomed below them. "This is where I grew up."

They were lucky the generators in the landing bay had worked. Of course, they had been left on sensor when the last miner had left so many years ago, but Shaun knew the rest of the machinery had been shut down as the inhabitants had come out of the mines and the living areas. There might be some fuel left in some of the generators, but the chances were minimal at best. He was grateful for the oxygen supply that still flowed through the caverns. Who knew how long they were going to be stuck down here? They were lucky to have made it this far instead of floating dead in space waiting for the Senate guard or, worse, the Ravigans to pick them up. With any luck, Ruben would come for them soon. Shaun checked once again to make sure the beacon his friend had given him was still working. He knew it would not penetrate the miles of earth and rock that stood above his head, but it would give Ruben a fix on their last known star position and his friend had enough sense to know that Pristo lay beneath it.

"So what do we do now?" Lilly tried not to let the shiver show as it worked its way down her spine. She was cold and the air was damp on her bare arms, but there was something else, something in the darkness that unsettled her.

Shaun felt it too; she could tell by the way he was peering into the gloom that there was something out there, something out of place, something that didn't belong.

"Let's see if anyone left some food behind." He extended a hand. "And maybe we can turn on some lights."

"Maybe we shouldn't."

"Why?"

"Because if the Ravigans come, they won't be able to see in the dark, and . . ."

"And I can."

Lilly nodded.

"Come on, Princess."

She took his hand, and they descended into the darkness.

How much of the way he knew by memory and how much he was actually seeing was hard to tell. Lilly stumbled along behind him, feeling as if she were totally blind. She had to remind herself that she wasn't blind, so great was the darkness that surrounded them. It felt as if they had been swallowed into the bowels of a great monster. Except for the dim glow that faded behind them, there was no light, no shadows, nothing except blackness.

Lilly caught a glow of silver and realized that Shaun was looking at her. "Use my eyes," he said.

She cast herself into his mind and looked through his eyes. She saw shapes and shadows without color and discovered they were following a wide tunnel that had been hewn from solid rock. The path lay straight ahead, but Shaun kept turning his head to the left as if he was hearing something or someone.

Lilly cleared her mind and listened through his ears as well as her own, but she heard nothing but their footsteps echoing hollowly from the walls. They came to a junction and he turned to the right, but his eyes looked to the left.

"What is it?"

"I don't know." They walked on. "Something's not right. . . ."

"Do you think someone knows we're here?"

"No, it's not that . . . it's something else."

They moved on until they came to a series of chambers. Rotten pieces of what had once been fresh canvas hung in tatters from rusty bolts punched into the rock walls over the openings. Shaun moved on, pulling Lilly with him, and finally stopped before one of the chambers. He slid the canvas away and ducked as a squeal and the slapping of skin came toward his head.

"Worrats," he spat out in disgust. "They always stayed away from the lighted areas."

Lilly crept closer, her skin crawling at the thought of the winged, ratlike creatures.

Shaun led her into the chamber and placed her hands on the cool metal surface of what felt like a table. The feel of the cold steel against her palms gave her an anchor in the never-ending darkness that surrounded them. She listened to the sounds of drawers sliding and doors opening and closing.

"Mother always kept candles," Shaun explained as he searched. "She liked their light better than the overhead." A tiny flame came into existence, and soon Lilly saw his face over the glow of a thick squat candle that was sitting in the middle of a plate.

"This was our home . . ." He held the candle up and circled the room around the table where she stood. The light bounced and dipped over the uneven surface of the ceiling of the chamber. There were more canvas curtains strung across, dividing the chamber into different compartments. Shaun gave her the tour. "This was where I slept . . ." He pulled back the curtain to reveal a narrow cot. Another revealed a bathing area, and then the third . . . "This is where my parents slept."

A wide mattress covered with a thick padded quilt covered two-thirds of a thick slab of rock. Stubs of candles were stuck in thick chunks of wax on both sides of pillows that were stacked against the wall curving up from behind the bed. It was an island of warmth and comfort in the middle of cold emptiness. She could almost see the wax melting down from the candles and cascading over the sides of the huge rock to be lost in the darkness of the floor.

"Father always said she would burn them up in their sleep with her candles."

Lilly could imagine the warm glow that made an intimate cocoon behind the privacy of the canvas as their son slumbered blissfully in his own cot beyond.

"They must have loved each other very much."

"They did—they lived for each other." He was lost in the shadows behind the candle, all dark except for the silver of his eyes.

"Do you ever wonder why they never had any more children?"

"I guess it was just too hard. This wasn't the best place to grow up."

"I can't even imagine."

"But Mother made the best of it. She was a wonderful teacher."

"You've never said what happened to them. I assumed that they died recently because of what Ruben said when we found him on Cathra."

"They died almost a year ago on Partin Five."

"You said the Senate decided to move the settlers?"

"Yes. Father wouldn't go. He had worked for years making a home for them, and he said he wasn't going to walk away from it just because someone across the galaxy told him to. They killed him because he wouldn't leave. Mother told me what happened before she died."

"They killed her, too?"

The sound that came from his throat was guttural and full of bitterness. He spat out the words as he continued. "They raped her and then they mutilated her body and her face. It was because they knew who she was and knew she had run away from her position. She had never lost her beauty, even after all the years of living underground and working hard, barely making a living."

Lilly touched her hand to his temple. "You don't have to speak."

He dropped his chin against his chest and submitted to her touch. She needed to know all of it. She should see what he had done and the reason why.

He had been home then. One of his visits between the smuggling runs with Ruben. He always made an effort to bring them something that would make life easier on the farm that had sprung up from nothingness under his father's hands. This time it had been a harvester that he had traded for and the thing had broken down on its first run, much to the amusement of his father. Ryan Phoenix had gone back to the homestead for parts while Shaun stayed to work on the faulty machine. Too much time had passed, and Shaun became worried that something had befallen his father on his way to or from the house. He became more concerned when he saw smoke rising over the ridge that hid the place from his view. He took off at a full run to his parents' home.

Lilly saw his father's body lying in front of the burning house. She felt the wail rise in her throat as it had in his on that day. Her chest pumped with the effort of his running as he raced down the ridge and knew without touching the man that he was dead, his eyes glassed over, sightlessly staring at the cloudless sky above.

She felt the heat from the fire as Shaun saw his

mother crawling out of the inferno. She swallowed the bile that rose in her throat as his mother's mangled face was revealed and her eyes focused on the face of her beloved son.

She heard the words that the dying woman uttered. "He would not leave here, even when they said they would kill him. And I chose to die with him rather than go back to their world, their deceit, their hatred."

Tears ran down her cheeks as the mother touched her son's cheek. "I'm so happy that we found you, Shaun. You have blessed our lives. I have had everything I could ever dream of." And then she died with her husband's name on her lips.

The grief that poured from his heart stunned her, and then anger surged in and rage filled the emptiness that the deaths had left. The killers could not be long gone, and he was filled with resolve as he gathered weapons.

Lilly saw the trail through Shaun's eyes as the five Legionnaires moved on to their next quarry. He caught up with them in a canyon before they reached the neighboring homestead, and quickly disabled their vehicle with a pulse from his father's rifle. Then he waited until darkness settled in.

He was quick and he was lethal. They never saw him coming. Two were dead before they even realized what was happening. The remaining three stood with backs together, weapons facing out into the darkness. They could not see him, and he finished them one at a time. The last one begged and cried and wanted to know why, and he told him before he snapped his neck. Lilly saw it all and understood.

Shaun hid in the caves of the canyons after that, knowing he had no way to get off the planet. They eventually found him and brought him to trial. His sentence was life on Rykers. And then the court congratulated itself on being merciful to the criminal.

Shaun realized he had been holding his breath and let it out slowly. The past year of his life had flashed into Lilly's mind in a few quick seconds. The flapping of a worrat brought her back to the present, and she jumped at the sound as the creature screamed at the light and quickly turned from its path. The sound of its wings could be heard as it echoed out into the halls.

"We need more light," he said, his voice hoarse from unshed tears. Lilly nodded in agreement, and Shaun lit the stubs of candles that remained around the bed of his parents.

"I'll see if I can find something to eat," he said, and went back toward the kitchen area.

The glow of the candles revealed a thick layer of dust covering the plush bedding. Lilly dragged off the covers and shook them out, which led to a series of sneezes on her part.

"I found something."

"What is it?" She swiped at her nose and replaced the bedcover, taking care to smooth out the wrinkles. The pillows needed airing also, and she shook them out, bringing on more sneezes from herself and Shaun as he came back with an open can and a spoon.

"Cleanliness can be deadly sometimes, you know," he said as he shook his head at her thoroughness.

Lilly stuck her finger in the can and drew out a

cherry dripping with thick juice. "Do you think it's safe to eat?" she asked.

"You tell me, Princess. The label says 'Oasis Cherries', the best in the universe."

Lilly plopped a cherry in her mouth and sucked the juice from her finger. "The label's right; they are the best in the universe."

"As hungry as I am, I'd think a worrat was the best in the universe." Shaun dug into the can with the spoon.

"I don't suppose you found another spoon while you were looking around?"

"Sorry, Princess, this is the only one." He offered her a spoonful and she let him feed her, then he took one for himself. Lilly stuck her finger in the can while he had the spoon in his mouth.

"Ouch!"

"What happened?"

"I think I cut myself."

"Let me see."

They sat on the side of the slab, and he held her finger down before a candle. "I can't tell if that's blood or cherry juice."

"It hurts, so it must be blood."

Shaun lifted her hand to his mouth and licked it. "A little of both." He brought it back down to the light and squeezed it, causing blood to ooze out. He returned it to his mouth and sucked on it, cleaning the blood from the wound once again.

"How bad is it?" The finger tingled now instead of throbbing.

"You tell me." He moved her hand down to the light again. The cut had closed.

Lilly looked up at the glitter of his eyes in amazement. "How did you do that?"

"How did you take the pain away after my fight with the giant on Oasis?"

"I just directed your mind away from the pain. I didn't heal you. Not like this."

"It's still there, Lilly. It's just not going to bleed anymore." He picked up the can and dipped in the spoon. "Here, eat." Juice smeared on the corner of her mouth and he wiped it with his thumb, placing his hand against her cheek. Her tongue slipped out and licked his thumb, taking the juice. With the quick, gentle glide of her tongue, his insides began to boil.

"Lilly . . ." He breathed her name and bent to kiss her. Her arms came up and wrapped around his neck, and his crept around her waist. The can clanked against the slab and rolled away. His mouth slashed across her lips, burning a brand against them. She answered him with her own, and her lips opened as his tongue found its way between and swirled against hers. She tasted blood, she tasted cherries, and she tasted Shaun. She wanted more. He was what she craved, and she had to have him.

He felt it and he saw it. The wall of her duty and obligation crumbled beneath the onslaught of his passion. He felt a momentary pang of guilt because he knew he was stronger than she, but then her will rose up to meet his. She wanted this. She wanted him as much as he had wanted her. She had been denying it, but it could no longer be denied. Her wanting was more than her reason. It was consuming her and had to be slaked or it would drive her mad.

Shaun rose up on his knees and pulled her up, too, matching her body against his. The length of her graceful thighs met the hard muscle of his. The flat planes of her stomach pressed against the bulging mass of his groin. The softness of her breasts was mashed flat against the hard ridges of his chest. Her head tilted back, and his bent to meet hers as his lips plundered her mouth and moved down the elegant curve of her neck.

The garment she wore crossed in the front and created a deep V between her breasts. He slid the tunic off her shoulders and down her arms, his mouth moving over the expanse of creamy skin as it was revealed to him. Her hands on his back moved up under his jacket and then pulled at the sleeveless shirt that was tucked into his pants. She found her way inside and her hands roamed over the smooth skin of his back, over his shoulder blades, and down his spine until they came around his waist and trailed up his sides. His mouth moved between her breasts, and the sleeves of her garment caught her arms so that she could not move them higher.

She needed to touch him. She had to feel him. She groaned her protest.

Shaun tore his mouth away and her fingers fumbled at the ties around her waist. She tore the hated thing off while Shaun shrugged out of his jacket. He pulled the short undergarment over her head, and she did the same for him.

The light from the candles was blocked by the

width of his chest and it cast a glow around his head and shoulders. His eyes glittered silver as he bent and caught her lips again. The heat from their skin coming together sent a current through her body, and her mind filled with him. His hands roamed over her, seemingly everywhere at once, but at the same time not where they needed to be. Her skin quivered with the anticipation of the next caress, and his hands could not move fast enough to slake her desire. She felt her pounding blood coursing through every inch of her body. She clung to his every touch, imprinting it in her memory as his hands roamed and sought and searched.

Lilly clawed at the waist of his pants and his hands dipped into hers, roaming over her backside and then coming around. She needed him to touch her. She was still wearing her boots and her pants, and she cursed them because they were a barrier between her body and what she desired.

With a growl he lifted her and flipped her onto her back on the bed. He pulled off her boots and yanked her pants off in quick jerking motions as her hands danced across his chest and over his stomach. Shaun knelt over her, and she looked up at him with eyes pale amid the shadows of her face.

"There's no turning back now, Princess," he said, knowing that once he had her he would never let her go.

"This is where I want to be." Lilly wrapped her arms around his neck and pulled him to her, raising her legs and wrapping them around his waist. He plunged into her in one swift motion, breaking the barrier of her virginity and claiming her as his. She arched her back and closed around him without pain as their foreheads touched.

She saw all of him and he saw all of her, but it was coming too fast for either one of them to absorb. There were flashes of time and the days of their lives spun together. He moved and she moved with him, and where their skin touched, it tingled as if electricity were flowing between them. A wail rose in her throat and he captured it with his mouth, sucking it inside his own and down into his core. The pressure came, and Lilly felt herself being drawn down into this being. He was the one moving inside of her, but yet he was drawing her into his essence. Stars swirled in her head, and she could not find a place in her mind where he was not present. She thought she would go mad with the presence of his mind, but she felt her soul rising and then the sun exploded and she was gone, whirled out into the darkness of space.

"Is it like that every time?" She was lying on top of him, and his hands were making wide circles on her back.

"I hope so."

Her fingers circled the depths of his pectorals. "I don't understand."

"It was different with you."

"What do you mean different?" She was suddenly terrified that she had disappointed him with her innocence.

"I've never felt it that way before."

Lilly pushed herself up to look at his face, her own eyes hidden behind the curtain of her hair. "You'll have to show me." She chewed on her lip. "I've never done . . ."

"Lilly, I have never felt so much passion before." His hands pushed her hair back from her face. "I felt like I was experiencing your feelings along with mine. At one point I thought it was going to kill me."

"So what does it mean?"

"It means we belong together. It means that we were meant for each other."

"They will never allow it."

"They won't have a choice."

"What are we going to do?"

"I don't know, and I'm too tired to think about it now." He rolled over on his side, dropping her into a spot beside him with her head resting on his shoulder. "Go to sleep, Princess." He kissed her forehead and pulled the bedding up and over their weary bodies. "I love you."

"I love you, Shaun."

"I know."

"I had to say it."

"I'm glad you did."

Chapter Fourteen

His sleep was restless. His movements awakened Lilly and she slid away from him, taking a candle with her to see if she could find some water. She found a liter when she stubbed her toe on it. Apparently it had been dropped in the haste to leave the place and forgotten just like the lives that had once played out on this dark planet. She drank deeply and returned to the chamber with the bottle, knowing Shaun would be thirsty also when he awakened.

He had rolled onto his stomach and lay with his arm thrown over her pillow. Lilly smiled at the thought that he had already missed her presence in the bed. He spoke in his dream, a mumbling of something unintelligible, and she placed a hand on his head and let it drift down over his rich dark hair. Her touch seemed to calm him, and she continued to caress his hair, letting her fingers test the thickness of the tresses as they teased the back of his strongly corded neck.

She felt ridges in his skin, a strangely irregular pattern, and she became curious as to what they could be. Lilly brushed the hair up with her fingertips and ran the pads over the ridges. She brought the candle in and held it over his neck as she pushed the longer locks of his hair up onto his head. Her light gray eyes widened as she realized the ridges were scars, probably placed there by a sharply pointed blade. The flame flickered back and forth as her brain refused to accept what her eyes were seeing.

Someone had carved his name in the back of his neck. The letters S H a U N were clearly visible, although the *a* looked more like an *o*. Why would someone do that to him? Had it been an Academy prank or hazing? Surely his parents wouldn't have done such a thing. She looked at the scars again, letting her fingertips trace the pattern. Why were all the letters done in strong uppercase except the *a*?

She jumped back so quickly that she almost dropped the candle. It wasn't an *a*. It was an *o*. It would have been easy for the hand that did this to slip while trying to complete the circle. Especially if it was done to a child that was crying out in pain.

The dream she'd had on the ship filled her mind. She had seen a woman using a knife to cut the back of a small boy's head. A boy with dark hair. There had been the sounds of generators running and they had been in a cave. Just like the caves that ran beneath the surface of Pristo. Caves that sustained life because of the huge generators that were kept running constantly. They would have surely drowned out the sounds of a baby crying out in pain and anguish.

His mother had done this to him. But why? He would have been too young to even remember it, but he had felt the pain as had his mother. Lilly remembered her tears in the dream.

Did he spell his name with an *o* instead of an *a*? Could it be Shoun? If his mother felt the need to place his name on his body, why not have it tattooed as it was on her shoulder?

Shaun's hand drifted up her leg and pulled her closer to him.

"What's wrong, Princess?" he asked sleepily.

"Nothing, I was just thirsty." She picked up the liter from where she had placed it on the slab.

"I see you got lucky and found something." He leaned up on one arm and took the bottle from her to drink.

"More like I tripped over it."

He placed the liter back on the slab and patted the mattress. "Come back to bed, Princess. It's cold out there."

Lilly slid between the covers and settled back against him. He quickly drifted off again, but she lay awake for a long time, her mind pondering the mystery carved on the back of his neck.

He was gone. Lilly woke up to an empty bed. She had slept deeply and her body protested against leaving the bed. There was no bright morning light such as she was accustomed to seeing when she rose. She called out his name, but there was no answer.

He had put on his clothes except for the jacket. Lilly quickly dressed in her pants and short upper garment, and after pulling on her boots, she put on his jacket. She picked up a candle, went to the entrance of the chamber, and called his name again.

The only reply was the screech of a worrat as it stirred from its rest.

Lilly cleared her head and sent her mind out to search for him.

He was in pain! She saw him sitting in the darkness, and tears were running down his face. He couldn't control the tears, but his hands were pressed to his ears to block out a sound. A sound that Lilly could not hear. She had to find him. Holding the candle high, she made her way back to the junction in the tunnel. They had taken the right-hand path before, but now he was in the left one. The candlelight barely broke the heavy darkness, but she pressed on, her feet flying as she felt herself getting closer.

A reflection caught her eye and she found her way barred by a metal gate. She knew Shaun was on the other side of the gate. She moved the candle around, looking for the opening. She found one on the side and easily stepped through, knowing that it had been a tight squeeze for someone of Shaun's size.

The air was fresher and warmer here. She felt, rather than saw, the roof open up above her. Shaun was close. She moved on, holding the candle high.

Her breath flew from her body as she hit the ground, and total darkness surrounded her when the candle dropped out of sight. Shaun rolled them over several times until she felt the solid presence of a wall in front of her. He was shaking.

"What happened?" she asked when she could speak again.

"Look." He placed her fingers on his temple and looked back over his shoulder. A huge chasm yawned before them, and she realized that she had come one step short of falling into it. "It's bottomless." His eyes flashed as he looked into her face. "Can you hear it?"

Lilly raised her head to listen and he sat up beside her. "No, what is it?"

"A woman is crying."

Lilly thought that he might have lost his mind. The power had come too quickly and sent him over the edge.

Shaun grabbed her hand again and placed it on his temple. "Listen!" he hissed.

She heard it then. Painful wails coming from the pit. They were heartbreaking and pitiful. There was no hope in them, only despair.

"Can you hear?"

"Yes, I hear her."

He looked back toward the pit. "She woke me up," he said in a childlike voice. "Make it stop."

He had gone mad. She had to help him.

"Shaun, look at me." She placed her hands on either side of his face. His eyes shone like twin moons in the darkness as they settled on her. "We're going to find out who she is, but I'm going to need your help."

He nodded in agreement.

"Follow me with your mind," Lilly instructed him.

She closed her eyes and took a cleansing breath. She willed her mind to leave her body, just as she had earlier when she was searching for him. She floated above where they sat in the darkness. She needed him to come with her so she could see. "*Come with me,*" she urged him with her mind. He raised his hands and touched either side of her face. He was with her; she felt the intermingling of their souls as he joined her in the quest. They floated out over the chasm and then suddenly descended as if their bodies had fallen in.

They felt the rushing of the air as their minds fell into the darkness of the chasm. The farther they fell, the louder the cries became, until they rang in a never-ending wail that echoed off the walls and surrounded them as they fell.

"Mother!" Shaun cried out.

With his cry they were lifted and propelled out of the chasm. Lilly's eyes flew open as her body came back to consciousness. The crying had stopped.

"I don't understand." His voice was normal again.

"There's a memory here," Lilly whispered. "And a lost soul."

"The woman?"

"You called her Mother."

The glimmer from his eyes turned toward the pit. "How can we find it?" The glow of his eyes settled on her again. "The memory."

"We go back and look for it. Just like when you showed me what happened on Partin Five."

"I have no memories of a woman in this place." His voice sounded so . . . lonely.

"Maybe it was before you can remember." Lilly said soothingly. "When you were a small child."

"You can see that far back?" The question sounded as if it had come from a small child.

"I can, if the memory is strong enough."

Once again she laid her fingers on his temples. She felt his mind open; the connection formed more easily after the passion they had shared. It was almost as if their memories had become one. Lilly saw the years falling away as the days flew into nights and the circle of time spun. His years as a youth flew before her eyes in an instant and she saw him as a babe, with his mother and father looking on adoringly. It was the beginning of his memories.

A cold wind stirred around Lilly, but she didn't feel it. Shaun's hands rose and grasped her wrists, and she willed his mind back beyond the time he could consciously remember. She saw a tiny boy with dark hair curling around his neck wandering in the dim light of the far tunnels. Blood streamed down his back, and a man gathered him up in his arms and looked on him in wonder.

Time spun backward again and she saw a woman holding a knife to the child's neck as she carved the letters. It was a different woman from the mother he had adored. Tears streamed from the woman's eyes. Eyes that were light gray between dark lashes. Eyes just like Shaun's.

The woman was hiding on a cargo ship with the boy. The ship had brought supplies to the colony of miners.

Lilly saw Oasis. Then she saw herself as she raised a knife to kill a child that slept in a cradle. A child with dark hair. Shaun. Only, he wasn't Shaun, he was Nicholas. The woman was his mother, Ariel. And the woman with the knife had been her mother, Zania.

Shaun jerked away.

"Someone's coming!" He yanked her to her feet, even as her mind protested the interruption.

"Did you see?" she cried. Her mind was still looking into his.

"Shh." Shaun flattened himself against the wall and looked out to where lights could be seen moving down the other tunnel.

"Your hand," Lilly gasped. The back of his hand was glowing. "It's the chip. It's leading them to us."

Shaun pulled his knife from his boot and cut open his hand. He popped the chip out with the tip of the knife and flung it into the pit. Then he sliced into his shirt.

"Tie it up so it won't bleed."

Lilly ripped a length from his shirt and tied it around his hand as he kept looking down the tunnel.

"Is there another way out?" she asked.

"No. We'll have to wait until they pass and try to sneak back to the landing dock." The shine from his eyes turned to her. "Maybe we can steal their shuttle."

"They'll have a cruiser waiting above."

"I know." His hand caressed her face. "It's our only chance, Princess. It's either that or stay in the tunnels until we starve to death."

"I'd rather face them than hide from them," Lilly said, hoping her voice did not betray her fear. For him.

They went through the opening in the gate and slid along the wall of the tunnel toward the junction. They could see the lights moving in and out of the chambers as they searched.

"The minerals in the walls are interfering with their reception," Shaun whispered. "They know we're here; they just don't know where."

"Is there some place we can send them?"

"Into the tunnels below," he replied.

As one they sent the image to the squadron that was searching for them. They watched from their place in the tunnel as the lights moved on past the living chambers.

"Let's go." He took her hand and led her back toward the landing bay. He stopped when they got close.

"Can you look ahead and see if anyone is there?"

"I'll try. It's hard if you don't know who you're looking for." She reached out with her mind, searching for life in the area around the dock. She tried to remember what it had looked like when they landed, but beyond the dim light and the rusted gate her memories of it were dim. It seemed deserted.

"It's empty."

They stepped forward into the bay and were immediately surrounded by Legion soldiers. The Circe Witch Arleta stood before them at the base of the ladder.

"Foolish girl," she spat at Lilly. "Did you really think your power could match mine?" Lilly threw up her wall. Arleta must not learn Shaun's secret. They would kill him immediately if they knew.

Arleta walked up to Shaun and looked into his eyes. "So you are the source of the disruption in our power. However did you come to be?"

"Why don't you tell me?" Shaun sneered. "After all, you're the one with all the answers."

He didn't know! Lilly had looked into his mind, but he didn't know. He had broken off contact with her before she had discovered that he was Nicholas, the heir to Oasis. Either that or he was stronger than she had ever imagined. Could he be hiding his secret that well? Could he hide it from the Mistress?

"Bind him!" the woman commanded. He struggled against the hands that held him.

"No!" Lilly cried. It was the collar. He would be mindless, under their power, under their control, without will of his own when they put it on. He fought them as Lilly fought the ones who held her.

"Fools!" Arleta called out. Her eyes narrowed and Lilly cramped up, falling limp between the arms that held her.

"Lilly!"

"It's a trick," she tried to tell him. *My mind is my own.* She gasped in pain. *No other may have it.* A burning started in her stomach and she cramped. *I will keep my mind.* She had to keep the wall strong. She couldn't let Arleta see. Her throat constricted and she gagged as she felt something moving up her throat from her stomach. She retched. *My mind is . . . my mind . . .* Blood poured forth from her mouth, and Lilly dropped to her knees. The guards released her and she fell to all fours. She was choking. *My mind is my own . . .* Something was wiggling and coiling within her. It was coming up her throat.

"You're killing her!" Shaun yelled.

"Submit." The Mistress arched her eyebrow as she spoke.

He bowed his head and stopped his struggles. It might be a trick of the mind, but Lilly was truly choking to death before him. He would not risk her life. Even if it meant giving up his own.

"It's a trick, it's all a trick." Lilly wanted desperately to warn Shaun, but the witch was blocking her. She couldn't get the words out.

The guards snapped the collar around Shaun's neck. His face relaxed and his light gray eyes darkened beneath the long lashes.

"No," Lilly sobbed as a pair of Legion soldiers hauled her to her feet.

"Bring them," the Mistress commanded.

"What about the men searching the tunnels?" one guard dared to ask.

"Leave them," Arleta said. "Go," she said to Shaun, pointing up the ladder. He obeyed her orders, quickly climbing up and then waiting for the Mistress before they entered the ship.

Lilly blindly climbed between her guards. At the top, the soldiers grabbed her arms again and hauled her into the shuttle. They threw her into the seat across from Shaun and strapped her in. They were angry about leaving their comrades.

"You could help them," she suggested, venturing into their minds. *"Help us."*

"Quiet!" Arleta hissed. She slapped Lilly across the face, turning her head with the blow. "Know this. Your lover's well-being depends on your cooperation."

Shaun, across from her, sat as if made from stone. He stared straight ahead, his face bland and blank as if he were dead.

Lilly felt the vibration of Ruben's beacon. It was still in the pocket of Shaun's jacket, which she now wore. He had found them, but what could he do against a Legion destroyer?

She didn't dare try to contact him while in such close quarters with Arleta. Ruben was a wily pilot. He made a career from smuggling. Surely he was wise enough to keep his distance.

"Patience . . ."

Lilly carefully kept her face composed as she looked at Shaun. The collar was blinking and his face was still empty. And yet it was his voice she had heard in her thoughts. His body might be submissive, but his mind was far from it.

Chapter Fifteen

Lilly quickly realized that Arleta was not going to take any chances with her. The Mistress stayed close by her side as she was led down into the bowels of the cruiser to where the holding cells were located. She did not know where they were taking Shaun, nor could she take the risk of trying to locate him with her mind. The answer was evident without jeopardizing his secrets. They would take him as far away from her as they could get him within the confines of the large ship.

"Time for a bit of reflection, my dear," Arleta said when the cell door opened as if on cue. "Ponder your sins and hope that forgiveness will be granted."

Lilly was shoved through the portal into a room empty of everything save a metal shelf attached low enough to the wall for her to lie on.

"If I were you, I wouldn't waste my powers on this ship. Best save them so that you can convince your husband-to-be that you are still a pure and worthy bride." Arleta sniffed the room as if the scent of it offended her. Or perhaps it was the scent of Lilly.

"Honora will not be pleased with this turn of events," Arleta informed her as she wrinkled her nose in disgust. "His smell is all over you and will be difficult to hide." The door slammed shut, and Lilly heard the slide of the rod through the lock that was controlled by an attendant at a station on another deck of the ship. Not far enough away that she couldn't contact the man, but far enough so that the Circe would know if she tried.

His smell. Lilly wrapped her arms around Shaun's jacket and let her nose take in the essence of his scent. If only it was his arms that kept her warm . . .

She could not go there. Even if they were both free to do as they wanted, she could not go there. If what she had seen in his mind was true, and she had no reason to believe that it wasn't, then Shaun was Alexander's son. Her uncle's son. Theirs was a liaison that could never be. It should not have happened. But they had not known.

How could something that had felt so right be wrong? They had connected on not only a physical level but a spiritual one also. Lilly, due to her inexperience, had no way of knowing if what had happened was right or wrong. Shaun had referred to the joining as something beyond what he had ever experienced before. He had said they were meant for each other. But they couldn't be, could they? The same blood ran in their veins.

She cared for him. She could not deny it. She loved

him. Even though it was taboo, she still loved him. It was a fitting punishment for her, after all. Her mother was the one who'd ruined his life and her daughter the one who found him—and loved him even though she should not.

"Control your thoughts, you fool," Lilly said to herself as she looked at the impenetrable door of her cell. What if Arleta was reading her mind at this very moment? Lilly couldn't feel her in her mind, but then again she had not felt her on Pristo either. Honora's second in command was strong indeed.

She knew the witch well enough to realize that Arleta was out for glory. She would be testing her powers on Shaun to find out the source of his power. Arleta wanted to break him before Honora saw him.

Lilly sat down on the metal shelf and pulled her knees up. She wrapped her arms around her legs and rested her chin on her knees. They had restrained Shaun physically, but his mind was still working. He had spoken to her on the shuttle in spite of his bonds. Surely he was strong enough to hold off Arleta's attempts to see inside his mind.

Lilly had no idea how strong he was. All she knew was that he continued to surprise her as his skills seemed to grow more powerful every day. He had thrown the Sacrosanct Mistress across the room merely by thinking it.

He was the forbidden son of a Circe. The daughters had always been taught to control their minds and their skills. But did not the more powerful witches hold the reins of the government of the Circe? Teaching the lesser witches to control their power was the same as keeping that power under their control. Shaun's power had never been controlled. It had been allowed to grow without his knowing it.

That was why he could see in the dark! His eyes had adapted and taught themselves to see.

And his powers of the mind, his control . . . once he had known that he had the power, there were no boundaries to stop him! He had never known he was anything more than the son of a soldier who had rebelled against his superiors. Ryan Phoenix had found him in the caverns and raised him as his own. He had called him Shaun because that was the name carved on the back of his neck. But why had Ariel carved those letters? Why not put Nicholas? Why do it at all? She'd known she was dying. Was the name an attempt to protect her son? Wouldn't she have wanted him to realize his destiny?

The letters! Strength, Honor, Obedience, Unity, Nobility. Why hadn't she seen it sooner? His name was the credo of Oasis.

"I was the catalyst," Lilly realized. The first time she had reached out to him, she had triggered his power. It had lain dormant for all the years of his life, but now . . .

"Be strong, Shaun," Lilly said to the walls of her cell. "Fight them."

Arleta placed a hand in the thick dark locks of Shaun's hair and jerked his head back so she could look into his light gray eyes. "You are an abomination," she said in disgust. She wrenched her hand from his hair. "What is the source of your power?"

"Pristo," she read in his mind. For someone who was such an enigma, his mind was strangely vacant of information, almost as if he were blocking her. But how could he? No man had the power. It was unthinkable.

Perhaps he was being controlled by another Circe. But who among them had that much power? Surely it was not Lilly. Because of her position on Oasis, the Circe had been careful to limit her power her entire life.

Shaun's face remained blank as he read the myriad of thoughts tumbling through Arleta's mind. The witch refused to believe that a man could have the power. She preferred to think that it came from another Circe instead of from him. So why not let her continue to think that way?

"Mistress, help me." He let the thought slide out into the deep recesses of his mind.

Arleta pounced on it the instant she read it.

"Who is your mistress?"

Shaun's eyes remained dead and dormant as he stared straight ahead, past the regal robes and the face twisted with jealousy and anger.

"What is her plan?" Arleta leaned forward until her nose was inches from Shaun's. "What is her interest in Lilly?"

He allowed the obvious answer to filter through his wall. *"Stop the marriage."*

"Why?"

"Mistress, help me."

Arleta slapped him. "We have ways to break through your barriers, you fool," she hissed in anger. "We will discover who is controlling you."

Shaun wanted to laugh as blood trickled from a cut in his cheek, but the collar kept him from doing so. He saw the flash of an ornate ring on Arleta's finger and knew now why she wore it.

"Does it hurt?" she said with a mock pout of concern. "I can fix it for you." The witch placed a finger on the cut and the sting immediately went away. "Or I can make it worse." She placed her hands on either side of his face. "I'll even let your screams be heard."

Shaun felt her mind enter his as if she held the sharp point of a knife and had bored it into his skull. He saw the image of the knives and felt the flesh of his face as it was peeled away. He knew in his mind it was false, but his nerve endings felt the exposure to the air, felt the scrape of the knife and the tearing of the skin. His mind was strained from the battle to keep his strengths hidden from the witch. Why fight this battle when he knew it was false?

The scream erupted from his throat and he saw the glint of evil satisfaction in the cold gray eyes of Arleta. Her mouth twisted in an evil smile as she made a soothing sound. "There, there now, it was all just a trick, see?" She ran her hand down the smooth skin of his cheek, unmarred except for the cut from her ring. "It's a game we like to play. Sometimes it's a trick, sometimes it's real. Did your mistress ever play this game with you?"

"No games with Lilly." He had not meant for that to be heard. He had to protect her.

"You care for Lilly." Arleta stated it as a fact instead of asking the question. "You do. You sacrificed your freedom to save her when you could easily have overpowered the guards."

He could have. He realized it now. He could have controlled the guard with his mind and broken Arleta's control over Lilly. He kept his frustration behind the wall, but Arleta sensed the discovery of it in his mind.

He should have acted instead of reacted. But hadn't that always been his problem? He had reacted to his parents' murder and wound up a murderer himself.

"No comment?" Arleta asked as she looked at him with a puzzled expression on his face.

He had just gone through a major soul-searching moment and the witch had missed it? She really did think he was of no consequence.

"Mistress, help me."

The beacon vibrated in the pocket of Shaun's jacket. Lilly pulled the device out and held it in her hand. *"Ruben, where are you?"*

Far enough away that he would not be discovered, she hoped. Surely he was smart enough and wily enough to stay away from the cruiser. He had to know that they were now prisoners on the ship. But where were they going? Would it be to Raviga for her wedding to Prince Ramelah? Or would they go by the Senate first? They had not made the jump to hyperspeed yet. Would Ruben be able to follow them once they made it to the port?

They would go to Honora first, she guessed. Even though the cruiser belonged to the Senate, the mission belonged to Arleta. She would carry her prize to her mistress and Lilly would have to face her also . . . an answer for her impudence.

The recalled vision of Honora sliding on her backside across the highly polished floors of the Prefect's private chambers brought a smile to Lilly's lips despite the gravity of her situation. It was a wonder that her ornate headpiece had stayed in place!

Perhaps there was a chance for Shaun. If Ruben got there first, then he could possibly free Shaun from Arleta. Lilly sat on the cold, sterile floor of her cell and began the process of clearing her mind in order to contact the smuggler.

"*Ruben?*"

She could feel him! She had placed a visual of him in her mind, one of him in the pilot's seat of his craft. How far was the distance between them? She had never attempted to cross such a great distance with her mind before. Could she do it? Could she hold on to it long enough for Ruben to get the message?

"*Lilly?*"

"*They're taking us to Honora. You must get there first and be ready to free Shaun.*" Her head pounded as she forced her mind to cross the distance of space.

"*And free you, too.*"

"*No, just Shaun. Free Shaun before they kill . . .*"

Lilly fell onto her side and clutched her hands to her temples as the blood pounded inside her head, building up into a great pressure that felt as if it would burst the confines of her skull. It didn't matter what happened to her. She couldn't be with Shaun, not now, not when she knew who he was, what he was.

She would marry Ram and bring peace and safety to Oasis and her people. At least if she married Ram she would be doing something worthwhile.

As long as she knew Shaun was free. Lilly felt the warm sensation of blood running down her fingers into the palms of her hands and was not surprised to see it.

"Free Shaun," she said once again, before the darkness overcame her.

Chapter Sixteen

Ruben watched from his hiding place as the Sacrosanct Mistress gathered her robes around her and walked up the ramp to the shuttle, followed by a few lesser witches and a masked minion, dressed in black. *Just my luck,* he thought to himself as he watched the woman disappear through the hatch. Instead of Shaun and Lilly being bought into her presence, she was going into theirs, taking a shuttle to the cruiser that waited in orbit above. Ruben's mind scrambled as he considered the possibilities before him. He could return to his ship, hopefully without being caught, and return to orbit in case the cruiser left without unloading its prisoners, or he could sneak aboard the shuttle and let it carry him up and hope that the witch with the big hat overlooked his presence.

Either way, he was pretty sure he was a dead man. The shuttle fired its engines as Ruben sprinted toward the back hatch that was used to off-load pieces of equipment. He jerked it open, knowing that it would trigger warning lights on the main control panel. Sure enough, the engine noise faded as the shuttle settled back onto its landing gear and Ruben searched for a hiding place. He could hear the sound of men complaining about the carelessness of others, and the hatch door was tested, then slammed shut without anyone taking a moment to look inside. Ruben let out a sigh of relief as he slid behind a row of benches that were used to transport troops from the cruiser. As the shuttle once again lifted off toward orbit, he decided to concentrate on being a nonentity instead of what he would do when he reached the cruiser.

Shaun felt the gentle shuddering of the deck below his feet as the cruiser shut off its engines and settled into orbit. He wondered what planet they were now circling. Arleta had finally left him alone to ponder his fate. She still thought another witch was behind his power and was frantic to find out who. Shaun had seen the fear in her mind too. Arleta's quest wasn't to help her mistress. Her desire was to be on the winning side. If another witch was going to challenge Honora, then she wanted to align herself with the victor.

Shaun longed to stretch and flex his cramped muscles. The collar had kept him stationary, something that he was not accustomed to. He had always been a man of action, and the inactivity of this confinement was frustrating. How did the collar control him? How could his mind still be his while his body was at the whim of another?

When he had joined minds with the Circe prisoner

in the stadium, he had thought he'd felt the man's fear. Now Shaun realized that he had barely tapped into it. He yearned to scream his frustration, but even his voice was captive to the collar.

Lilly. Was it safe to think about her now? Did it even matter if he did? He didn't care that they knew about his feelings for her. He'd shout his love to the Senate if they would let him. He loved her, and Oasis and the Senate and the Circe could all be damned.

She loved him, too. No matter what she said, he knew that she felt it. How could she not after what they had shared on Pristo? Shaun had made love to more women than he could count on two hands, but he had never felt what he had shared with Lilly before.

Funny how being totally paralyzed makes you more introspective, Shaun mused to himself as he realized that he had never actually made love with a woman until Lilly. His feelings for the women in his past had been nothing more than sexual attraction. He had left them all as casually as he had left the Academy, and spared them nothing more than a passing thought. They had filled a temporary need while he searched for something more.

Lilly was the answer. She was the one he'd been searching for, why he had always been restless. He had sensed that a part of him was missing or that he was somehow misplaced in the universe. So if Lilly was the answer, why did she bring so many more questions?

Why did he have the same power as the Circe? What was it about Lilly that had triggered it? Some of the answers he sought lay deep in the chasms of

Pristo, but the Legion had come before he had found them.

Or had they?

Lilly had still been deep in her trance when the soldiers came. She had sought the answers in his past, and Shaun recalled his entire life unfolding in his mind as she had probed for things long forgotten. She said she could see back to the beginning, even to before his conscious memories. What had she seen?

Shaun felt someone coming. Did he dare hope that he and Lilly would be taken down to the planet on the same shuttle? He needed to see her. He needed to touch her. He needed to grab her and run as far away from the evil and the intrigue as the boundaries of the universe would allow him.

The gentle hiss of the cabin door opening filled his ears and he was met with the sight of Arleta and the Sacrosanct Mistress dressed in her full regalia. Several witches and a masked, black-clad male slave stood behind her, awaiting her orders.

"Did you fix yourself up just for me?" Shaun couldn't help thinking as he watched the woman go through the process of arranging her robes.

"Don't be ridiculous, you fool," Honora retorted. Her righteous anger boiled beneath the surface of her carefully composed features. She had to subjugate this prisoner before it became known that a mere male had bested her before the Prefect. This one would suffer greatly for the injury to her pride and her backside, which was somewhat bruised from her sudden journey across the polished marble floor of the Prefect's private quarters. He would suffer indeed. Honora almost wished that the prisoner could move so she could watch him cringe before her wrath.

"Who is your mistress?" she asked as she stood before his chair in a regal stance. "Look at me," she commanded.

Shaun raised his light gray eyes to look up at the imposing face of the Sacrosanct Mistress.

"How did you come by your eyes?" Honora demanded as she slowly bent to look into his long-lashed eyes.

"I was born with them."

Honora read the answer in his mind and let out a hiss. "Impossible!" she exclaimed. She fought back the urge to claw them out with her sharp nails. If she showed her anger, then she would lose the upper hand. She must remain calm and collected. Someone had the audacity to challenge her and was using this . . . male as her weapon. She needed to squash this rebellion quickly. She would grind whoever it was under the heel of her shoe. Honora needed answers, and this fool of a man would be forced to produce them. Terror had always been her favorite weapon. She would use it now.

"Take him to the palace," Honora commanded as she regained her imperious stance. "And bring me his eyes!" She swept from the cell, followed by a smirking Arleta and the lesser witches. The black-clad male slave stepped forward, his face unreadable behind the mask but his intention clear. He must follow the orders of his mistress or he would soon be wearing the collar.

Shaun had felt his stomach drop as the witch issued

her orders. How could he fight when he couldn't move? Could he use his mind to control the other man just as Honora and the other witches used theirs?

Think, Shaun. Think, he told himself. Panic began to set in. He had never felt so lost or helpless; even when he was being hunted by the Legion he had still felt himself in control. During the farce of the trial, he still knew what he was capable of and knew that he had the chance of escape. He had never in his life felt the nameless terror that was settling into his mind now, numbing his brain, making coherent thought impossible. The witch wanted his eyes, and the man approaching him would take them because that was what his mistress had ordered.

Move, move, move, Shaun urged his body, but nothing happened. The other man cocked his head as if listening for sounds in the corridor, as a drop of sweat beaded at Shaun's temple and trickled down his cheek, stinging the cut left by Arleta's ring.

The slave rolled his hand and a knife slipped into it. Shaun felt his pupils widen in shock.

"Don't, please don't," Shaun sent out with his mind.

"How did you do that?" Ruben asked as he removed the mask from his face.

"Get this thing off me!"

Ruben studied the collar for a moment, then slipped the point of his knife into the lock, popping the hated contraption apart. Shaun jerked it from his neck and flung it in the corner.

"Where's Lilly?" he asked as he stood and stretched his cramped muscles.

"Still on board, as far as I know. She told me to get you away from here."

"She told you?"

"With her mind. Like you just did." Ruben looked at his friend and wondered how he was going to stop him from charging down the corridors of the cruiser to find Lilly. "How did you do that?" Comprehension spread across Ruben's features. "Your eyes."

"You can't have them," Shaun said dryly.

"Are you one of them?" Ruben asked.

"*No,*" Shaun protested, and then ran his fingers through his hair in frustration. "I don't know," he sighed in exasperation. "I'm still trying to figure it all out."

"When did this happen?"

"When I met Lilly. All kinds of bizarre things have been happening to me since I met her. I've been blown up, shot down, chased, beaten, chased some more, and paralyzed."

Ruben placed a comforting hand on his friend's shoulder. "Don't worry about it. We all have our bad cycles," he said with a cocky grin. "Actually sounds pretty much like one of our runs."

"I can't lose her, Ruben." Shaun's pale gray eyes looked earnestly at his friend. "I won't."

"We've got to get out of here."

"Not without Lilly," Shaun said as he flexed his hands. They ached to hold a weapon. "How did you get here?"

"I knocked out the slave on the shuttle. He was sitting in a separate cabin so he wouldn't contaminate the witches," Ruben said with a sneer. "After that, I just kept saying 'must obey the Mistress' in my head over and over again, and they pretty much ignored me."

"They think all men are idiots," Shaun said in disgust.

"So prove them wrong."

"What?"

"Do you honestly think you can get Lilly off this cruiser without getting both of us killed?"

"I appreciate the offer, Ruben, but I don't expect you to go with me."

"And how do you plan on getting the two of you off the ship?

"Steal a shuttle?"

"And get shot out of the sky?"

"So what do you suggest?"

"Let's get out of here and see what happens next. We need to come up with a plan."

Plan instead of react, Shaun told himself. But how could he run away when every part of his body screamed for Lilly?

"Lilly?" he cast out with his mind.

Lilly wondered if her head would hurt less if she rose to a sitting position. It certainly couldn't hurt any worse than it did at the moment. She pushed herself up on the cold, barren floor of her cell.

The attempt to reach Ruben had been difficult and risky, but at least she had gotten through to him. A headache was a small price to pay for Shaun's freedom. If only she could know he was free, she would go to her fate and be content.

She wondered how long she had been unconscious. Long enough for the blood to dry and crust on the side of her face. She briskly rubbed her skin after dampening her fingers in her mouth. She couldn't risk Arleta guessing that she had been in communication with someone.

"Lilly?"

"Shaun?" He seemed so close. She could almost feel him beside her, touching her, comforting her, loving . . .

"I'm coming for you."

"No!" Why wouldn't he just go and leave her alone? He had to go. It was the only way.

"Ruben's with me." His voice in her mind was gentle and reassuring. If only she could go with him. If only everyone in the universe would go away and leave them in peace. But even that wouldn't help. They still could not, should not be together.

"I won't go. Please get off the ship while you can." She could see Ruben through Shaun's eyes, saw the minion uniform he was wearing, and would have hugged him if they weren't separated by decks and walls.

"Why won't you go?" His voice in her mind sounded tragic, heartbroken. She couldn't let him know, not while he was on the ship, not while the Circe were so close. They must not find out his true identity. They would kill him without hesitation, without remorse.

"Go back to Pristo. You'll find the answer." She sensed the presence of Honora in the corridor. *"Go!"*

Lilly quickly sealed her mind against him. He was free to escape, and she would not be responsible for his recapture.

"What did she say?" Ruben asked.

"She said to go," Shaun replied, his mind spinning. He knew she loved him. Why wouldn't she go? He knew the answer as well as he knew his feelings for her. She would not go because of her devotion to her planet and her people. She was a shining example of self-martyrdom because of the evil her mother had done.

Funny how they were both so stubborn. She had a one-track mind and so did he. Unfortunately their tracks ran in opposite directions.

"So where are we going?" Ruben asked.

"Back to Pristo," Shaun barked.

"Think we should get off this ship first, or were you planning on taking it with us?"

"Let's go," Shaun said in a somewhat gentler tone. It wasn't Ruben's fault that he and Lilly were stubborn and foolish.

Ruben picked up the collar and handed it to Shaun. "Put this on."

"Are you crazy?"

"It won't be activated, but if you're wearing it, maybe we can just walk to the shuttle bay."

"That's your plan?"

"You got a better one?"

Shaun hated to admit that he didn't. He placed the collar around his neck. "Let's go."

Lilly arranged her features into a calm facade as she heard the release of the bolt on her cell door. In the entryway was the Sacrosanct Mistress, arrayed in her robes and hat. Lilly saw Arleta and some of the lesser witches standing behind her.

"I will talk to the child in private," Honora informed them in a deceivingly gentle tone, and the door slid shut behind her.

"I am no longer a child, Mistress," Lilly said as she stood before the woman.

"So I've noticed," Honora replied, twitching her nostrils in disgust. She sensed the presence of the man on Lilly's body. It sickened her to think of the things they could have done. "You have strayed from your purpose, daughter."

"How can it be my purpose when I had no say in it?"

"Foolish child, have you not known that your life was never your own?" Honora did not even bother to hide her mounting anger. "Your life was granted by the benevolence of your uncle and given over to us by the same benevolence. You have been trained and raised to a purpose, and that purpose has come to fruition."

Lilly looked at the woman with dawning realization in her eyes. "You seek to rule the universe through me," she stated calmly.

It all made perfect sense. Oasis supplied the food, and whoever controlled the planet would command tremendous power. Alexander had chosen not to wield that power. Honora would be very different.

"How long has the plan been in the making?" Lilly asked, afraid of the answer.

"Generations," Honora responded.

Lilly was astounded to see that the woman was pleased she had figured it out. She almost seemed proud of her.

"It started with Ariel," Honora said. "We raised her for that exact purpose."

"And she was supposed to have a daughter who would be the rightful heir to Oasis."

"The foolish girl fell in love with her husband." Honora said it with disgust. Love was not something she understood or tolerated. "She refused to destroy the son he gave her."

"A male Circe would be beyond your control, so you sent in my mother."

"Zania." Honora nodded. "She was my finest apprentice. I knew she would not fail me." Honora smiled benevolently at Lilly. "It pleases me that you resemble her," she said tenderly. Or what passed for tenderness in Honora.

"But she did fail," Lilly said, dismissing the gentle words. "She died."

"That was a chance we were willing to take to eliminate the heir."

"Which she did." They must never guess that she hadn't.

"And gave us you in the bargain." Honora took a moment to arrange the wide sleeves of her cloak. "Of course, there was a time when we were concerned that the Sovereign would put her to death before you could be delivered to us. It was a chance we had to take. We dared not ask him to spare you, since his feelings toward us were not charitable at that time."

"Did you start the war?"

"We advised the ruler of Raviga that it would benefit him to enter into an alliance with us."

"Therefore giving you an army," Lilly concluded. "Does the Prince know about this?"

Honora laughed, surprising Lilly, who had thought her incapable of such a feat. "Don't be ridiculous, child. He is of no consequence. He is merely an instrument, a means to an end. You can kill him, for all I care, once you are with child and certain of an heir to his throne." The woman chucked her finger under Lilly's chin. "You might even enjoy it. The killing, not the other part."

"The Senate?

"Fools who concentrate more on posturing than power."

"My uncle?"

"The Sovereign," Honora said with an unattractive grimace. "It was a surprise when he attempted to kill you. That's how much he hates us, child. He pretended to agree to the alliance, then arranged your death so the Senate would have to step in. He would rather see you dead than let us win." Honora placed an arm around Lilly's shoulder. "We are your family, Lilly. We will take care of you."

"Only if I do what you wish."

The change that came over the Sacrosanct Mistress was so rapid that Lilly was unprepared for the crack of the hand across her cheek.

"You will do as I say. You have no choice in the matter."

"Don't I?" Lilly tasted blood on her tongue. The salty bitterness of it strengthened her.

"We have your lover. It's up to you whether he lives or dies."

"You would make promises and kill him anyway. That is your way." Lilly hoped her impudence would distract the witch long enough for Shaun to escape from the ship. She felt the presence of Honora in her mind and concentrated on her wall.

"There are lessons that we have overlooked in your education, Lilly," Honora said with false regret.

Lilly almost sighed in relief. The witch had given up on delving into her mind.

"You must learn obedience."

Or had she?

"Who is controlling your lover?"

Lilly stood silently before the woman.

"What is her purpose?"

Lilly suppressed the urge to laugh in the woman's face. Years of suffering had bought the Circe women mental superiority, and yet they made the same mistakes the men of their planet had made all those years ago. The men of the past had determined the women to be of no consequence. Now the women were doing the same thing.

"It is amazing that he has eyes such as ours, is it not?"

Lilly thought Honora resembled one of the great hooded snakes of Cathra that hypnotized its prey before swallowing it whole. She hoped she would not be so paralyzed.

"I've taken them from him," Honora said casually.

No, you haven't.

Horrified, she realized she'd let the thought escape. She had so wanted to wipe that smug smile off the witch's face. Honora's eyes widened.

Lilly fell to the floor of the cell as the witch filled her mind with horrible images of Shaun. She saw him burning, saw him disemboweled, saw his skin being scourged from his body as her mother's had been. She saw his face screaming in terror and felt the screams filling her mind. It was a trick, it was not true, yet it would be if he was caught. She clutched her hands to her head and screamed in agony.

"He will not escape, and neither will you," the woman hissed as she whirled for the door. "Arleta! The man is escaping!"

Arleta snarled and pounded the communicator on the wall.

"Bring her," Honora said, nodding her head toward the sobbing heap on the floor. "Collar her!"

Chapter Seventeen

It had been easy. Shaun and Ruben had walked through the corridors of the cruiser as if they did it every day. Shaun neglected to tell Ruben that he had mentally commanded everyone they passed to ignore them. He had been afraid that Ruben would relax if he thought that Shaun had everyone under control. He wasn't even sure if he could do it, although as the shuttle bay came into view, it looked as if he had.

"You'd better pick one out now and go straight to it," Shaun said as they passed through the hatch. "If you look lost, they'll be on us in a minute."

"I've got it." Ruben jabbed Shaun in the back as if he were still a prisoner and turned him toward a small shuttle sitting near the entrance of the bay. Shaun concentrated on being submissive while they crossed the wide open deck of the launch bay. He felt the hair on the back of his neck stand on end and knew they were being watched from the window that overlooked the bay. It took every bit of his willpower not to break into a run, and he could sense that Ruben was having the same issue.

"Run!" It was Lilly. Her voice in his mind was full of despair. *"Go,"* she urged.

She was suffering. He could feel it. How could he leave her? He couldn't.

"No," he said simply.

"Don't do it," Ruben cautioned. The shuttle was just a few feet ahead of them.

A siren sounded. Shaun turned. Ruben swung and hit Shaun in the temple with the hilt of his knife. He caught his friend as his eyes rolled up into his head.

"Halt!" Soldiers poured in through the hatch as a siren screamed and a red light flashed.

Ruben dragged Shaun to the shuttle and heaved him through the hatch.

"You sure did pick a fine time to take a nap," he complained as he slammed the door shut behind them and jumped into the seat to fire the engines. He had chosen this shuttle because of the model's speed and maneuverability. The wide shield above the controls revealed the slow closing of the bay doors. Ruben felt the impact from a pulse rifle against the side of the shuttle as it lifted from the deck.

"I hope there's no one waiting for us outside," he said to the controls as he punched the stick forward and the shuttle blasted toward the shrinking opening. The shuttle screamed from the bay as a battery of shots from the gun towers exploded around it. Ruben turned the stick toward the multitude of satellites that circled the planet.

"What happened?" Shaun asked as he lurched into the seat beside Ruben.

"You were being stupid," Ruben replied as the shuttle vibrated beneath his control.

"There's a first time for everything," Shaun retorted.

"With you it's starting to be a trend," Ruben replied casually as he dipped behind a satellite.

"Your turn will come." Shaun punched up the chart for the planet. "Let's get back to your ship."

"Already on it. Why don't you see if you can convince our friends to leave us alone," Ruben said, pointing to the blips on the circular screen located on the instrument panel.

"I'm not sure if I can. I've never tried reaching out through space."

"Lilly did it."

She had, Shaun realized. He also didn't know what he was capable of, and he had nothing to lose but his life. He took a deep breath, closed his eyes, and concentrated on sending an image of the shuttle in a different position.

"It worked," Ruben announced. "Too bad we didn't know about this hidden talent years ago. We'd both be rich men."

Shaun ignored his friend. He closed his eyes again and reached out.

The collar wasn't so bad, Lilly decided as she followed meekly behind Arleta. She did not have to cast out with her mind to know that Shaun had escaped. The confusion and anger that pulsated from the Circe was a sure indication that he had.

It was easy with the collar. She had no choice. Her body had to obey even though her heart rebelled. It would keep her from doing something foolish. If only she had been wearing it earlier, she would not have run off with Shaun. She would not have experienced ecstasy and passion. The collar made it easy. If only she could wear it for the rest of her life.

Her life. That was a sobering thought. According to Honora, it had never been her own. She had belonged to the Circe even before she was born. She had been part of a plot, the instrument in a bizarre plan to take over the universe.

So what should she do about it? What could she do about it?

Nothing as long as she wore the collar. The collar made it easy.

"Too bad your male escaped," Arleta whispered in Lilly's ear as she boarded the shuttle. "Now you will have to answer our questions."

I will not betray him. Lilly repeated the litany over and over again in her mind. She must not betray his secret. She must not betray him again.

He had escaped.

"What is it you're looking for?" Ruben asked as he skillfully guided his ship into the cargo bay on Pristo.

"Answers," Shaun replied. "Stay here with the ship. I don't know how many guards were left behind."

"I'll guard it with my life," Ruben said with a grin. He saw the set of Shaun's jaw. "Good luck."

Shaun took the extended hand of his friend. "I won't be long."

"Good. You know what I always say."

"Yeah, time is money, I know," Shaun said on his way out of the ship.

He cast out with his mind as he reached the ladder that descended into the caverns. How many men had been left here to fend for themselves after his and Lilly's capture? There was too much at stake to risk coming across them.

Shaun could not feel their presence in the darkness below. Nor did any light shine up from the depths. That was fine with him. He knew where he was going and he needed no light to guide him. He made his way down the ladder and into the darkness.

The twists and turns were as familiar to him as the back of his hand. He walked without hesitation toward the left branch of the tunnel and the chamber that held the chasm.

A woman had died there. He had heard her cries when he had been here with Lilly, but now all was silent. Had she found her peace in those few moments when the two of them had joined and dipped down into the yawning abyss that went all the way to the core of the planet? What had the woman been trying to tell him?

She had been seeking him, Shaun was sure of it. Lilly had not heard the cries until she entered his mind. Who was she? When had she died? Shaun could not recall anyone falling into the chasm in his lifetime, nor had his father ever mentioned it happening. Surely he would have if he had known.

He heard it then. A muffled weeping as if her tears were used up and she had nothing left to give. Shaun squeezed through the narrow opening in the gate and went to the edge of the rift in the planet.

He took a deep breath and closed his eyes. His head spun as vertigo came over him. Shaun blinked and threw himself backward, landing in a puff of dust on the floor of the cave. He looked up at the ceiling that disappeared beyond his enhanced vision into darkness so black that it seemed no light could penetrate it.

I would still be falling. He closed his eyes again.

"Who are you? What do you want from me?"

"You know who I am—you know and yet you deny me still."

"Mother?" He had said the word before when Lilly had guided him into the chasm. He remembered it but did not understand it.

"Yes."

"How? Why?"

"Look inside yourself, my son. The answers are in your memories."

Shaun's eyes flew open once again. *The answers are in my memories?* His head whirled and spun once again as he felt the dizziness overcome him. He turned over onto all fours and scrambled toward the safety of the cavern wall, taking in great gulps of air as he crawled. Why couldn't he breathe? What was wrong with him? Was this . . . terror . . . he was feeling?

Get control. He must have control. *"How?"* he repeated as his breathing became normal again.

"Look inside."

Shaun took a breath as he had seen Lilly do, closed his eyes, and let his mind go.

"Look inside."

"How do I do that?"

"Look inside."

Shaun formed a picture in his mind. He was sitting in the cavern and Lilly was with him, her hands on his temples. She had unfolded the scenes of his life. She had opened his memories.

"Where do I go?" he asked the voice.

"The beginning," she replied.

The beginning. What was the beginning of his memory? Suddenly he was a boy again, a small boy, walking and talking, running and playing, falling against stone, skinning his knees, bumping his head. His mother comforted him. His father encouraged him. He slept in his cot under the warmth of the quilts and knew he was loved. He was Shaun.

The memory of the child from his dream intruded. The child wandered the tunnels of Pristo. The child was lost. The child was crying and there was dried blood on his neck and back. Shaun watched as his father picked up the child and looked at it in wonder.

"Where did you come from?" his father asked.

The child was Shaun. His mind did not have time to absorb the shock as the memories spun into an ever-tightening circle, as if the days of his life were moving in reverse.

He was in pain. The source of his comfort and joy was hurting him, and her tears mingled with his own as he fought against the hand that held him down while the sharp point of the knife pierced his skin. Why was she hurting him? Always before she had come and made the tears go away, but now she was causing them. Where were they? Why was it dark?

Where was the light and the warmth that he had always known?

The woman was holding him close against her as they hid in the noisy hold of a ship. The noise was so loud it hurt his ears, and the woman was frightening him. He could feel the sticky wetness that dampened the back of her cloak.

"Shh, my darling. Don't make a sound. Mother is here. Mother will protect you."

Mother had always cared for him. But this time she didn't. This time she hurt him and then she abandoned him.

As he sat alone in the darkness of the deep cavern watching the events of his early life unfold, tears escaped from his tightly closed eyes and traced a pattern down his chiseled jaw.

He saw Lilly's face in his mind. But instead of the quiet beauty he was accustomed to finding there, this face was twisted with evil. It terrified the child that he had been. Then he saw the beloved face of his mother as she shoved the evil Lilly aside and gathered him into her arms.

"You'll not have my son, Zania," his mother declared.

"Give him up, Ariel. They will never let him live." Zania held out her arms to take him.

"You will not have him," his mother said, and turned to leave.

He watched over his mother's shoulder as the other woman came after them with a knife in her hand. She swung the knife, and he screamed in terror as it struck his mother in the back. Ariel gasped in pain and then kicked her away. Zania fell against the wall, striking her head and sliding to the floor. Ariel ran and Shaun felt her heart pounding against his head as she held him close, desperate to escape Oasis. She had to get her son away. The Circe would never let him live.

Still the memories went back in time. He was lying on his back and reaching for the brightly colored flowers that danced above his bed. The next thing he saw was the face of his father as he stood with his mother over his crib and then kissed him good night.

The Sovereign Alexander of Oasis.

Shaun threw back his head and roared his frustration. The sound swirled out from his throat and bounced off the cavern wall before it swelled up into the roof. The worrats that slept in the high reaches screeched their angry retort and descended in an angry mass of flapping wings and nipping teeth as they beat their way down into the chasm before surging up again toward the entrance. Bodies beat against the metal gate as some made their way over and through and others crashed into it.

"Mother?"

"The proof is on you, Nicholas . . ."

Shaun touched his hand to the back of his neck. He knew the scarred letters were there but had never understood why. Until now.

"Strength, Honor, Obedience, Unity, Nobility." The credo of Oasis. It had been scratched into the back of his neck by his mother.

This isn't even my real name, Shaun thought bitterly as he rose to his feet.

"I'm so happy we found you, Shaun." His mother's

dying words. Only, she wasn't his real mother. Ryan Phoenix had found him. The hidden heir to the most powerful planet in the universe.

And his real father was trying to kill the woman he loved.

Shaun rose to his feet.

"What do you want of me, Mother?"

"You must return. You must return to your father."

He wanted to kill his father.

"And do what?"

"Defeat the Circe."

Had she ever loved him? Or was he just an instrument for revenge?

"Will you be at peace then?" he asked.

"I am at peace now."

He saw her then, in his mind. He watched as she wandered through the dim light of the tunnels, bleeding from her wound. He saw her weaken in the darkness, saw her stumble, watched in horror as she fell into the abyss and disappeared without a sound into the darkness.

She was at peace. The crying was gone. The voice had gone with it. His mother, Ariel, was at peace.

He wasn't.

Chapter Eighteen

How long will they wait? Lilly pondered her fate even as she embraced it. She had been put in seclusion in one of the many small chambers that made up the interior of the Circe palace adjacent to the great congress of the Senate. No doubt Honora was making wedding arrangements for her even as she sat in the solitude of her cell.

They had removed the collar. Lilly wished they hadn't. It had made things so much easier. Do as we say. Move here. Stay there. Sit. Stand. Obey.

Obey. Except for her one moment of rebellion with Shaun, she had been obedient her entire life. And her one moment of rebellion had been the only moment in her life when she had felt alive.

Alive. If only she hadn't felt so alive. If only she hadn't felt the giving and the taking. If only she hadn't felt the meeting of their souls. If only she hadn't felt the passion.

How could it be wrong? It was wrong, wasn't it? The union of two so closely related was forbidden. Their fathers had been brothers.

How could something that felt so right be so wrong?

If only they could make her forget him. Maybe then the hurt would go away. The despair would disappear and there would be contentment. Was that too much to ask for? Didn't she deserve a reward for being obedient?

Shaun had escaped; wasn't that reward enough? That was all she had asked for. That he would escape. That he would be safe.

She would be obedient.

Yet Honora had questions for her still. The witch was determined to know who had gone against her but had not guessed it might be a man. In her logic, it had to be another witch. It had to be someone who was as greedy and vicious as she was. It had to be someone who shared Honora's aspirations to be ruler of the universe.

"Arleta." Lilly's mind pounced on the thought greedily. Could she convince Honora that Arleta was behind it all? Surely the motive was already there, buried deep inside the bitter mind of the witch. Surely Honora would sense it if she looked into Arleta's thoughts. Surely Arleta had entertained the idea of overthrowing her mistress at one time or another. She was too ambitious not to have thought it. The diversion would certainly take the Mistress's mind off of Shaun, whom the witch considered to be nothing more than an insignificant pawn in the political game.

The Circe must never find out who he really was.

Yet Lilly herself had sent him to Pristo to find out that very thing.

What would he do once he found out that he was Nicholas, heir to Oasis? Would he go back and claim his kinship with her uncle? Would he take control of the government and lead his people in the war against Raviga?

But there would be no war once she married Ram.

And the Circe would not let Shaun live once they found out who he was. Even if he was sitting on the throne of the most powerful planet in the universe, they would still go after him. Their order would not permit him to live. It went against everything the Circe believed in.

They were coming for her. Lilly felt the presence of the minions as they entered the corridor of her prison. Of course, she would be summoned to the Sacrosanct Mistress. The witch had deigned to come to her once. She would not do it again. This time, Lilly knew what to expect.

She only hoped she was strong enough for the coming battle.

"From the look on your face, I'd say you found what you were looking for," Ruben commented as he watched his friend climb the ladder to the launch port hidden beneath the surface of the gas-covered planet.

"You could say that," Shaun grunted as he hopped over the top step and joined his friend on the platform.

"Anything you want to share with me?" Ruben

asked as they walked shoulder to shoulder toward his waiting ship.

"Remember the story you told me about the missing heir to Oasis?"

"Yes." Ruben hesitated as Shaun walked on with his long stride.

"It's me."

A wide grin spread over Ruben's face. "I figured it was something like that," he said.

"If you did, then you were way ahead of me," Shaun growled as he slumped into the copilot's seat.

"It started to add up, considering the color of your eyes and that special talent you have," Ruben said as he went through the ignition series.

"Seeing in the dark?"

"That, and the recent mind capabilities. I imagine there would be some very angry witches if they found out." Ruben stopped flipping switches and looked at his friend. "Lilly knows, doesn't she?"

"Yes, she does. She found out when we were here earlier."

"Thus the sudden shutdown."

"What do you mean?"

"You're cousins. That's taboo, or have you forgotten?"

A wide grin spread over Shaun's face. "So that's why she was in such a hurry to run me off. She doesn't want the witches to know, but she also thinks that we can't . . ." Shaun reached over to Ruben's panel and finished the ignition series. "We're going to Oasis."

"It will be nice having friends in high places,"

Ruben said with a cocky grin as the ship blasted from the bay.

"Don't count your credits yet," Shaun said in reply.

The ship quickly made the jump into hyperdrive and the stars of the galaxy streaked by as one continuous light. Shaun hardly noticed; his mind was still reeling from his recent discovery. In just a short amount of time he had gone from being a convicted murderer to the heir of the richest planet in the universe. Come to think of it, he was still a convicted murderer, but he should be able to get around that sentence now that he knew he was so well connected. Wealth and power could get you anything.

"I wish you'd dropped me off at Rykers when I had the chance." He sighed as he leaned back in the seat and looked up at the overhead panels of the ship.

"No escaping destiny," Ruben replied with a grin. "Or so my father always says."

Shaun looked at his friend in surprise. That was the first time he ever recalled hearing Ruben mention a family of any kind.

"So what's your plan?" Ruben said quickly before Shaun had time to ask him any personal questions.

"I don't know, I'd thought I waltz into the palace on Oasis, introduce myself to my father"—Shaun sneered over the word father—"who is trying to murder the woman I love, stop the wedding, stop the war, keep an entire planet of witches from plotting my death, and live happily ever after?"

"I never considered you to be the ambitious type."

"I was saving it all for now." Shaun scrubbed his

hands through his hair. "Do you have any suggestions?"

"As a matter of fact, I do."

Shaun gave his friend a quizzical look.

"I think you should talk to Michael."

"Did you save the code that Lilly used?"

"Do you even have to ask?" Ruben replied as he started punching the com.

"This lost sailor is coming home," Shaun said to the stars as they whizzed by.

The air in Honora's formal chambers was crackling with anticipation. The Sacrosanct Mistress awaited Lilly in an ornate chair on a dais, not unlike the one the Prefect used in the Senate. She wore her most regal robes and her impressive hat sat atop her brow like a crown. Arleta stood at her right side, her hands folded into the deep sleeves of her robe. Lesser witches stood around the perimeter of the chamber, each one focusing all her attention on their mistress in case she had need of any of their insignificant powers.

As if she would. Lilly knew she was in for the fight of her life, but she also knew she was safe. They could not harm her. After all, without her they couldn't rule Oasis or Raviga. She was the key. Prince Ramelah would not want his bride to be marred in any way. Make that any obvious way. Lilly was certain Ram would overlook the fact that she was no longer a virgin in exchange for the riches of Oasis.

As long as Shaun was safely away, the Circe had no hold on her. All she had to do was keep his secret and convince Honora that Arleta was behind the deception. Lilly took a cleansing breath as she entered the chamber. She was in for the fight of her life.

"I would have a word with you before you leave for Raviga," Honora began.

Lilly fought the impulse to roll her eyes as she stood submissively before the Mistress. Why must they pretend that all was well? It had not even been a full cycle since she had been dragged from the cruiser with a collar around her neck. She was sick of the lies, sick of the deception, sick of being a pawn in the Mistress's political ambitions. Lilly glanced sideways and saw the gleam in Arleta's cold pale eyes.

Lilly decided she might as well enjoy herself.

"The Prince is still content with the arrangement?" Lilly asked meekly, her eyes now obviously darting to Arleta.

Honora tilted her head, trying to read what was inside her mind. "He bears you no ill will," she said.

"I am grateful, then," Lilly replied, playing her role as was expected. She felt the lesser witches testing her, each one hoping she would find Lilly's secret and therefore advance herself with the Mistress. Lilly kept her wall in place. She couldn't let the information out too easily. After all, she was protecting someone. "Will my uncle be present?"

"Everyone you hold dear will be present," Honora continued as she sifted through the layers of Lilly's mind. "The ceremony is to be held on Oasis, and the Prefect will be in attendance, as will I."

Lilly allowed herself to smile as if flattered by the attention. Of course, Ram would want the ceremony to be held on Oasis. It would put him that much closer to everything he desired.

"It is a great treaty for everyone." Honora smiled indulgently.

You mean for the Circe. Lilly allowed the rebellious thought to come to the surface. She must not appear to be too submissive. She watched in satisfaction as Honora's nostrils flared.

Lilly willed her face to remain impassive as the Mistress snatched gleefully at the bait. The witch moved quickly despite the heavy robes she was wearing. She jumped from her dais and snatched Lilly's head by the temples, placing her palms against her face and squeezing hard until Lilly's knees hit the floor.

"I will have your secret, child," Honora hissed, her voice low, seductive.

Lilly knew she had only one chance. If she failed, all would be lost, for Honora would not let her go until she had emptied her mind of everything. Distraction was her only weapon.

"*Why have you abandoned me?*" The pressure against her temples was unbearable, but with determination Lilly was still able to turn her eyes toward Arleta, who was watching the proceedings with evil glee transforming her sharp features into a caricature of wickedness.

"Traitor!" Honora shrieked. She turned toward Arleta, whose eyes suddenly widened at the strange turn of events.

"She lies," Arleta cried out, guessing what Lilly had done. "It is a trick!"

"Who else would have the power but you?" Honora demanded as she approached the witch.

"Even now she has tricked you," Arleta tried to explain, pointing to Lilly, who stood with her head bowed submissively, willing her mind to stay focused on one thought only. *Arleta has betrayed us. Arleta has betrayed you, Mistress.*

Lilly fought to keep the adrenaline rush suppressed as she realized that she had beaten the most powerful of the Circe. And it wasn't the power of her mind that had done it; it was the power of her logic. Honora saw only what she wanted to see, because anything else was unthinkable. No man could have the power; therefore, it came from a woman.

Lilly wanted to laugh at the absurdity of it. She wanted to smile gleefully as Arleta had just smiled in anticipation of her punishment. Now Arleta cowered on the floor before Honora, her mind scrambling for a way out of her sudden predicament.

Lilly felt the power of her own mind. No one even noticed as all eyes focused on Arleta, who fell to the floor with her hands to her head, shrieking at the top of her lungs.

Honora turned from her victim, her face flushed and her pale eyes glazed.

"Your bridegroom awaits," she panted. "Take her to him." She turned away, her full attention focused on Arleta.

The masked minions, always waiting, stepped forward to escort Lilly from the chamber.

They think I want to escape. Lilly looked straight ahead as they marched her down the corridor. They did not realize that she was happy to be going.

Chapter Nineteen

"Welcome, visitor. Are you a trader?"

"No, I'm a sailor lost at sea," Shaun replied to Michael's code. Lost was a good word for it. He didn't have a clue as to what he should do next, but Ruben's idea of talking to Michael first had been a good one. Shaun just hoped that the truth he had seen in Michael's mind would hold more power than any other allegiance he owed.

Blood would tell.

"Lilly?" Michael asked in response to the password.

Shaun wondered if anyone else was listening on the other end.

"No," he said finally. He didn't know where she was or how she was doing. But one thought gave him comfort. They wouldn't hurt her. They needed her.

He needed her.

"Same coordinates as before," Michael snapped into the com.

Shaun slumped back in his seat as Ruben deftly guided the craft down to the planet.

"Looks like everything is in a holding pattern," Ruben commented as they slowly descended into the atmosphere. As soon as they had come out of the hyperport they had noticed that the Ravigan and Oasian battle cruisers in orbit were standing down along with the smaller fighters that were now quietly patrolling the perimeters of their territory.

"Yes," Shaun agreed. "But what are they holding for?"

"Maybe something's about to happen," Ruben said cheerily.

"Something is about to happen, all right," Shaun grunted in response.

"Come on, don't you think that dear old Dad is going to be glad to see you?"

Shaun considered pitching Ruben through the hatch and watching him fall to the colorful patchwork surface of the planet below. The fact of the matter was, he didn't know what to expect, didn't know how he felt about the Sovereign. . . . He refused to think of him as his real father, even though he realized that Alexander had not wanted to lose his . . . him.

What drove Alexander? Was it revenge? Was it sorrow? Was it bitterness? What would drive a man to try to murder the only family he had? Did he see Lilly as an enemy? Did he see her as an extension of her mother? Did he hate his enemies more than he loved his family?

What would his reaction be when Shaun presented himself as his son? Would Alexander even believe him?

What proof did he have to offer the Sovereign beyond the letters scratched on the back of his neck? It was not as if he could walk in and let the Sovereign look into his mind for the proof.

Ruben switched on the landing gear as they approached the dock.

"There's another set of eye shields in the console," Ruben said as he maneuvered the craft onto the pad. "It's midday and the sun is high."

Shaun popped the console open to retrieve the shields. A mirror inserted in the door caught his attention and the answer to his dilemma stared back at him.

All he had to do was show Alexander his eyes. They were the testimony that he was Nicholas, heir to Oasis. They were all the proof he needed.

Michael was waiting for them.

"Are you here for the ceremony?" Michael's tone was not pleasant as Shaun and Ruben came through the hatch.

"Ceremony?" Shaun asked, knowing the answer and dreading it also.

"The treaty between Oasis and Raviga," Michael began. "The union of our two planets." He spat the words out.

"Lilly and Ram," Shaun finished for him.

"What happened?" Michael demanded. "You promised to protect her!"

He had. The last words he had spoken to Michael had been a promise to protect her. But he had also promised something else.

"We need to talk," Shaun said. "How long do we have?"

"Not long enough. The Ravigan delegation is already here. All we're waiting for is the groom and the . . . bride." Michael nearly choked on the word as he led the two men into an office in the port. "Something happened before you left with Lilly," he said without preamble as he closed the door firmly behind them.

"I saw your secret," Shaun said.

"How?" Michael asked. "Why?" He looked up and once again realized that Shaun's eyes were the same color as Lilly's. Michael slumped down against a table. "Who are you? What are you?"

"I'm Nicholas," Shaun stated. "I'm the missing heir . . ."

"Come back to claim his destiny," Michael finished, quoting the legend. "So I didn't imagine it. You were in my mind. You saw things. Where have you been? What—"

Shaun held up his hand to stop the sudden barrage of questions. They didn't have time for explanations now. The important thing was stopping the wedding. He had to save Lilly, and at the same time he had to save Oasis. For her. "I don't want the throne, I don't want the planet, and I don't want the riches."

"You want Lilly," Michael said, understanding dawning in his eyes. "But the war. We have to stop the war."

"Did you ever figure out who was responsible for the attempt on Lilly's life?"

"The Ravigans?"

"No. Alexander."

"That doesn't make sense."

"It does if Alexander will do anything to keep the Circe from taking power."

"What do the Circe have to do with it?"

"They formed an alliance with Raviga. They encouraged Raviga to start the war and persuaded the Senate to look the other way,"

"In exchange for tribute." Michael caught on quickly. "And afterward, the Circe could control Oasis through Lilly. But why would Alexander want Lilly dead?"

"Without her, there's no way for an alliance to be formed. He could prevent the Circe from gaining power, and with the death of a princess, the Senate would be forced to take an active role in ending the war."

"And I sent her to them," Michael said in disgust.

"You had no way of knowing, Michael. You were doing what you thought best for the planet. You were obeying your orders." Shaun meant to comfort the man, but he realized there was contempt in his tone nonetheless.

"Damn them all," Michael said. "Damn him."

Shaun smiled bitterly. That didn't even begin to cover what he was feeling.

"So what do we do?" Michael asked in exasperation.

"Bring in our secret weapon," Ruben replied.

"The heir to Oasis." Michael looked at Shaun, daring to hope for the first time in a long time.

"I believe it's time for me to meet my father," Shaun replied as he adjusted his shields over his eyes.

As Michael led them through the corridors, Shaun wondered what it would have been like growing up with pageantry and riches instead of poverty and hardship. Would he have turned out different if he had known that whatever he wanted was simply his for the taking? He had never needed much, nor had he ever seemed to want much as a child. He had never longed for a special toy or felt jealousy over another's possession. He and his parents had always made do and used whatever was on hand. There was no limit to his imagination when he was playing, and his mother had a way of making stories come alive.

His adopted mother.

But as he grew older his contentment changed. He began looking for a place to fit. His father saw the restlessness and sent him to the Academy. He excelled there but never felt the military life as a calling. He always thought it was because of his father's history, something that the students and instructors never allowed him to forget. His father had turned his back on the brotherhood and abandoned his post.

His adopted father.

After that Shaun had wandered, going to new frontiers, new settlements, thinking that what he wanted was the adventure of building and discovering, but still he was unsettled. He hooked up with Ruben, smuggling supplies beneath the noses of the Legion to avoid the heavy taxes levied by the Senate. Shaun discovered he didn't care about the credits they amassed; it was tweaking his nose at authority that gave him a thrill. He thought he had gotten that attitude from his father. He never would have guessed that he was supposed to be the authority.

Would he be a different man if he had grown up as

the pampered son of a Sovereign? Would he have idolized Alexander as he had the man he'd thought was his real father? Would Ariel have trained him in the Circe ways even though it was forbidden? Chances were he wouldn't have survived to adulthood. The Circe would have seen to his assassination, one way or another. They would have done anything to keep a man from wielding the power.

He had the power. What would he do with it?

Shaun took a deep breath as Michael opened the door that led to Alexander's suite of offices.

"Do you want me to go with you?" Ruben asked.

"I think I'd better go this one alone," Shaun replied.

"I'm here if you need me."

"I know." Shaun reached out his hand to shake the one proffered by his friend.

"I guess you do at that," Ruben said with his sly smile.

Michael led the way through the outer office where the frantic preparations for the coming wedding were being made. One of the Ravigans in attendance looked up from the list that he was going over with one of Alexander's secretaries and gave Shaun a cold, hard stare. Shaun ignored him. He had one thought on his mind as he walked through the richly appointed room.

Would he have loved Lilly if things had been different? He knew he would.

Would she have loved him? She would, but only as a cousin. Shaun focused his attention on Michael, whose back was held rigidly erect, a soldier down to his very core. Yet even he had had his moment of weakness and a secret that he had carried all these years.

What had happened to make him betray his liege? Had it all been a part of Zania's plan or a desperate attempt to become pregnant after Victor failed to produce an heir? Had she seduced Michael or had he gone willingly to her bed? All these years Michael had thought he was protecting Lilly by letting everyone think she was Victor's daughter. And now Lilly was about to pay the price for the safety of being of royal blood.

"My lord?" Michael rapped on the door. "There is someone here to see you."

Alexander looked up from his work, relief appearing on his face at the interruption. The light in the room was dim, the only illumination coming from a lamp on the huge ornate desk, but still Shaun was able to see the look of relief change to puzzlement when he stepped into the room. Michael ducked out without a word and shut the door behind him.

Shaun refused to wonder what his father was thinking. He looked into his mind instead. The first thing he saw was dread. Had Lilly's protector discovered that he was the one behind the attempt on her life?

"I know what you did," Shaun answered the silent question as he walked toward the desk where Alexander sat, his face now a blank mask. "And I know why you did it."

He sensed Alexander's confusion.

"You hate the Circe more than you love your niece."

"What gives you the right to question my motives or even my actions?"

"You're still seeking revenge against them after all these years."

"That is none of your concern," Alexander said as he rose to his feet. He looked beyond Shaun toward the door.

"He'll come if you shout," Shaun said, knowing that Alexander was frightened.

"What do you want of me?" Alexander asked, confusion now taking over his features as Shaun came closer. "How do you—"

"I ask nothing of you," Shaun interrupted him. "I have one purpose, and that is to stop Lilly from sacrificing her life to help you and your planet."

"But the war—we must stop the war," Alexander declared weakly.

"You're still planning to kill her." Shaun saw it all. He saw his father's plan to kill Lilly before the ceremony and blame the treachery on the Ravigans. It was the only way to keep Oasis out of the hands of the Ravigans and out of the hands of the Circe.

"I won't let it happen." Shaun stopped as his thighs came into contact with the desk. He raised his shields, placed his palms down on the surface, and leaned across until his face was inches from Alexander's.

"Who are you?" Alexander asked, his voice barely a whisper as he looked into Shaun's gray eyes, the light from the lamp heightening the contrast between the pale pupils and the black centers.

"Don't you recognize me?" Shaun said in disgust. "I'm your son."

Chapter Twenty

The first thought that flashed through his father's mind was that Shaun was some sort of Circe trick designed to ensure Circe rule of Oasis.

"My son is dead," Alexander said as he pushed his chair away from the desk and the large looming body of his son. "Nicholas is dead."

"Your wife, my . . . mother . . . hid on a transport that took us to Pristo. She died there." Shaun watched Alexander's face as he told the story. "Before she died, she marked me so you would know."

"How? Where?"

Shaun felt as if he were about to put his head on a chopping block. He lowered his body across the desk until his cheek lay against the cool surface of the marble inlay. With his hand he lifted the hair from the back of his neck and turned so the lamp shone upon his scars.

"Here," he said.

Alexander rose from his chair and tentatively took a step toward the desk. Shaun heard his gasp and wondered for a moment if the man held a knife in his hand. Then he realized that if Alexander meant to kill him, he would sense it. He forced himself to relax as his father turned the lamp and walked around the side of the desk to better view the scars.

"It is our creed!" Alexander exclaimed.

Shaun raised himself and self-consciously rubbed the scars. Alexander's eyes were wide with wonder as he looked in earnest at Shaun's face.

"You resemble her," he said.

"I know I have her eyes," Shaun said, suddenly disgusted with the discussion. Why did he feel the need to explain himself to this man who even now was thrilling at the prospect that he had a secret weapon in his war against the Circe?

"Your face resembles hers also," Alexander said as he studied him. "I should have seen it before."

"You had no reason to."

"You kept your eyes hidden when you were here before," Alexander realized. "Why? Why did you not tell me then who you were?"

"I didn't know. I've just found out. Lilly . . ."

"Lilly guided you into your past."

"Yes."

"Her powers are greater than she realizes."

"You suppressed them," Shaun said. Alexander had suddenly started blocking him as he walked around to the front of the desk. Shaun turned to face him and leaned against it with his arms folded casually as he studied the man.

"We had to. I believed she was born to serve a high purpose."

"You mean serve you."

"Why shouldn't she? It was by my grace that she was allowed to live. I could have killed her mother while she was still in the womb."

"Instead you kept her to be a weapon against the Circe."

"It was her destiny," Alexander said with a casual shrug. "I was hoping for a male, like you, my son."

"I won't be your weapon."

"Why not? With your powers, it would be easy to convince the Prefect that the Raivgans and the Circe conspired to murder Lilly. The Senate would have to step in and defend the planet. You could even convince the Prefect that her assassination was part of a plot to murder him . . ."

Shaun slammed his fist against the desk. The force of his rage split the wood across the top to the edge of the marble inlay. "Lilly is not your pawn. I will not allow you to kill her."

Alexander looked in awe at the damage done to his desk. "Why do you care for her? She is your cousin and can be nothing more. She will serve the greater good by sacrificing her life. It is the least she can do to . . ."

"Lilly did not kill my mother," Shaun ground out. "She had nothing to do with it."

"But she is one of them."

"So am I!" The awareness of his identity washed over Shaun at the same time that he shouted the words

to his father. He was a Circe. He had the power. What would he choose to do with it?

"They fear you," Alexander stated.

"They think I'm a pawn, nothing more. They deny the possibility that I exist."

"We can use their disbelief to our advantage. We can defeat them."

Shaun could tell by the look on his father's face that Alexander was plotting something. His own mind was in too much turmoil to concentrate on finding out what. Besides, he knew that Alexander would block him. Years of paranoia about the Circe had caused him to develop that skill to the highest level.

Shaun rubbed his temples with his hands. What did he want to do? What should he do? Defeat the Circe? All he wanted was to take the woman he loved as far away from this beehive of intrigue as possible. Just as his father had done. His adopted father.

A knock on the door interrupted his thoughts.

"The Prefect's carrier has just come out of the hyperport," Michael reported.

The two men in the room looked at him, both suddenly remembering what was about to take place.

"Lilly is with them. And so is the Prince."

This will certainly take all the confusion out of what to wear in the future, Lilly said to the mirror in her cabin. She was swathed from head to toe in a white cloak, courtesy of her bridegroom, who had generously provided her with the proper costume for a Ravigan wife. Lilly refused to think of it as anything but a costume. After all, the entire wedding was nothing but a masquerade. This ceremony would celebrate not the joining of a man and a woman, but a transfer of power.

Ram had actually swaggered when he had presented her with the chest containing her new garments. He was already tallying the riches that he would acquire when he took over leadership of the Oasian government. After all, there was no one else to assume the role once the Sovereign passed on. Lilly didn't even have to delve into her future husband's mind to know that plans were being made to assure the quick assassination of her uncle. She wondered what Ram would say if he knew that the Circe expected Lilly to rid herself of the burden of a husband.

It was almost comical to step back and watch them scurry about and work on their plans, each of them thinking he or she would emerge victorious. The Prefect was certain that he would become stronger with the tribute from Oasis. Ram and the Ravigans were certain that they would be controlling the universe when they controlled Oasis. The Circe saw both as fools and knew that they would be the ones secretly pulling the strings.

Lilly envisioned stuffing all of them in a reactor and watching them separate into innumerable particles.

The headpiece she wore chafed the skin of her forehead, so she dropped the cloak back and readjusted the bead-encrusted cap that fit low over her brow. Fringe hung from the cap over her eyes, obscuring her vision. She fought the desire to rip the thing off and fling it in the corner of her cabin.

What would Ram think if she did? She realized that she didn't even care.

He lusted after her planet and he lusted after her. Perhaps she would make him think that he had had her between the sheets. She could plant that thought easily enough. She would make him believe she was lacking so he would go seek his pleasure elsewhere and leave his bride alone.

She was so alone. But at least she had the satisfaction of knowing that Shaun had gotten away. She hoped he was on the opposite side of the galaxy by now. Surely he would have gone on once he realized that they could never be together. Wouldn't he?

The tremor of the deck beneath her feet gave notice that they had come out of hyperspeed. They had reached Oasis. She had come home.

Her uncle had tried to murder her. What part would he be playing in the masquerade? What about Michael? What would his role be? Had he known what her uncle had planned? Lilly could not imagine him going along with such a plan, but she never could have imagined her uncle wanting her dead, either.

How would the people of Oasis receive her? Had she let them down? Would they see her as a traitor as they faced the prospect of Ravigan rule, or would they realize that it was the only way to stop the senseless slaughter that would occur if the war was not stopped?

Whatever they thought, it no longer mattered. The issue was soon to be out of her hands. Lilly's eyes opened wide as she looked at her reflection in the mirror. She had gone to the Senate to fight for her people. But instead of fighting, she had fallen in line with everything that had been prearranged for . . . generations!

Lilly was angry. Frustration boiled up from her gut as she glared at her reflection in the mirror. She ripped the cap from her head and threw it in the corner and jerked the pins out of her hair. The cloak followed, billowing out as it floated toward the bed. She started on her vest and then stopped.

Think, she said to the mirror. Her face was flushed and she was panting. She needed a clear head to think this through. How often had all the important characters in this masquerade been together in one place? The Prefect was on board, as was Honora. There was Ram, of course, and his father was already on Oasis with his contingent of ambassadors. Then there was her uncle. All of them assembled to watch the union of the two planets.

She took a cleansing breath and looked in the mirror once again. "It's time for you to save your people," she said to the reflection. A pair of pale gray eyes beneath dark lashes looked calmly back at her. It was time.

Chapter Twenty-one

Had the capital ever looked so beautiful? It seemed that every flower on Oasis had bloomed as if prearranged in honor of her wedding. The myriad of colors were breathtaking against the pristine white of the city walls. The stones in the walls sparkled as the midday sun shone down upon the entourage that made its way through the streets. The shuttle had been directed to the farthest port from the palace so that the honored members of the wedding party could be paraded through the streets and the assembled throng could see their honored Prefect, the leader of the Circe, and the future leader of Oasis in person. Each one in the parade graciously waved to the people as the crowd cheered them on.

Lilly sensed that the cheers were merely polite. She had seen the Ravigan carriers assembled in orbit, anxiously awaiting their chance to level the planet if the wedding did not proceed as planned.

Countless thoughts ran through her mind as she silently stood in the small hover pod with Ram beside her, resplendent in his blood-red leather and silken cape. His eyes were not even even squinting in the strong rays of the sun; they were accustomed to its brightness. His thick forehead was the result of thousands of years of evolution, protecting the eyes that were in deep shadow beneath the brow.

Lilly was grateful for the heavy fringe that hung over her eyes. They protected her eyes from the sun, but also kept Ram from seeing how her eyes darted to and fro, checking for protectors in the crowd, taking note of where soldiers were located, where Ram's father had placed his troops, there under the guise of peacemakers.

Ram had commented on how exquisite she looked in her Ravigan garb. If only he knew how close he had come to seeing her in complete disarray, a far different picture from the carefully composed bride who rode beside him. After all, it would not do her plan any good if she tipped her hand too early.

They passed through the gate with the words "Strength, Honor, Obedience, Unity and Nobility" carved over the arch. Her hands longed to reach up and touch the letters as she had when she was a child, safely carried upon the breadth of Michael's sturdy shoulders. She would have need of all of those qualities. On the steps she saw her uncle, dressed in his most royal garb, as he greeted the Prefect. Michael stood behind him and to his right, and on his other side was . . .

Shaun. It was Shaun. He was here, dressed in the

uniform of protector and wearing his shields. Honora stepped down from her hover pod, and he regarded her casually, looking as if he owned the place.

"Hello, Princess." The words curled through her mind like a soft caress on her body. Lilly felt a tingling begin, deep within the very core of her being, as she fought to keep her face composed. *"Nice day for a wedding, isn't it?"*

He never could be serious. Even under the most trying of circumstances, he couldn't go without having something smart to say. If she weren't so deliriously happy to see him, she'd give his mind a good scare.

Why was she happy that he was here? She shouldn't be. He should be far away from this mess, not standing right in the middle of it. Surely he knew that they couldn't be together.

You think for too highly of yourself, Lilly, she chastised herself. He had found out he was heir to the richest planet in the galaxy and had come to stake his claim. Why else would he come?

Well, if he wanted the planet he was going to have to fight the Ravigans for it.

"Funny, I was just thinking the same thing, Princess," he said in her mind as a curse from Ram filled her ears. Shaun had sounded amused. Ram was furious.

"What is he doing her?" Ram firmly gripped her upper arm as he leaned over to whisper in her ear. "I shall present his dead body to you as a gift."

"Touch her again and you will die."

Ram's head flew up and his nostrils flared as the words he'd heard in his mind struck him. Lilly had heard them also, and she waited anxiously as Honora climbed the steps to be greeted by her uncle.

Shaun ignored the Sacrosanct Mistress. He just stood there and ignored her as she tried to probe him with her mind. Lilly could feel the witch's surprise and annoyance from where she waited. The witch longed to grab him, but all she could do was follow protocol while her former prisoner stood at attention as a good protector should. Lilly wondered briefly how Arleta was faring after Honora's probing and decided she didn't care. Whatever the witch had suffered, she deserved it.

How could Shaun just stand there so casually?

"Don't tempt me. I might just have to kiss you," he said in her mind.

Lilly didn't know if she should laugh or cry. How could he be so . . . nonchalant?

"At least you didn't make fun of her hat," Lilly replied in her mind, more to calm her nerves than anything else.

"Didn't make fun of yours either."

Lilly self-consciously touched the ridiculous beaded cap that was clamped on her head.

"I will demand his head from your uncle," Ram declared as their pod came to a stop. "His presence is an insult and an affront to my authority." He held out his hand to assist Lilly in descending from the pod.

"You have no authority here." Lilly smiled sweetly at Ram, batting her lashes beneath the fringe.

"That's the way, Princess. Go right for the throat," Shaun said encouragingly her. His body remained

poised and at attention, his countenance remote, as a protector's should be.

"You will pay for that remark soon enough," Ram threatened. "My authority will be granted quickly, I assure you."

"I will kill you," Shaun assured him.

Alexander grasped her hands and planted a generous kiss on top of her cap. For the first time in her life, Lilly dared to look inside his mind. His wall was strong, but the foundation that held it was based on hatred for all Circe, including her.

How could someone carry that much hate and not be damaged by it? Had he been consumed with such anger all these years? She realized she'd always been afraid to look too closely. She moved past Alexander, and he turned to greet Prince Ramelah of Raviga, whose father anxiously awaited his presence within.

Lilly's eyes flew wide when Michael touched her arm as she passed. Her mind swam in circles at what she had briefly seen. Surely she'd misunderstood. There was too much going on, too much to think about, too much to do.

"When will you make your move?" Shaun asked as the entourage moved into the palace.

"At the public ceremony," she replied. *"Does Alexander know who you are?"*

"He accepts me as his . . . weapon."

"Why did you come back now? Why didn't you wait until it was safe?"

"I came back for you, Princess. If you don't believe me, ask your father."

The train of her cloak tangled beneath her feet and Lilly tripped. Michael was at her side in an instant, catching her arm before she fell to the ground. Tears filled her eyes as she looked into his handsome face. On it she saw the terrible loneliness he'd suffered to protect his secret.

"Father?"

Michael's eyes narrowed. It was not the time or the way he would have chosen. But she knew.

"Tell her," Shaun encouraged.

"I am."

Only Honora noticed the exchange, so quickly had it happened. It mattered not to her who the child's father was. She had sent Zania to Oasis to produce a female heir, and Lilly was accepted as such. The man who now laid claim to her parentage could be taken care of easily enough. He was insignificant and did not matter.

Nor did it matter that the protector was here. Honora supposed he had come back to Oasis and the limited protection it offered. She would have to take him back with her and present him to Arleta as proof of her mutiny. And before she killed the witch and the man, she would demand the secret of how he had been trained. She had never come up against a wall as strong as his. It must be created by some sort of transference of power. And the power was so strong that there had to be more than one witch involved. Honora sniffed the room as if searching for the treasonous witches among the Circe acolytes there. Any and all involved in the scheme would have her full attention as soon as this wedding nonsense was done.

The Prefect settled into the Sovereign's chair and the wedding guests gathered around, exchanging greetings and congratulations on an excellent conclusion to difficult circumstances. The Prefect was applauded as a man of great wisdom, worthy of the confidence that the Senate and the universe held in him. The Sovereign and the Ravigan king were congratulated on the match that was about to be made and the treaty that would be signed upon the sealing of the marriage. The bride's and groom's assets were proclaimed to all within hearing distance, and those fortunate enough to be present at the momentous occasion applauded.

Lilly was oblivious to the celebration in the room, even though she smiled graciously and played her part as was expected. Her mind was still reeling over the revelation that Michael was her father.

Which meant that Shaun was not her cousin. Her eyes searched him out among the throng in the room and found him standing at attention by the door, as a good protector should.

"I told you we were meant to be together."

"We might not survive the battle to come."

"It's a chance we have to take, for the people."

How many times had she said the very same thing when he was urging her to run away with him? And now he was here, ready to lay down his life to save his people. People who didn't even know he existed. He was born of royal blood. He had an obligation.

"You have taught me well."

Lilly realized that she would have gladly laid down her life for Oasis earlier in the day, but now she wanted very much to live. She wanted to survive. She wanted to be with Shaun. But she also knew that she shouldn't expect the people of Oasis to lay down their lives to fight off the Ravigans, unless she was willing to do the same thing.

"It is time," Alexander announced. The assembled guests moved as one toward the door, leaving the bride, groom, and their respective parents alone in the room so that the ceremony could begin. Shaun and Michael remained at their posts.

"This moment will go down as one of the greatest in the joining of our archives," proclaimed Ram's father, the king of Raviga.

"Let the record show that what I do, I do for my people," Lilly stated in reply.

An awkward silence filled the room. Lilly noticed that the protectors tensed their bodies to keep from laughing out loud at the discomposure showing on the faces of the Ravigans.

A herald sounded the hour and Ram left the room, accompanied by his father. Alexander offered his arm to his niece with a word of caution. "It would be best, niece, if you entered into this union with compliance."

"When have you known me to be anything but compliant, Uncle?" she replied sweetly.

"I love you," Shaun gently proclaimed into her mind as he and Michael fell in behind the pair.

Lilly stepped out onto the grand balcony that overlooked the main square of the capital. She felt the warm comfort of Shaun's presence in her mind and knew that he would help her through what she must do. The players in the masquerade had all taken their positions. The Prefect and the Sacrosanct Mistress were seated in chairs from which they could watch the proceedings and bestow their blessing upon the union. Below, in the square, the populace pressed in, standing shoulder to shoulder beneath the bright sun of early afternoon.

In the entire planet of Oasis, Lilly could honestly say that this was the only spot where she felt uncomfortable. She hated this place and consciously avoided it except for the momentous occasions that required her presence. Her mother had died in this square; her bloodstains on the dazzling white stones had remained long after her execution. Being here always reminded her of what her mother had done and what her uncle had suffered. Was that why the wedding had been arranged in this very spot? To remind her of her obligation to her uncle and the people of Oasis?

Ram was waiting for her by the banister of the balcony. Flowers of every variety known on Oasis had been woven into a vine and draped around the banister and columns. Their heady scents filled the air as she stepped to the rail to look out upon her people. The silence was deafening as they waited with hushed expectation for the ceremony that would place them under Ravigan rule.

Ram reached for her hand as she faced the crowd, but she jerked it away and grasped the rail as if she were afraid of falling. With the other hand she pulled off the hated cap. Her hair, free of its confines, drifted up like a banner in the stiff breeze that suddenly filled the square.

"People of Oasis," Lilly shouted to the crowd. "There are present today those who would shape our destiny." She heard the sharp intake of breath behind her and felt the hot anger of Honora as she came into her mind. "I say that the destiny of Oasis belongs to its people." She fought to stay upright as Honora attacked her from within. At the same time she felt Shaun's presence in her mind, joining with her to hold off Honora as she went on to inspire her people. "If you want to control your destiny, then you must fight for it! Better to die than to live under Ravigan rule!"

The crowd drew in a breath and released it as if the onlookers were of one mind. A howl erupted from somewhere as the Ravigan peacekeepers nervously handled their weapons. In the next instant the square exploded into violence as the people attacked the Ravigan positions.

Lilly could not move. She felt the battle going on in her mind as Shaun and Honora struggled against each other. She could hear the angry shouts of the Prefect as his guard surrounded him. Ram's father calmly pulled out a voice com and issued an order to the ships waiting in space to attack. Michael pulled his weapon and placed it against the temple of the Ravigan King.

"Consider yourself our guest, Your Highness."

"Traitorous witch!" Ram snarled, and grabbed her arm. Shaun broke off his internal battle with Honora and reached for Ram, who pulled a hooked blade from his boot and pressed it against Lilly's throat.

She felt the pressure of the blade against her jugular and sensed the dark presence of Honora in her mind, slithering about like a snake, searching for a way inside so she could work her poison. Behind her were the screams and shouts of battle as the populace stormed the Ravigan guards. The Oasian army, caught off guard, scrambled for position, not sure if they should be putting down the insurgency or aiding it. The skies above boomed with the sounds of falcons, launched from the cruisers to attack the farms and fields.

Shaun stopped as Ram's blade threatened.

"Help the people," Lilly implored. *"They need a leader."*

Above the noise of the battle, Shaun heard the crazed laughter of Alexander.

"Lead the people."

Ram backed toward the door, using Lilly as a shield. He spared a glance at the Ravigan King, who was paralyzed by the threat from Michael.

"Come to me!" Ram commanded his father's guard, and the men quickly surrounded the prince and his bride.

Lilly took advantage of the moment to gather her strength, certain that if she could confuse Ram and his soldiers, Shaun would be strong enough to overcome them. She closed her eyes and took a breath. But instead of the power she sought, her mind was greeted with darkness as Ram brought the hilt of his knife down hard against her temple. She slid down into oblivion and into Ram's arms.

"No!" Shaun yelled as the prince faded into the palace with his guard covering his flight. He turned away in frustration as the realization of what Lilly had started sank in. He had to lead the people.

Chapter Twenty-two

Honora shrieked as her contact with Lilly was broken. "You will pay for this!" she ranted at whoever would listen. The Prefect joined in, only he directed his tirade at Alexander, who seemed to find the entire event amusing.

"Did you plan this?" Michael asked Shaun incredulously as he kept his hold on the Ravigan King.

"Not really," Shaun replied as he quickly scanned the riot going on below the balcony.

"We're going to be wiped out, you know," Michael said, looking to the heavens above.

"Maybe not," Shaun said as he jumped onto the banister. The wedding guests shrieked and screamed as they fought to get into the safety of the palace. "Tell your fleet that you are our hostage," Shaun instructed the Ravigan King. "Tell them to stand down or you and your son will die."

"On what authority do you give such orders?" the Prefect screamed.

Shaun pulled off his shields and leveled his gaze on the Prefect, then Honora, who was still spouting her anger.

"On my authority," he said. "By the authority of Nicholas, son of Alexander and heir to the throne of Oasis." His voice rose in volume as he spoke until it was roaring over the screams of the crowd and echoing against the buildings that surrounded the square. Beneath him, the fighting stopped as the import of his words sank in to the people.

"It is Nicholas come back to claim his legacy," the crowd murmured. "Look at his eyes. He has the eyes of his mother. The eyes of a Circe."

Shaun stood on the banister and let his eyes roam over the crowd. The closest ones could see, and the word passed back that he did indeed have the eyes that had cursed the child Nicholas to death.

"It is not true!" Honora cried.

Shaun turned his eyes upon the witch. "It is true, Witch. I am that which you abhor. I am your curse. Look inside and you will see the truth of who I am, as I have seen the truth of who you are."

Honora leaped into his mind eagerly. She would know who was behind this treason, and while she was at it, she would conquer this . . . male . . . who attempted to destroy the plans of several generations of Circe. She spread her mind into his as if it were a poison. She would destroy him. Those who fought against her would learn the price of their revolt when they saw the vegetative remains she would leave as an example to all who dared to cross her.

A scream was ripped from her throat and her eyes widened when she saw the power that lay coiled and waiting within him. In his mind she saw Ariel's face and witnessed the victory written upon it.

"I'm done with you," Shaun said, dismissing her probe as if it were nothing. Honora felt his wall go up like the slamming of a door, and she shrieked against it.

"You will not survive," she promised.

Shaun rolled his eyes in disgust and looked at Michael.

"The Ravigans are ready to talk," he said, handing Shaun the com.

"Find an escort for His Highness. We've got to make sure Ram doesn't get off the planet," Shaun barked. "And see if somebody can do something about my father." Shaun ducked into the door of the palace. Sovereign Alexander stood against the banister with arms open wide, as if he were embracing his people. The crowd below cheered.

The son had returned. They were saved.

"Talk to me, Ruben," Shaun said into his com.

"Can't talk now, big guy." Ruben's voice crackled over the com. "Got my hands full."

"That should be slowing down," Shaun replied as he raced through the hallways of the palace.

"Are we negotiating?"

"We've given them something to think about. . . ."

"Hang on," Ruben said, and Shaun heard the sound

of blasters over the com. "Sure could have used you up here."

"How is it?"

"We did okay. Hate to think what would have happened if we hadn't been ready for it. What's the word on your end?"

"We've got the Ravigan King in custody."

"And the Prince?"

"Need you to keep an eye out for him. He's got Lilly."

"I'm coming back toward the port. If he comes off planet, he'll have to get through me."

"Thanks, buddy."

"Ram's left the palace with Lilly," Michael reported as he caught up to Shaun. "Whatever guard they had left in the city has joined up with him and they're fighting their way toward the port."

"We can't let him off planet, Michael."

"I know. I've alerted the guards, but what can they do if he uses Lilly as a shield?"

Shaun felt a sinking sensation in his gut. Lilly was well loved and her people would not risk her life. Nor could he blame them. He himself had surrendered on Pristo when he saw her life was in danger.

Shaun looked at the other man's face and saw the anguish written on it. He placed a comforting hand on his shoulder. "Tell them to do what they can to make sure she is safe."

Michael nodded. Shaun didn't want to think about what would happen if Ram got Lilly off planet. He didn't have to delve into Michael's mind to see that he was thinking the same thing.

"I'm afraid I must protest these events!"

Great. Just what he needed. More politics to deal with. Shaun turned to face the Prefect, who no doubt had been sent after him by Honora. The Sacrosanct Mistress had followed him down the corridor with her acolytes scurrying behind her.

"Can you tell me exactly which event you want to protest?" Shaun said icily. "Do you wish to protest the fact that Oasis has fallen out of your control?" He looked at Honora. "Did you really think the Circe would let you have a say in governing it? Or are you more upset about the credits that will not be coming your way now?"

The Prefect had not gotten his power by being foolish. "Can you prove that you are the heir to Oasis?"

Shaun turned away in disgust. "Ask your witch; she knows the truth," he flipped over his shoulder as he and Michael walked away. Lilly's life was at stake and the Prefect was still trying to figure out where the best profits lay.

"I believe you," the Prefect shouted after him.

Shaun turned, a dark eyebrow arched in question. Honora, standing behind the Prefect, looked as if she were ready to explode. If only she would. Michael took a cautious stance beside him, his hand poised against his weapon.

"So whose side are you on, Prefect?" Shaun asked. He had already looked into his mind and seen that the man was merely playing the odds. At the next moment, he might cast his lot with the Ravigans again. But for now, Shaun could use him.

"You are the heir. I'm with you," the Prefect said,

placing his hands down and out at his sides in a willing sign of agreement.

Shaun tossed the Ravigan com to the man. "Then tell your former allies that we are ready to negotiate."

"Negotiate?"

"We will return their King and Prince in exchange for an immediate cessation of aggression toward Oasis."

"You have the Prince in custody also?" Honora asked.

"Tell them," Shaun said, ignoring the witch.

"What if they don't agree?" the Prefect asked.

"Then there will be nothing left of this planet for you to fight over. I will tell the people to burn the crops as they stand in the fields. There will be nothing here worth taking." The steely sound of Shaun's voice made clear his determination.

"But you will starve," the Prefect protested.

"We will survive," Shaun assured him. "Your main concern should be the other planets under your jurisdiction. My people are more than willing to sacrifice and go hungry in order to ensure that we continue to rule our own planet. Are you willing to sacrifice as much? What will you tell the Senate when they ask you where the food is? Will you tell the people of the universe that they are going hungry so that you could have some extra credits in your account?"

The Prefect looked at Shaun as if seeing him for the first time.

"Are you a man of the people, Prefect?" Shaun asked, hiding his impatience. He felt like throwing the man against the wall. He didn't have time for talk; Ram was escaping with Lilly. Shaun needed to move, he needed to fight; he felt the urge to kill something or someone with his bare hands. Instead he stood in a quiet corridor of his father's palace talking politics with the underhanded leader of the Senate.

"I'll do what I can," the Prefect said.

Playing it safe, Shaun wanted to snarl at the man. "Tell them what I said and leave it at that," he commanded.

Ruben's com blipped in his hand. "We've got a problem," Ruben said over the static. Shaun felt his heart sink, but his face never betrayed his pain as he kept his eyes steady on the Prefect.

"Tell them."

Lilly's head throbbed. Especially the side that was pressed against the deck. The vibration of the engines pounded against the lump over her temple as waves of nausea swirled in her stomach. The fact that a sturdy boot was pressed against her back didn't help the matter at all. She blinked against the noise and confusion and saw a leg covered in red hovering in her peripheral vision.

Ram. She was on a shuttle with Ram. Apparently against her will, since he was holding her down and she had been knocked unconscious.

Then she remembered.

She had started a revolt on her home planet. She had told her people that it was better to die than to live under Ravigan rule.

Yet here she was, still alive and very much under the rule of the Ravigan Prince. How many of her people had died because she had foolishly urged them into a fight that could not be won?

Was Shaun still alive? Wouldn't she know it if he wasn't? She recalled the look on his face as he came after Ram, who had been holding a knife against her throat at the time. She had told him to lead the people. They needed him more than she did.

She had lied.

Her mind raced as the power of the thrusters lifted the craft from the Oasian Port. Where were the Sky Fighters that patrolled the space above the planet? Had they all been blown to bits as they went up against the Ravigan Falcons? Were there any left to keep Ram from escaping?

What should she do? Ram had knocked her unconscious to keep her from controlling his mind. If she showed that she was awake, then he would just knock her out again; it was the only way he could control her. Lilly willed her body to remain as still as possible as the craft shot into the atmosphere and climbed into the vivid blue of the Oasian sky.

Shots were fired from the planet's surface. Shots that went wide or fell short.

They're trying to save me, Lilly realized.

"There's a group of fighters coming for us," the pilot informed Ram.

"Blast your way through them," Ram commanded. Lilly felt him squirming in his seat as his foot pressed harder into the small of her back.

"Our Falcons are coming," another voice said.

"They will cover our escape," Ram said gratefully.

Lilly felt the anxious group of soldiers aboard the shuttle relax as the sounds of fighters engaging in battle filled the sky. The Falcons were well known for their superiority in the sky, and the Ravigans were confident that their escape was made.

Lilly kept her eyes shut tight and cautiously drew in a cleansing breath. She willed her mind into the pilot's so that she could see the battle. Maybe she could do something to help.

The Oasian Sky Fighters were now engaged with the Falcons. One Fighter quickly eliminated the Falcon on his tail and took out another that was just about to blow a fellow pilot out of the sky. The Fighter then came on a straight path toward the shuttle.

It was Ruben. Lilly felt him as she watched through the pilot's eyes.

"We've got one coming straight at us," the pilot announced.

"Use your weapons," Ram commanded.

She had to stop them. Lilly quickly jumped into the mind of the soldier sitting in the weapons seat. His hand reached to fire, but she stopped him. Ruben was still coming straight for them.

"Fire!" Ram commanded, and Lilly fought to maintain her hold on the soldier. She felt Ram's foot lift off her back and she opened her eyes. Ram was looking at the soldier as he sat paralyzed at his controls. The next thing she saw was a blood-red boot coming toward her head. She threw her hands up and tried to roll away, but the confines of the shuttle defeated her. She saw stars, and then a flash of light before the darkness consumed her again.

Ruben felt the impact of the blast as it hit the wing of his Sky Fighter. He spun out and spiraled away from the shuttle, shielding his face with his hands as his console shorted out.

"Let the shuttle go!" he yelled into the com attached to his helmet. "The Princess is on board!"

Ruben grabbed the stick when the fireworks stopped and finally leveled out the fighter.

"Looks like you're done for the day, Star Shooter," came another pilot's voice over the com.

"Tell me something I don't know," Ruben shot back as he firmly gripped the stick.

"You're going to make it down, no problem," crackled over the com.

Ruben felt his body relax. He had not been able to see the damage, and since his console was gone, he had no way of telling how bad it was.

"Thanks, Eagle Eye. We'd better go home and see what the damage is."

"We'll keep you company," Eagle Eye informed him, and the group of remaining fighters formed an escort around their injured companion.

Ruben flipped the channel on his com to contact Shaun.

"We've got a problem," he said, hoping his voice would carry through the static.

"Tell him," he heard Shaun say.

Ruben tapped the side of his helmet as he wondered if perhaps his communications had been damaged in the blast.

"Ruben?" Shaun said.

"Coming in hot, big guy."

"Lilly?"

"Sorry."

"Will you make it?"

"Don't I always?"

"First time for everything."

"This isn't it."

"Good," Shaun said, relief evident in his voice. "I'll see you on the ground."

Chapter Twenty-three

"So how bad was it?" Shaun asked Michael. They had assembled around a table in one of the larger chambers adjacent to Alexander's offices.

"Our losses could have been worse," Michael informed him. "We lost some Sky Fighters, around five percent of our ground force, and close to a thousand civilians."

"In the capital?"

"Planetwide."

It wasn't so bad when he looked at the numbers, but any loss of life was too much. "What about the ports?"

"We lost one of our major shipping ports in the sky attack, but our military port is still intact, along with the one here. The Ravigans still control the hyperport. All of the Ravigan Peacekeepers are in custody and the fighting is over. All you'll see in the streets now is celebration."

"With the Sovereign right in the middle of it?"

"He's celebrating, all right," Michael added. "We convinced him that it was best to do it inside for his own safety."

Shaun folded his arms and leaned against the large table. He tilted his head back to look at the thick beams, hewn from the great trees that still forested the planet. The people of Oasis never took a tree without planting two more to take its place. They had never laid a forest bare; instead they carefully culled it, choosing a tree to take down so that the others around it would have a better chance to reach their full potential. Generations of careful thought and planning for the future had kept this planet fruitful until it was the primary source of food for the universe.

But it could so easily have been destroyed due to greed and hatred.

Ruben sauntered in and flipped him a salute. Shaun lifted an eyebrow at him as he made his way to a side table that was well stocked with the best wines and ales from the planet. He poured himself a stout glass of ale and downed it in one gulp.

"What's the news?" Ruben asked as he wiped the froth from his mouth with his sleeve.

"We're waiting," Shaun grunted in response. Waiting. That had always been the hardest part for him. All he could think of was how to get Lilly back.

The Prefect had conveyed his terms to the Ravigans, but that was before Ram's escape with Lilly. The stakes were higher now. What would he do to get her back?

It all depended upon what they asked for.

The com taken from the Ravigan King vibrated against the wood of the table. Shaun looked down at it with his heart jumping into his throat. He nodded to Michael, who picked it up and switched it on.

It was Ram.

"I have something of yours."

Shaun's hands curled into fists. If only he could place them around Ram's thick neck and choke the very life from him.

"We have something of yours also." At least Michael had enough control to talk calmly.

Ram responded with laugher. "You have my father. Keep him and I will be the ruler of Raviga. Kill him and I will use his death as an excuse to wipe out your planet."

"Attack our planet and we will burn the fields. There will be nothing left for you to take," Michael assured him.

"We have starved for a long while. We can go hungry until the fields are replanted."

"I'm sure the Senate will be happy to hear that. Do the rest of the people in the universe agree with your plan?"

"We care not about them."

"I will be happy to inform the Prefect of your plan."

Shaun jumped up from the table. More politics. He took the com from Michael.

"What do you want in exchange for Lilly?"

Ram laughed again. "Finally we get to the heart of the matter," he said. "I want you."

"Fine."

"A battle."

"Yes."

Ruben waved his arms in an attempt to keep Shaun from walking into a trap.

"The two of us, winner gets everything."

"Winner does not get everything," Shaun replied. "No matter what the outcome, Lilly walks away free."

"You flatter yourself to think I would want your leavings."

Shaun fought the urge to throw the com across the room.

"Lilly walks away."

"Only if you win."

"There has to be a better way," Michael insisted quietly.

Ruben's face had a look of impending doom.

What could he do? Ram was callous enough to abandon his father. He knew he was in the position of power. But he was also so arrogant that he thought himself invincible. Shaun, however, had seen his weakness and knew how to use it against him.

"When?"

"Tomorrow."

"Where?"

"The Senate, so everyone will be witness to our . . . treaty."

"So be it." Shaun snapped off the com.

"Are you insane?" Ruben asked incredulously. "You know what the battle will be."

"I know."

"I've seen you pull a lot of stunts in our time together, but this . . ."

"Thanks for the support, buddy."

"What are you talking about?" Michael asked, suddenly very nervous.

"Our esteemed Prince here has just agreed to fight the Murlaca," Ruben informed him.

Michael slumped against the table. He opened his mouth to speak but was interrupted by the doors of the chamber swinging open with a rush.

"How much longer am I to be kept prisoner here?" Honora fairly screeched as she flew into the room.

"Pack your bags, witch. We're leaving now," Shaun said as he walked out of the chamber, dismissing her presence with the flick of a hand.

Ruben and Michael watched with subdued amusement as she opened her mouth to speak and then clamped it shut before sweeping out of the room.

"Are we in trouble?" Michael asked Ruben.

"It's looking fairly bleak," Ruben replied. "But then again, I've seen him get through worse."

Somehow that didn't make Michael feel any better.

They had given her something to keep her sedated, which was fine. Lilly was fairly certain that she didn't want any more blows to the head. One side of her face was already bruised and swollen, while the other sported a lump the size of an Oasian plum. The only problem was that the drug created a skewed perception of reality. It wasn't her fault that she had laughed out loud when Ram had come into her room and told her how he was going to slice Shaun into a million pieces. It wasn't as if she found the idea of Shaun's death amusing, it was just that Ram had looked so funny strutting around and waving his arms in imitation of the strokes he would use when he dealt his death blow. If only Ram's face hadn't seemed so . . . distorted when he leered over her and promised that Shaun would die a slow and painful death.

Lilly decided she really needed to get a grip on things. Ram had drugged her to keep her from attacking with her mind. At least he respected her powers. She giggled at the thought. She had powers.

So get a grip on reality and figure out how to use them. Lilly concentrated on keeping her brain from turning cartwheels and spinning itself into paralyzing dizziness as she struggled into a sitting position. At least she thought she was sitting. The cell did have an upright appearance to it.

Think! The drug must have been forced on her when she was unconscious after the second blow to her head. She had been on a shuttle then; now she was on a planet somewhere.

Ram and Shaun were going to fight the Murlaca. The sudden realization brought her mind to a sobering halt. Everyone in the universe knew that Ram was champion of the Murlaca. He had never been beaten. Never. Few of his opponents even survived the battle. She could count the survivors on one hand. And the only reason there were any was that he had been feeling generous at the time.

Lilly had serious doubts that he would be feeling generous when he fought Shaun.

Why had Shaun agreed to this? He held the Ravigan King as hostage. Why didn't the opposing forces make an exchange and go their separate ways?

She knew why. Ram's pride would not allow it. He cared not whether his father was returned. He had been scorned by her publicly at their wedding. He also knew that Shaun had slept with her. He could accept the fact that he was getting damaged goods. But he would not rest knowing that he had held the most powerful planet in the universe in his grasp and allowed it to be wrested away.

He would not feel generous at all.

If only her stomach would quit rolling and her head would quit spinning. It had to have been a Circe drug to cause such effects. No doubt courtesy of Honora or one of her acolytes.

What could she do? What should she do? Even if Shaun could best Ram in the Murlaca, the Circe would be working against him. They would use every trick they knew to confuse him, to defeat him. It would be an easy way out for them. Let Ram remove the most powerful male in the universe. They would not be to blame. With one slash of the blade, the power they wanted would be back in their grasp.

And the Senate would sit back and watch to see which power they would support.

Lilly sensed a presence in the cell and quickly resumed the careless sprawl that she had been in when awareness had first come to her again. She knew that this would be her only chance.

It was Martia. Had she been spying for the Circe or for Ram? Lilly quickly smothered the thought beneath her wall and filled her head with inane musings. Martia pulled a needle from her pocket and reached for Lilly's arm.

The witch wasn't even probing her! Lilly quickly sent an image into Martia's mind and patiently lay still as the witch squirted the contents of the needle into the air beside her arm.

It had worked. Martia was convinced that she had given Lilly the drug. All she had to do now was maintain the charade for as long as possible.

As Martia left the cell without a glance behind her, Lilly wondered how long that would be.

Chapter Twenty-four

"Rumor is that this match is the biggest thing to ever hit the pits," Ruben declared as Shaun picked up the weapons that had been generously supplied to him by Ram.

"Is that supposed to make me feel better?"

"Hey, it's your first time and already you're the headliner."

"You make it sound like I'm the main course at a banquet."

Ruben grimaced and looked away. Actually he had heard the very same thing when he had been outside placing his bet.

"I don't even know if this stuff works," Shaun said as he flung the gauntlets down in frustration. Why had he agreed to this?

Because it was the only way. He had seen Ram's weakness in the Murlaca. He knew the man would be overconfident in the ring. All he had to do was wait for the right opportunity to strike.

Of course, he had to survive long enough for the opportunity to present itself. And he would also have to fight off the powers of every Circe witch present. He'd be lucky if he survived the ringing of the bell.

"I've got some help for that part at least," Ruben replied. He didn't have to read his friend's mind to know the concerns that were going through it. He opened the door to admit one of the female warriors of the Murlaca.

"This is Laylon," Ruben said, introducing the woman. "She's going to help you get . . . ready."

Laylon picked up the gauntlets with the curved blades and immediately began checking along the length of the leather. Shaun wasn't surprised when one of the razor-sharp blades came off in her hand after she tugged at the base of it. Laylon snorted in disgust and went into the corridor to retrieve a bag she had left there.

"Overconfidence is his weakness," she informed Shaun as she pulled a chest protector from her bag. "Strip," she commanded. "Your clothing can catch on the blades and inhibit your movements."

Shaun shrugged out of his jacket and sleeveless shirt. Laylon placed the thin black armor on his chest and back and adjusted the straps over his shoulders and beneath his arms. Next she placed the black armor over his thighs. Shaun looked down at the design scrolled into his chest protector. The feral eyes of a black panther looked back at him.

"Where did you get these?" he asked Laylon as she made sure the thigh protectors were secure.

"From a great warrior of the Murlaca."

Shaun placed a hand on the top of her head and saw the history of the man. He had been Laylon's lover and Ram had killed him in the ring.

"I am honored to wear them," he said.

Laylon kept her eyes down for a moment to regain her composure before she reached into the bag again and pulled out a pair of silver armbands.

"These will keep the blades from tearing the muscles of your arm." She handed them up to him while keeping her eyes down.

Shaun slipped them into place but was dubious about how much protection they would offer.

Next she handed him a pair of boots that came over his knees. Shaun sat down to put them on and was pleased with the fit. They would not rub, nor would they slip.

"You are similar in size," Laylon commented as Shaun stood again.

"Shouldn't he have something to protect his, uh, assets?" Ruben asked.

Laylon wordlessly produced an oval-shaped cup from the bag and handed it to Shaun, who turned his back and stuffed it into place.

Ruben whistled and arched an eyebrow. "Impressive."

Shaun merely rolled his eyes, but he noticed that a flush had crept into Laylon's cheeks. He resisted the urge to adjust himself as she dug into the bag once again.

"These blades will serve you well," she said as she held up the gauntlets.

They were evil-looking, Shaun had to admit. He was certain they would hold. The blades glistened and gleamed, telling all that they had been well cared for. He held out his arms for Laylon to attach them.

Last came the heavy black gloves. They were reinforced with metal bands and edged along the bottom part of the fist with hard metal bars sewn into the lining.

"For adding a strike," Laylon explained.

Slash and strike. He would remember it, if he lived that long.

"Any other advice?" Ruben asked.

"Stay alive," Laylon said. She closed up the bag and left without another word.

"Ruben." Shaun stood with his arms held straight out at his sides. He didn't know what else to do with them. "Get Lilly out of here when . . ."

"I've already got it taken care of."

Shaun didn't question how. He trusted his friend enough to know that he would do it.

Besides, he had his own worries.

Martia guided her to her seat. Lilly realized that she felt sorry for the woman. She had been working closely with Arleta and was now under suspicion, too. Martia was so frightened that she didn't take the time to make sure that Lilly was really drugged. It was easy for Lilly to keep up the facade as she was led to a seat next to the Prefect.

After all, she was the prize. Well, actually Oasis was the prize, but she was the decorative ribbon it was wrapped with. She was a symbol, nothing more, and a somewhat disheveled one at that. She still wore the hated Ravigan wedding garment, but had been given a fresh cloak; the white one had been soiled by the floor of the shuttle. Her ash-brown hair hung in complete disarray around her face and down her back. Lilly couldn't risk shoving it out of her eyes. She might give herself away.

She kept her eyes down and her face blank, along with her mind. She didn't have to look to know that Honora was seated on the other side of the Prefect. She sensed the woman's presence as easily as she could smell the bloodlust of the crowd. Lilly was also sure that Michael was there, along with Alexander. This was all too important for them to wait for the outcome on Oasis.

Why, oh why, had Shaun agreed to this? Why hadn't he just gone away when he had the chance?

Because he wasn't that kind of man. He would stay and fight because it was the right thing to do. Because the people of Oasis needed a leader. Because it was the only chance they had. It was the only chance she had. Because he was courageous.

And because he was also stubborn, foolish, and just a bit headstrong.

She knew him well enough to know that he would rather die facing Ram than give up without a fight. This way, at least there was the chance that he would win it all.

And there was that chance. Was that what fate had dealt them that day when she stepped onto the ship and felt his presence? Did they have a chance?

She was about to find out.

The roar of the crowd was deafening. The lights were dimmed and the spotlights shot into the air, dancing off the ceiling of the dome. Lilly took advantage of the distraction to cautiously glance around and was encouraged to see that all eyes were on the ring. They were ignoring her. Even Honora was leaning forward in her chair, eagerly awaiting the demise of her hated enemy.

To her left Lilly saw the anxious faces of Michael and Alexander. To the right was the Ravigan contingent. She recognized Ruben's tall, lanky form in the crowd as he and a tall, muscular woman moved through the mass of stomping and clapping people to a spot somewhere behind her.

Everyone had taken his place. The lights went dark and a hush of expectation filled the arena. Smoke rose around the pit, disguising the entrance of two shadowy figures that rose into the ring on two separate platforms elevated from below.

The crowd exploded into screams of anticipation that turned into a roar, sweeping up into the dome. The light returned with such brilliance that Lilly was alarmed for Shaun. It would blind him!

But then she saw that he was wearing his shields. Ram could protest, but he didn't, sure he was going to kill him anyway.

Lilly didn't even bother pretending that she was drugged. Everyone had forgotten that she existed. And with the roar of the crowd, she would have to be dead not to notice what was about to happen before her eyes.

The evilly hooked blades on the gauntlets stretched from the wrists to the elbows. Ram waved his arms above his head for all to see. Shaun watched him from his corner with his arms held out at his sides.

Ram observed his pose and grinned broadly at the crowd as if he were sharing a secret. "I see that you looked elsewhere for your weapons," Ram said, loud enough for only Shaun to hear.

"I found that these suited me better," Shaun replied.

"You should have chosen some that did not have such a tragic history," Ram said, and turned his back on him to pay homage to the crowd.

Shaun patiently waited for the posturing to be done. After all, this was Ram's show. He watched grimly as Ram stepped into the middle of the ring, shook his raised fists at the dome, and enjoyed the accolades of the roaring crowd. The Ravigan Prince brought his arms down to his sides and looked eagerly at Shaun. He was ready to do battle.

Shaun forced his gaze to remain impassive as Ram gazed avidly at him. He could not let his opponent know how terrified he was. He had been in plenty of sticky situations before, but never had so much been at stake. The fate of an entire planet depended on the outcome of this battle. Lives were at stake. His own life was at stake. Shaun had quickly come to the realization that losing his life wouldn't be so bad if he didn't have so much to lose.

Lilly was somewhere in the crowd. He didn't have to search the screaming faces to know that she was present. And if he lost, Ram would soon be gazing upon her face with the same ferocity he was now focusing on him.

He couldn't let that happen. Shaun took a deep breath as Ram came at him with arms crossed, ready to slash and hack him into countless pieces. Shaun crossed his arms to meet him, and both men met and pushed the attacking arms away.

Ram countered by slashing down. Shaun jumped back and blocked as Ram's other arm swung up toward his chin. Shaun blocked again and managed to drive his fist into the underside of Ram's chin.

The Prince staggered back a step and arched his eyebrow in approval. "At least you can make the proceedings a bit more interesting."

Shaun knew that he would never defeat the Prince by blocking. Somehow he would have to attack. This fight would not be over until one of them was dead. Shaun could only hope that he would last long enough for Ruben to get Lilly away to safety.

"You cannot win." The voice echoed from the deep recesses of his mind. *"Best surrender now and let the end be quick."* Why did Ram suddenly look taller, heavier, his blades more deadly as he approached again?

"Be strong, Shaun."

"Lilly?"

"Your arms are heavy and slow."

Shaun shook his head as he blocked again. One of the witches was in his mind, tricking him, confusing him. Ram quickly countered his blocks and slashed again, his blade hooking on Shaun's left armband and gouging a hole as Shaun ducked beneath another slash and drove his fist into the armor covering Ram's stomach.

It wasn't enough to really hurt the Ravigan, but the move earned him a respite as Ram played to the audience, which had gone crazy at the sight of the blood dripping down Shaun's arm.

Who was in his head? How could he concentrate on blocking when he had to fight off mental attacks as well?

"I'm here." He felt her then. Lilly came into his mind like a whirlwind, closing off the avenues that Honora had used to distract him. She formed a bond with his mind and placed a strong wall up against intrusion. Shaun saw himself through her eyes and felt her fear for him. She would do what she could to protect his mind. It was up to him to protect his body.

Ram was still celebrating the drawing of first blood. Shaun went after him with a downward slash that Ram blocked at the last minute. Shaun slashed again with the other arm and followed it with a downward strike of his fist. Ram's arm moved down and away, and Shaun slashed across the armor, gouging a path into the carved ram's head on the chest shield. Ram looked down in surprise and snarled, coming back with an attack on Shaun's head and shoulders.

Ram and Shaun were as graceful as dancers as they attacked and defended, slashing and blocking, dodging and feinting their way around the ring.

Honora gasped in disbelief when she came up

against the wall in Shaun's mind. Who dared to defend him? Her nostrils flared as her pale eyes searched the crowd, looking for the source of power and protection. Surely it was not Lilly. The twit was not strong enough, nor was she aware—or was she? The Sacrosanct Mistress looked over the Prefect, who was trying to keep a dignified manner despite the excitement of the match, and saw Lilly peacefully sitting in her seat with her eyes closed. Her hands betrayed her, however; they clutched desperately at the arms of her chair.

"Traitorous child," she hissed, and prepared herself to attack.

Lilly felt Honora slam into her mind with a boiling mass of poisonous thoughts. The impact of her joining was the same as if the breath had been knocked from her body.

"My mind is my own," Lilly began. *"No other may possess it."* So deep was she entranced in her battle that she did not realize Ruben and his woman friend had moved down behind her.

"I will keep my mind and use it to overcome my enemies," Shaun repeated with Lilly as he slashed and blocked.

Honora shook her head in disbelief when she realized that defeating Lilly was going to be harder than she had originally thought. She would take a more direct path. Quickly she summoned Martia with her mind.

Ruben nudged his companion and indicated Martia with a nod of his head. Laylon easily moved through the crowd and grabbed the acolyte's arm before she had a chance to join her mistress. Honora's lip curled, but before she could gather her powers, a blow to the back of her head slumped her back into her seat.

"Lilly." Ruben knelt behind her seat to be heard over the crowd. "It's just the two of you now. We got the rest."

Lilly heard him, and through Lilly's mind, Shaun heard him.

"Lilly, you've got to get out of here," Shaun said as he dodged and blocked. Sweat was pouring off his body and stinging in the multitude of cuts that crisscrossed his upper arms. At least his shields kept it from running into his eyes. Ram was having his own problems. His dark, deep-set eyes seemed to be glazed.

"I will stay with you."

The floor of the pit was damp with the sweat that streamed off their bodies as the two men slashed at each other, their arms becoming heavier with each attempt. Shaun's foot slipped as he tried to dodge and the end of a blade caught him in the cheek and ripped the skin back to his ear. Shaun struck out, reacting to the pain, and caught Ram's forehead, tearing a gash from his hairline to his temple. Both men staggered back, with chests heaving as they tried to suck in air. Blood poured from their wounds and fed the frenzied screams around them.

"Lilly, go while you can," Shaun begged with his mind as he gulped for air.

"I will never leave you."

"I can't beat him."

"You can."

"He's stronger than me, he's better."

"Use your strengths."

Was she asking him to cheat? Had she dared to suggest that he use his mind to distract Ram?

Yet hadn't Ram done the very same thing when he'd sent the defective equipment for him to use?

His father had taught him to be fair and honorable. Yet there was no honor here where politics ruled the day.

Each warrior in the ring had his weaknesses. Each had his strengths. Ram was skilled at the Murlaca. Shaun could see in the dark. Ram had the crowd to his advantage and Shaun had his mind.

He had a choice to make. Could he live with himself knowing that deception had won the day? Could he live at all?

Shaun wanted very much to live. He knew it when he saw Ram coming at him again. Shaun arched his belly back as Ram slashed, and Shaun slashed back, knocking Ram's arm downward. He gathered himself and jumped while Ram was bent. He arched over Ram's back in a flip, slashing at the back of his leg as he landed.

Shaun felt the satisfaction of his blade tearing through flesh, muscle, and ligament as Ram's leg buckled beneath him. As he fell, Ram swung downward with his arm toward the back of Shaun's neck. Shaun rolled away and felt the blades catch in the buckle of his armor. He pulled against it and the buckle gave way, releasing the armor.

Shaun kept rolling until he came against the side of

the pit and jumped to his feet. Ram pushed himself up and stood awkwardly, his right leg useless beneath him.

Shaun realized that he was bleeding from a gash across his shoulder blades. The two men stood sucking in air and taking inventory of each other's injuries.

Ram was crippled. But Shaun was vulnerable. His chest and back were exposed; all it would take was one good blow to a vital organ and he would be dead.

The crowd quieted until the only sound in the arena was the heavy breathing of the warriors.

"You can beat him."

"I can beat him." How? Neither warrior could go on much longer. The floor of the pit was now covered with sweat and blood, making the footing treacherous. Shaun's arms felt as if they were covered in heavy bonds instead of the gauntlets. It was similar to the feeling the collar had given him. He very much wanted to move them but wasn't sure if he could. Ram had to be as worn and weary as he felt, but he wasn't showing it.

He looked very much as if he was about to deal a deathblow.

Ram lunged then, launching himself off his one good leg and coming straight at Shaun with his blades curving out. All he had to do was connect. There were multiple targets; his heart, his lungs, his jugular, any or all of his organs could be struck as the blades penetrated his body, carving a path of death and destruction. Shaun spun to the side and slashed blindly with one arm as he sought to shield his torso with the other. Ram crashed into the wall and pushed off it.

The weight of his body caught Shaun's arm as he slashed, and the two men tumbled to the floor of the pit as Shaun desperately fought to keep Ram's blades, as well as his own, facing away from his unprotected chest and abdomen.

Ram's eyes shone with victory and then shock as Shaun felt a sudden gush of blood spraying across his chest and face. With all his strength he shoved, and Ram was flung over on his back. His arms were spread wide as his eyes stared up to the dome overhead and blood poured from the wide gash across his throat. He tried to speak but couldn't. The damage was too deep. Shaun, on hands and knees, looked down at his face in shock and saw the hatred that filled the Ravigan Prince's features as he fought to take a breath while his lifeblood poured out and dripped over the sides of the ring.

Shaun leaned back on his haunches and watched in amazement through blurry eyes as a young woman with a heavily painted face caught the drops of blood in her fingers and smeared them across her cheeks. She looked up at him with an insane smile plastered on her face and pointed. Shaun looked down and saw that his chest was covered with blood. It was running down his body, tracing a path through the heavy ridges on his abdomen and dripping to the floor of the pit, where it mingled with Ram's.

The crowd roared with renewed frenzy and a riot began as the watchers raced toward the river of blood, trying to catch it in their hands. Those in the front fell beneath the feet of the onlookers behind them and their own blood mingled with that of the Prince's, which had formed a pool on the floor of the pit.

Shaun backed away from the onslaught as hands sought to dip into the blood in the ring. Some became caught in the wire of the net, and flesh was torn as they reveled in the defeat of the former champion.

"Lilly?"

"I'm here." She sounded so far away.

"Where?" He looked but could not find her. Attendants from below had come up through the floor and pulled him to his feet. They walked him around the ring and held his arms up in victory. He had not the strength to do it himself.

"Lilly?"

"I'm with you." He could not see and he could not breathe. He wanted to push his shields up, but realized he could not without further injuring his face.

"Take this off," he said, but his words were slurred with exhaustion. Somehow the attendants understood, however, and they quickly unbuckled the gauntlets and removed the gloves.

"Lilly?" Did he say it or think it? Shaun pushed up his shields, and blood smeared across his eyes from the cut on his cheek. His shoulder and his chest stung and burned; his arms were leaden weights. The noise was deafening.

"Shaun." She had said it. She was in front of him, on the other side of the net that surrounded the ring. Ruben and Laylon were standing on either side of her and Michael was behind her, protecting her from the push of the crowd. The net separated them. Shaun looked at the wire and coils that kept them apart as if seeing them for the first time. He grasped a section in each hand and pulled. The pieces tore as if made of the sheerest fabric and Lilly fell into his arms, or he hers; he did not know or care as he slowly floated to the ground, safely caught by her love.

Chapter Twenty-five

Peace. It was a strange feeling. Shaun wasn't sure if he was dreaming it or feeling it. The hands on his body felt real enough. And for someone who had been in a great amount of pain not too long ago, he felt amazingly rested.

Had he dreamed the battle? Why did he feel no pain or exhaustion? Why was he content just to lie in this state of semiconsciousness and let others take care of him? He sensed that his body had been cleansed, his wounds tended, his pains relieved. A cool hand brushed the hair back from his forehead and gently moved across the skin, checking for signs of a fever.

He couldn't just lie here, could he? What if it had been a dream? What if Lilly was still with Ram, or worse yet, with the witches? What was happening on Oasis? Had the witches gotten to him and drugged him?

Dark lashes blinked hard over bronzed cheeks as his

pale gray eyes fought to open. Something tickled against the bare skin of his chest and a gentle hand placed a finger against his temple.

Instantly his eyes opened and focused on the peaceful face of Lilly smiling down at him. Above her he recognized the richly woven fabric that formed a canopy over the bed in her Senate apartments. A quick glance around the room let him know that it was night. A lamp on the table by the bed put out a soft glow that was easy on his eyes. The sheets were cool and soft against his nude body, and his aches and pains seemed to be nothing more than a distant memory.

"Welcome back," Lilly greeted him with a soft smile. She wore a gown of pale lavender that matched the color of her eyes in the dim light. It slid precariously low over one shoulder as she dipped in to place a soft kiss on his lips. Her unbound hair drifted over the bare skin of his chest as she moved back to her place on the edge of the bed.

"Have I been out long?" Shaun reached for her arm. He had been without her too long and wanted to make sure she would stay.

"Not really. I made you sleep so I could tend your wounds."

Shaun looked down at his chest and saw the multiple slices in his skin, now closed and healing. His other hand touched his cheek where it had been laid open and found the same. The wounds were there, but he was miraculously pain free.

"You're already healing."

"More Circe tricks?" Shaun asked with a hint of a devilish smile at the corner of his mouth.

"There's good in everything if you look hard enough," Lilly informed him with her own impish grin. "You can even find goodness in a convicted murderer." She traced a finger down the middle of his chest.

"Make that an escaped convicted murderer."

"You won't be able to lay claim to that for long. The Prefect is expunging your record."

"In exchange for?"

"You've only been a prince for how long and you're already jaded?" Lilly teased.

"I knew that the Prefect was corrupt long before I became a . . . prince," Shaun replied. His hand went to Lilly's cheek. "Do you mind that you're not a princess anymore?"

"I am more than willing to sacrifice the benefits of the title to get what I want."

"And that is?"

"You."

Shaun's hand moved behind her head and he eased her down until their lips brushed. Lilly's hand crept around his neck.

"It's not over yet," she sighed against his cheek.

"We'll worry about that later." Shaun's mouth moved across her cheek to her ear.

"We will?"

Shaun rolled them over, placing Lilly on her back. His hand stroked her cheek and moved down her neck. He splayed his hand in the valley between her breasts and stroked down to her stomach. Her muscles bunched and contracted beneath his touch as if an electric current had been sent through her body.

"We will," he answered her, and bent to kiss her again. Lilly's arms crept around him, one of her hands tangling in his hair as the other moved over the muscles in his back.

She felt the current again, as she had the first time they made love. It moved over them as if a gentle breeze caressed their bodies. Lilly's skin tingled in anticipation of his touch. Somehow her gown dissolved into nothingness; she felt it go, and yet neither of them had taken the time to remove it. Lilly wondered briefly, as Shaun's lips moved over her body, whether it would be possible for them to melt together. She felt as if she were going to at any moment. She tried to hold back, but she wanted to touch him as he was touching her. She wanted him to feel the rapture that was coursing through her body, making her blood boil and every fiber of her being swell up in longing to have more . . . of Shaun.

"Can you feel it?" he whispered hoarsely against her throat.

Lilly arched her back in response. She couldn't speak. She was afraid to. It was almost too much, almost too powerful; she was afraid their joining would kill her, and also afraid that it wouldn't. She had to have more; she couldn't get enough.

"I love you," he whispered as he eased himself inside her and she rose up to meet him, wrapping her legs around his hips. Shaun wrapped his hands around her face and she opened eyes that had been held tightly shut.

"Hold on," Shaun said. Her pale gray eyes locked onto his as she grabbed his shoulders. Lilly felt her hair rise up around them as if they were caught in a heavy wind. It wrapped around their heads and twisted wildly as he moved against her. Every part of her being raced to meet him. She felt the wind move over them and then felt as if they were being carried up by it.

"Hold on," Shaun gasped again. He threw his head back as she gripped him tighter with her legs, and she watched in awe as his eyes flashed with a silver glow.

How could she not hold on? If she let go, she would be lost; she would disappear into his essence. Her head swirled with a myriad of images as his forehead dropped to touch hers and she saw herself through him, felt the gathering in his loins as she felt it in hers. She would die from the coming explosion, she was sure. She did not know and did not care where he ended and she began. The whirlwind settled over them, and she saw that it came from their joining. She was being sucked into it and she didn't care. The world exploded and she went with the wind, spinning away into innumerable particles scattered in space.

"I love you," she said when she could speak again. Her head rested on his shoulder and her body was shielded from the world by his as she lay within his embrace.

"And I love you," he replied. He stroked his cheek against hers, too weary to move any other part of his body.

"They still won't allow it." Lilly felt the need to voice her fear. They still had a battle left to fight.

"Who won't allow what?" His response was distant, as if he were too content to make much effort.

"The Circe. Us."

"I don't care what the Circe want or don't want," Shaun said. "I don't care about what the Prefect wants or your unc . . . my father, or the people of Oasis, or even Agatha, who I'm sure is lurking in the hallway outside the door."

Lilly grinned against his neck at the mention of her maid.

"All I care about, right now, is this." He squeezed her tighter against him. "And until whatever passes for daybreak comes through that window, that's all I'm going to care about."

"We'll worry about it later?"

"Much later," Shaun said with a sigh.

Lilly reached down for the sheet and blankets that had gotten shoved away in their passion and pulled them up over their bodies. She could already feel the even breathing that meant Shaun had fallen asleep. So much had happened to them since they had met, it was no wonder that he was mentally and physically exhausted.

Lilly lay within the soft, safe cocoon of Shaun's arms and willed her mind into a state of relaxation. They would both need all their strength come the morning.

Lilly, as always, awoke as soon as Agatha pulled open the door. The false light of morning poured through the large window of her chamber. At least on the Senate planet you never had to awaken to gloomy skies or bad weather. The artificial sun was always there to greet you, no matter what time you chose to rise.

If only the prospect of the day were as cheery as the weather seemed to be.

"Mistress?"

"Yes, Agatha," Lilly replied from the bed. She was much too comfortable to worry about any embarrassment Agatha might feel at the sight of her mistress naked and in the arms of a man.

Who is supposedly my cousin. Lilly's face flushed a deep pink when she realized what must be going through her maid's head. She jumped from the bed and hastily wrapped the sheet around her body as she went to greet the maid. Agatha's discomfort was obvious; she kept her eyes focused on the floor as Lilly approached her.

"Be assured, Agatha, that all is not what it seems," Lilly said to the maid as she gathered up the end of the sheet.

"He is not the heir?" Agatha's face showed her confusion as she looked up.

"He is. I'm not."

"Mistress?"

Lilly chewed on her lip as she pondered exactly what she should say to the maid. The fact that Michael was her father was not yet public knowledge. She had not yet had time to talk to Michael about it. She didn't even know if her uncle knew. Lilly realized that she could just ignore Agatha and let her think what she wanted, but the woman had served her well and deserved some consideration.

Lilly took the woman's hand in her own. "He is the heir and he is the one you now serve . . ."

"By continuing to care for your mistress," Shaun added from the bed.

Lilly turned to see him sitting up with a blanket placed discreetly over his hips. Agatha bobbed her head in his direction, still unsure of what had changed.

"Your uncle . . . father is waiting," she said, not knowing whom she should report to.

"Tell him I will join him soon," Shaun replied. Agatha dipped and backed from the room. "As soon as I find something to wear. . . ." He looked around the room and then at Lilly, who quickly went after Agatha.

"Was this a trick to keep me at your mercy?" Shaun's face held a wry smile when Lilly came back into the chamber.

"Strictly an oversight," she replied saucily. "What you were wearing when they carried you in here was not fit to be worn again." She sat down on the edge of the bed.

"I was carried in here?"

"By Ruben and Michael."

"I'll never hear the end of that one," Shaun said as he rolled his eyes.

"We were all worried about you, including Ruben."

"I heard him when I was fighting Ram. I heard him through you." Shaun ran his hand down the length of her ash-colored hair. "What did he do?"

"Knocked the Sacrosanct Mistress unconscious." Lilly tried to keep a straight face but couldn't suppress a smile.

"He what?" Shaun asked incredulously.

"We were fighting for you, or over you."

"She was trying to distract me."

"Yes, so I went after her. We were battling for control in your mind. Ruben figured out what was going on and hit her on the back of the head. She was still out when the fight was over. I don't know what happened to her after that."

"I'm sure we'll all be hearing about it before long."

"Yes, we will." The temptation of having him close was too much, especially after the passion they had shared. Lilly's hand reached out of its own accord and traced a path up his heavily ridged stomach and chest. She watched in fascination as his muscles contracted under her touch. She raised her eyes to find his burning with longing.

"Shaun," she breathed though lips parted with anticipation. His response was quick as he jerked her close and covered her lips with his own.

"We can't," she gasped. "They're waiting."

"Duty calls?" he growled in protest.

Lilly pushed herself away and caught her breath at the hunger that flamed in his eyes. "Agatha will be back soon with your clothing."

"I know." His hand smoothed her hair. "But be warned. I will never have enough of you."

He moved in and out of her mind so quickly that Lilly wasn't sure it had happened except for the fact that she saw his hunger for her, and felt it, as if someone had stuck a knife into her abdomen and twisted it around.

The Circe would never allow their marriage.

Shaun placed his hands on either side of her face.

"They have no power over us." His words were meant to comfort her, but Lilly heard them as a challenge.

Would they ever be left in peace?

She turned to dress, but a hand on her shoulder stopped her progress. "Why don't I have this mark?" he asked.

Lilly looked over her shoulder at her tattoo. "It's a rite of passage," she explained. "It's given when you complete the training of your rank. I received it when I was eleven."

"You were so young," Shaun commented.

"I was the only heir."

"Was it painful?"

"Yes. It was." He knew she meant more than the tattoo; it was her life that had been painful. Shaun rose on his knees and wrapped his arms around her from behind.

Lilly leaned back into his body and wrapped her arm around his neck as he kissed the lily held within the paws of the lion. "It's nice to know that I have a father now."

"You've always had one."

"I have." She turned to look at him. "When I was small, I used to dream that Michael was my father. It made me feel less lonely. But there was always this strict formality whenever anyone else was around that reminded me he wasn't and that I didn't have anyone who cared."

"I promise that you'll never feel that way again."

Agatha came in with Shaun's clothing, and Lilly went to meet her.

"Have you talked to Michael at all?" Shaun asked when the maid had left.

"Not really. We haven't had time. . . ."

"And?"

"I looked inside." Lilly's face flushed with embarrassment, as if she had committed a terrible crime. "I wanted to know what happened, how I came to be. I should have waited to ask him . . ."

"You had a right to know."

"My mother tricked him. I don't even think that Michael knows how it happened. All he recalls is waking up in her bed. He doesn't know how he got there, but she gave him the memory of my conception. He knew from the start that he was my father."

"Victor must have been unable to get her with child."

"So she picked someone who was convenient."

"She picked someone who would take care of you."

Lilly nodded in agreement while fighting back the tears. "I always wondered if she would have cared for me if she had lived, or if I would have been just another instrument to get what she wanted, what they wanted."

"They?"

"Everything that happened on Oasis was part of a plan created generations ago by the Circe to gain control of the universe. I don't think your mother even knew that there was a plot. From what I've learned through the years, I know that your parents' marriage was a love match, but the Circe saw it as an opportunity to gain control of Oasis. But your mother refused to go along, and when she had a son, it angered the Circe even more. So they sent in my mother to set things right again accordng to the Circe plan. I saw it all in Honora's mind. Honora let me see it."

"The plan failed." Shaun rose from the bed and went to her. "The Circe failed. We know their tricks and we know what to expect." He placed his hands on her shoulders.

"They won't give up."

"Neither will we." Shaun dipped his head to look into her eyes. "As long as we stay together, they can't beat us. You have to stay strong, Lilly. You beat her when I was fighting Ram."

"With help from Ruben."

"You were beating her before that. I heard you. I felt you long before Ruben came in. You were stronger than Honora."

"I was?"

"You are."

"Mistress?"

Shaun and Lilly both turned to see Agatha standing uncomfortably in the doorway, eyes down and hands clenched together. Shaun looked down and realized that he was naked. Then he noticed Ruben's wide grin over the maid's head. He picked up the tail of Lilly's sheet and wrapped it around his hips as Ruben sauntered past Agatha into the room.

"I wouldn't worry about having a protector with that maid around," Ruben said cheekily.

"Thank you, Agatha," Lilly said to the maid as she bobbed out the door. Lilly was beginning to feel sorry for the woman. Agatha had already had more excitement this morning than in the entire time she had been in Lilly's service.

"I'd rather have a lock on the door," Shaun growled, and cocked an eyebrow at Lilly's amused grin.

"Such is the price of nobility," she said, and tried to move away. Shaun was still holding the sheet, and her escape was cut short when she realized that moving any farther would expose her body to Ruben's rakish grin.

"Don't mind me," Ruben said evilly.

Shaun's eyebrow went higher as he looked at his friend. "What do you want?"

"So this is how you show gratitude after I hauled your bleeding carcass in here?"

Shaun handed Lilly the sheet. She picked up the end and dashed into her bathing chamber to dress.

"From what I hear, you did a lot more than that," Shaun said as he looked dubiously at the clothing that Agatha had carried to him.

"Just helped out where I could."

"By knocking the head witch unconscious?"

Ruben laughed. "That was the best part!"

"And now there will probably be a price on yours," Shaun continued as he dressed.

"I was hoping that my well-placed connections could help me out with that." Ruben sprawled into a chair in the sitting area of the chamber.

"Ruben. You know that the Circe will be coming after us and anyone close to us." Shaun pulled on a shirt and grimaced at the fit.

"Life has never been dull around you."

Shaun, shirt still hanging open, sat down across from Ruben.

"Maybe it's time for you to move on," he said. "And take Laylon with you."

"Laylon will be fine. I doubt that they even know who she is. And I'm not going anywhere . . . yet."

Shaun extended his hand to his friend. "You've been a good friend, Ruben. I won't forget it."

Ruben grabbed Shaun's hand and shook it. "I always knew you'd pay off someday."

"You just kept me around so you'd feel safe."

"I always said you were the brawn and I was the brains."

Shaun punched his friend in the arm, and Ruben rubbed the injury as if he were in a great deal of pain.

Shaun ignored his antics and pulled on a pair of boots. Ruben picked up the coat that Agatha had carried in and let loose an admiring whistle.

"What?" Shaun asked.

Ruben held up the dark blue coat to show the adornment of braid and medallions.

Shaun let loose a curse when he saw the ornamentation.

"Such is the price of nobility, big guy," Ruben said, and held the coat for Shaun to put on.

"Is it too late to take me to Rykers?" Shaun asked as he shrugged into the coat.

Chapter Twenty-six

Lilly wasn't surprised in the least to see the Sacrosanct Mistress at her usual station in the Prefect's office with her acolytes gathered behind her. She was dressed, as always, in the uniform of her station, complete with the large ornate hat that overshadowed her features. Lilly wondered if the lump on the back of her head was uncomfortable beneath it. Shaun's lips twitched in suppressed humor as Lilly sent the thought into his mind.

Shaun looked rather uncomfortable himself in the uniform borrowed from his father. Its length was fine, but the fit was tight across the chest and shoulders and he was unable to button the shirt at the neck. The added braid and epaulets looked strangely out of place on his broad frame. Lilly decided she preferred him in simpler clothing.

"I agree," he said into her mind, and sent an image

of the two of them locked in an embrace, without a stitch of clothing between them.

"Be serious," Lilly returned as the Oasian contingent, consisting of herself, Shaun, Alexander, Michael, the Ambassador, and his secretary, took their places in the Prefect's office.

Also present was the Ravigan King, in obvious mourning and flanked on both sides by his surviving sons. Behind the King stood his Ambassador and a few of the officers of his court.

"It is time to put an end to your hostilities," the Prefect began. Lilly resisted the urge to roll her eyes at his empty words. It was long past time for the hostilities to be over. "Let us put the antagonisms that led to this war behind us and move together toward peace."

"There were no antagonisms," Lilly wanted to scream. *"It was just a case of simple greed on everyone's part."*

Honora arched an eyebrow as she read the thoughts in Lilly's mind.

"Too much blood has been shed," the Prefect droned on, and his scribe furiously scratched at his keypad, recording the words for posterity. They were all witness to the infamous conclusion of the Oasis-Raviga war that came down to a death match between the heirs of both planets. The Prefect had to have his part in it, however. That was why they were all gathered together for another act in the continuing masquerade that everyone in the universe mistook for a governing system.

He had seen the sudden shift of power and thrown his lot in with Oasis.

"The treaty has been prepared," the Prefect continued.

So literally nothing had changed except that innocent people had been killed and now there would be promises made that the same thing would not happen again. Until greed once again overcame reason and her planet once again became a target.

But a more immediate sense of foreboding filled Lilly's mind instead of relief that the entire thing was over with and they had survived.

Perhaps it was the look on Honora's face that caused it.

The Ravigan King was filled with hostility and grief at the loss of his oldest son, but he concealed it well as he signed the treaty and took his leave with his entourage. At least the Oasians had the assurance that he was a man of honor and would keep his word, although Lilly was not sure about the two sons who cast a final glance in Shaun's direction as they left the offices of the Prefect. The King would not live forever, and it was rumored that he had more sons than credits for them to inherit.

The Prefect bestowed a generous look upon the Sovereign Alexander, who was well versed in the posturing of the Senate.

"It pleases me that you have your son restored to you, Alexander," the Prefect began.

"I am afraid that we have an issue with that very matter," Honora interrupted.

The Prefect and his staff were rendered speechless by the daring of the Circe witch.

"His very existence is contrary to all we hold sacred." The Sacrosanct Mistress stood as she spoke. "He must be returned to us, or we will withdraw our support of your office," she challenged.

"By all means, withdraw away," Shaun growled in return.

"What you are asking is unthinkable," the Prefect protested. "It would be as if we were sanctioning his murder."

"Is he not a convicted murderer himself? Would it not appease his victims' families to know that he has been eliminated?"

"Excuse me," Shaun said. "I'm standing right here."

"You must choose, Prefect. You must choose between the Circe and this"—she looked at Shaun in disgust—"curse!"

Shaun crossed his arms and looked at the Prefect. "You heard her. Choose."

Lilly clearly understood the Prefect's dilemma. He had reached his position by careful maneuvering and powerful alliances. His alliance with the Circe had given him the power to see into his enemies' minds and would be a great loss. On the other hand, he could not afford to lose the support of the people, and without Oasis, the people would starve.

"He's going to stall," Lilly warned Shaun.

"We might have to make a run for it again," Shaun returned as they watched the Prefect struggle with his decision.

They both saw what he was thinking. With Shaun in his power, he could hold both Oasis and Circe captive to his whims. Shaun would be held hostage until one or the other gained the upper hand, and the hostage would be a peace offering to the victor, either to rule or be killed.

"You've got to be kidding," Shaun said as he read the man's thoughts.

Lilly revealed the Prefect's thoughts to Michael.

"I'm afraid that is not acceptable to us," Honora proclaimed as she saw them also.

"That is not for you to decide," the Prefect declared.

They realized without seeing the small signal button that the Prefect had summoned his personal guard to the office.

"This is not acceptable." Honora's words were slowly enunciated, as if she were talking to a child. "The male Circe must be eliminated."

"You mean murdered," Michael challenged.

Honora arched a brow in contempt. "*You dare to speak in my presence?*"

Lilly saw the thought and wondered what the woman was hiding behind her wall.

"You're going to have to choose, Prefect, because your plan is not acceptable to me either." Shaun's rigid stance dared the man to make a move against him. The Prefect looked about nervously. He had not forgotten how Shaun had thrown the witch across the room or the way the doors had slammed tightly behind him when he made his escape with Lilly.

"I have summoned a collar," the Prefect warned.

"I'm anxious to see how it fits you," Shaun retorted.

The sound of the guard could be heard in the corridor.

"*Hold the doors,*" Shaun directed Lilly.

Was she strong enough? Shaun believed she was. If she could hold the doors, it would leave him free to fight Honora. Lilly concentrated her thoughts on the doors. She sensed the movement of the Ambassador and his secretary as they tried to blend into the walls of the office. The Prefect's staff had also moved away, leaving the man in a vulnerable position in his chair on the dais. The only ones who did not seem nervous about the coming confrontation were the Circe acolytes who had gathered in closer behind their leader.

The door shook as the guard pounded on it. It would only be a matter of time before they used something to blast it apart.

Michael stood on the balls of his feet with his fists clenched. His duty was to protect the royalty of Oasis, and he would gladly give up his life to do so. He had failed once in his job. He would not fail again.

The Sovereign Alexander seemed confused by the latest turn of events. Had he not defeated the Circe's quest to have Oasis? And his son had been restored to him. Why was there now an issue?

How did Honora do it? Lilly's mind remained focused on the door, but her eyes saw the slowing of time as the acolytes moved to attack as one being. They ran toward Shaun in a shrieking mass, and his response was as slow as if his body were laden down with heavy weights.

The acolytes slashed with their knives, and the three men tried to blocked and shove them away. All three were weaponless, a standard requirement for entering into the Prefect's chambers.

But Lilly saw the attack as a distraction. The acolytes were there to take the brunt of the men's strength, to sacrifice themselves if necessary for the common good of the Circe. Honora was the true assassin and she relished the thought of placing her knife into Shaun's heart.

The men could not see her coming. She used the acolytes as a distraction to blind them to her presence.

Lilly tried to scream out a warning, but Honora had deafened their ears. They saw nothing but the attack.

Honora raised her knife.

Lilly released her hold on the door and cast a warning into the minds of the men.

Alexander saw the witch as her arm slashed down, and he stepped into the blow. Blood sprayed out as the knife pierced his heart.

"No!" Shaun yelled, and caught his father as his knees weakened and he began his descent to the cold marble tile of the chambers.

Michael struck Honora's hand and the knife went flying. The acolytes looked up in surprise as Lilly entered their minds forcefully; they dropped their weapons and backed away.

The Legion guard rushed into the room. The Prefect, who had taken shelter behind his chair, rose and pointed to Honora.

"Place the collar on that witch and place her in a cell," he commanded.

Honora shrieked in protest and attempted to gather the powers that had been dissipated during her attempt on Shaun's life. Shaun turned his silver eyes on her, and in the next moment she was trembling on the floor.

"Finish her," Lilly said to Shaun, who was looking on the witch in disgust.

"I would rather she had years to contemplate what she has lost," Shaun said as he looked down into his father's face.

Lilly took the collar from one of the guards as two of them hauled the witch to her feet.

Honora gazed at Lilly with cold, pale eyes. "You have always been a disappointment to me, Lilly," she murmured as Lilly placed the collar around her neck. "It saddens me to know that my daughter died so that you might exist."

Lilly hesitated for only a moment before she snapped the collar together.

"You will have plenty of time to think about it, Grandmother," she said as the guards took her away. "Go back to Circe and choose another leader," Lilly told the acolytes. "And I suggest you choose one who is capable of making peace out of this situation."

The acolytes scurried from the room with their heads down and a great sense of relief sweeping over them. Lilly did not spare them another thought as she knelt by Shaun's side.

"Can we stop it?" Shaun asked her as the blood spread over the dark maroon of Alexander's coat.

"Not this," Lilly said as she picked up the Sovereign's hand. He jerked it away and grabbed at the lapel of Shaun's coat.

"Your mother died saving you, Nicholas," he gasped. "I could only do the same."

"You saved me . . . Father."

Michael, kneeling on the other side of Shaun, covered his face with his hand.

"It's up to you to lead the people. To take care of Oasis."

"I will."

"I never stopped loving you," Alexander gasped. His eyes fluttered and his head lolled to the side.

The Sovereign Alexander of Oasis was dead.

"I have summoned my personal physician." The Prefect stood over them, wringing his hands.

"It's too late," Shaun informed him. He gently lowered his father's body to the floor and rose to his full height so that he towered over the man.

"Does this mean you choose me, Prefect?"

Shaun turned on his heel. The chamber doors swung open as if in anticipation of his leaving and slammed shut behind him.

Michael placed his hands over Alexander's eyes to close them.

"I have failed you twice," he said quietly.

Lilly placed her hand on his arm. "Both Alexander and Victor died to save someone they loved. Would they have wanted you to stop them?"

"I should have died in your fa . . . Victor's place."

"What would have happened to me if you had? Would Victor have loved me, knowing that I was not his daughter? Would he have left me to die in my mother's womb?"

Michael shook his head. He did not have the answers any more than Lilly did. He opened his arms, and Lilly moved into the safe circle of them as she always had when she was small and wished for things that could not be. But this time her wish had come true. Michael was her father.

"They will never leave us in peace, will they?" Lilly had traded the safety of Michael's arms for the bliss of Shaun's. They had moved up to the satellite in preparation for their trip back to Oasis. And because they felt safer there. There was always the chance that the Circe would make another attempt on Shaun's life or hire assassins. And the Ravigan threat could not be dismissed either. There might be a treaty between the planets, but that did not rule out the fact that Ram had a lot of brothers who might want vengeance for personal reasons.

Alexander's body had been displayed in the Senate Rotunda so that all of the politicians and officers of the government could pay their respect and meet the newly discovered heir. Shaun had borne it all, standing at attention by his father's bier and reading the thoughts behind the condolences.

They were all wondering about him. They wondered if he was the true heir or a trick of the Oasians to keep control of their planet. They wondered if he truly held the power of the Circe. They wondered if he had really defeated Ram in the Murlaca or if it had been a Circe trick. Mostly they wondered if he was having an incestuous relationship with his cousin. Shaun did not mind the thoughts. He now knew who the friends of Oasis were, and more important, who were its enemies.

"I'm afraid they won't," Shaun replied. Lilly's

quarters on the satellite were no less luxurious than those she had on the planet below. It would be a lot for her to sacrifice for his safety.

"Do you think we'll be able to totally disappear?" Lilly's hand traced lazy circles on his bare chest.

"It depends upon how much of a price they put on our heads."

Lilly rolled up so that she could look into his eyes. They glowed the customary silver in the dim light of her quarters.

"Will they do that? Are they that desperate to kill you?"

"Think about it, Lilly. What if we have children? Think of how powerful our son or daughter could be."

"As long as we're together, we're a threat to the Circe's existence."

"We are." His arms pulled her up close so that her head rested beneath his chin. "We'll just have to be stronger than they are. We'll never be able to let our guard down."

"And our children will have to grow up knowing that they never will be safe."

"We'll protect them somehow," he assured her.

"So where will we go?"

"Michael is working on a plan. He's not anxious to lose you, you know."

"Nor I him."

"And how do you feel about the revelation that Honora is your grandmother?"

"Happy that I escaped her evilness. She sent her own daughter to kill you, knowing that she would probably be captured and killed also. I'm thankful that Alexander hated the Circe so much that he did not send me to them. I can even understand why he could never love me. I—I look so much like my mother."

"You have some of your father in you too."

"I do?"

Shaun's hand caressed her chin. "You have this stubborn tilt here that I've noticed on Michael. And your smiles are alike."

"I'm surprised that you've even seen him smile."

"He was smiling when I beat the giant."

Lilly laughed. "I'm sure he was."

"No more worrying about the past, Lilly." Shaun's hand stroked her back as he spoke. "You are not responsible for your mother's evil deeds or even your grandmother's—"

"I'd rather not use that term," Lilly interrupted.

Shaun's smile stretched across his face. "As a matter of fact, you are responsible for undoing the evil that they did."

"I am?"

"You found me, remember?"

"I think it's more like you found me."

"How is that?"

"When I walked onto the ship, I could feel you. It was almost as if you were calling out to me."

"All I remember is that it was almost as if my unconscious mind awakened. Even though I was asleep, I could see your face when you walked up to the tube. I thought I was dreaming until I crashed through my tube and saw you sleeping in yours."

"Isn't it strange how fate stepped in and brought us together?"

"I prefer to think of it as a higher being taking the time to right some wrongs."

"Then I owe whoever it is my undying gratitude."

"For the rest of our days."

Epilogue

Ruben was waiting for them the next morning to take them back to Oasis. Shaun and Lilly were to attend Alexander's funeral and then Shaun would publicly hand over the day-to-day operation of the government to Michael.

Michael had found a safe place for them to go: an ancient villa located on a mountainside deep within the rain forest on Oasis. The only way in was by air, and the villa led into a series of tunnels and caves that ran deep through the mountain. It was located on the other side of the planet from the capital, but at least they would remain on Oasis.

"And knowing the Circe, this will be the last place they'll look," Ruben exclaimed as Michael showed them the diagram of the villa.

Agatha was sent on ahead with a few other trusted servants to make preparations.

For Shaun and Lilly, it was as good a place as any to go into hiding. At least it would feel like home.

They hit the hyperport and a great feeling of relief washed over them. As far as Shaun was concerned, he couldn't get far enough away from the Senate's politics and intrigue.

"So you're feeling pretty good about the way things turned out?" Ruben asked as Shaun leaned back in the copilot's seat and stretched his long legs out onto the console.

"With the exception of a few deaths," Shaun growled, wondering why his friend was wearing such a cocky grin.

"It would have been nice if you could have gotten to know your father."

"Yes, it would have. Although it was hard to get over the fact that he tried to kill Lilly." He reached back and took her hand in his.

"So now you've got the mind-reading thing, you've got the royal blood . . ."

"What are you driving at?"

"Just don't want you to get all cocky on me, big guy."

"And why is that?"

"Just don't want you to think you have a monopoly on royal blood in this partnership."

Shaun's feet hit the floor as he reached over and flipped on the autopilot. "I'm going to hold him," he said to Lilly. "Do you think you can beat it out of him?"

"Why don't you just look inside and find out?" Lilly asked as Shaun wrestled Ruben from his chair.

"Because this is a lot more fun."

SUSAN GRANT
THE STAR PRINCESS

Ilana Hamilton isn't an adventurer like her pilot mother, or a diplomat like her do-right brother; she's a brash, fun-loving filmmaker who'd rather work behind the camera than be a "Star Princess" in front of it. Heiress or not, she's a perfectly normal, single woman . . . until Prince Ché Vedla crashes into her life.

With six months to choose a bride, the sexy royal wants to sow his wild oats. Ilana can't blame him—but fall for the guy herself? Hotshot pilot or no, Ché is too arrogant and too old-fashioned. But when he sweeps her off her feet Ilana sees stars, and the higher he takes her the more she loves to fly. Only her heart asks where she will land.

AN ORIGINAL SIN

NINA BANGS

Fortune MacDonald listens to women's fantasies on a daily basis as she takes their orders for customized men. In a time when the male species is extinct, she is a valued man-maker. So when she awakes to find herself sharing a bed with the most lifelike, virile man she has ever laid eyes or hands on, she lets her gaze inventory his assets. From his long dark hair, to his knife-edged cheekbones, to his broad shoulders, to his jutting—well, all in the name of research, right?—it doesn't take an expert any time at all to realize that he is the genuine article, a bona fide man. And when Leith Campbell takes her in his arms, she knows real passion for the first time . . . but has she found true love?

___52324-8 $5.99 US/$6.99 CAN

Dorchester Publishing Co., Inc.
P.O. Box 6640
Wayne, PA 19087-8640

Please add $1.75 for shipping and handling for the first book and $.50 for each book thereafter. NY, NYC, and PA residents, please add appropriate sales tax. No cash, stamps, or C.O.D.s. All orders shipped within 6 weeks via postal service book rate.
Canadian orders require $2.00 extra postage and must be paid in U.S. dollars through a U.S. banking facility.

Name____
Address______________________________________
City____________________State______Zip__________
I have enclosed $__________ in payment for the checked book(s).
Payment must accompany all orders. ☐ Please send a free catalog.
CHECK OUT OUR WEBSITE! www.dorchesterpub.com

SHADOW FIRES

CATHERINE SPANGLER

Jenna dan Aron lives a solitary existence, shunned by her people because she can see the future. She even foresees her own destiny: to be a human offering, a mate for a savage Leor warlord. When two Shielder colonies have to be rescued and the Leors who are their only hope demand a bride for their leader in return, Jenna steps forward.

Arion of Saura finds mating outside his race abhorrent, but he has no choice, as his kind faces extinction. Bound to him, Jenna faces a life of barbarism with a mate who seems more beast than man. Jenna and Arion wage a battle of wills until they discover that the heart is mightier than any weapon—and that love will forge shadow and fire together.